BEING "SY"

by David M. Antebi

RoseDog ❧ Books
PITTSBURGH, PENNSYLVANIA 15238

RoseDog Books
585 Alpha Drive
Pittsburgh, PA 15238
Visit our website at *www.rosedogbookstore.com*

ISBN: 978-1-4809-7559-0
eISBN: 978-1-4809-7582-8

1

A PLEASANT DREAM

I awoke this morning to find I was seventy-five years old, thirty pounds over-weight, but otherwise in fairly good condition with a full head of hair. I have maintained most of my faculties, except for some minor memory lapses, which started happening in my late forties. There is no redeeming quality to aging that I know of, other than the fact you are still alive for a few more years, before you will be dead for eternity. Where did my life go? Was I aware of it as it was happening? Did I feel it along the way? A long life span is complicated. Things occur that are not planned for. Surprises pop up all along the way. One doesn't always have the answers as to why events happen, but you try to explain them anyway to keep your sanity, by saying things such as, "It was meant to be," or "There are no coincidences," or even, "Bad things always happen in threes." Sometimes I wish my logical mind could lean more toward simplistic answers, but that is not who I am.

Many of my contemporaries have died, Sammy Levy and I being the sole survivors of our "Pack of Four" group of inseparable childhood buddies. Now Sammy, a heavy smoker all his life, is dying of lung cancer. The longer you live, the more people you know pass away. Approaching the end is not fearful for me, only gloomy. Each day I strive to find something that pleases me and urges me to go on living. There are solace and joy in my children and grandchildren.

I was born into the Syrian/Jewish community of Brooklyn, known as the SYs, a very close knit group that avoids drawing any attention to it and has come a long way since my youth in Bensonhurst, Brooklyn. My father, Ezra

Dweck, having landed at Ellis Island in 1921 from Aleppo, at the age of fourteen, with his parents and two older siblings, went straight to work, as did many other new SY arrivals. Pop landed a job at a company owned by one of the richest Syrian businessmen at that time, Judah Cohen. Mr. Cohen made his fortune manufacturing men's and ladies' handkerchiefs in a factory on lower Broadway before moving his production to the Philippines.

Mr. Cohen was a sponsor of many of these immigrants, guaranteeing them a job with his firm. He supported many organizations that arranged for the immigration of the SYs and was a founder of *Rodfe Zedek*, a burial service that ensured a plot and proper religious interment for every member of the SY population. He fought for the purchase of additional burial land to accommodate the growing community and won. Ironically, when he died, he was the first person to be interred in the new area. I remember in my early teens working for Mr. Cohen's company on Sundays for $1 an hour, but the best part was we got to order anything we wanted for lunch from Lou G. Siegel's kosher deli.

By the time he was twenty, my father was promoted to shipping manager of Mr. Cohen's company. Pop married at the age of twenty-four, late, by SY standards, and my brother Jacob was born in December 1933.

Mom, Pop and my three older siblings, Jacob, Michael, and Esther, are gone. The two brothers died six months apart, and my sister passed the following year. The surviving members of the Dweck family are me, my sister Marilyn, who is five years older and still living with her partner in Brooklyn. My brother, Al, born thirteen months before me is living out his retirement with his wife, Marie, in Aventura, Florida. There isn't much contact between Al and me, hasn't been for quite a while, ever since I recovered from alcoholism thirty-two years ago. It seems he was more embarrassed by my disease rather than proud of my reclamation of sobriety.

When I awoke today, it was from a pleasant dream about me, at seventy-five, playing with my three young children. It was delightful to see all of them, as toddlers, frolicking in our small Brooklyn apartment. Adele, my first wife, so beautiful and vibrant, shushed the kids to lower their voices, lest the downstairs neighbors complain. I could even smell the wondrous aroma of Adele's signature SY meal, *Yabrack*, grape leaves rolled up with ground meat and rice, and cooked in a savory mixture of tamarind juice, dried apricots and lemon.

The strangest part of aging is that everyone else around you grows old, but in your mind you still feel young. My eldest son, Ezra, that cute baby bouncing around in my dreams, will be fifty years old in two months. How weird is that?

Suddenly, everyone in the dream disappeared, and I was now on a luxury cruise ship full of SYs, surrounded by couples dancing to Arabic music, joyfully clapping their hands as they gyrated around the dance floor to Mohammed El-Bakkar's popular song, "Port Said." It reminded me of any one of hundreds of SY weddings or Bar Mitzvah parties I attended over the years where as many as one thousand guests would attend whether they were invited or not. The joke of these affairs was the invitations, calling for "Ceremony at 6 p.m." They never began less than three hours late. Weddings and Bar Mitzvah parties were taboo on Saturday night because they started and ended too late. Most affairs were held on Thursday or Sunday evenings. At my son Ezra's Bar Mitzvah celebration, I put "7 p.m. American Time," which sent the message to get there early.

My daughter Tuni's wedding, held in the Share Zion synagogue, which has on average a thousand worshippers on Shabbat, was such an affair. She was nineteen years old and is now forty-three and the mother of three teenage kids.

Adele and I were divorced at the time of the wedding. She handled all the details, and I wrote the checks. The flower arrangements alone cost me a hundred grand. The lighting: thirty. Catering was two-ten. And when you added in all the extras, such as silk bunting streaming across the ceiling, the DJ, the photographer, etc., etc., it came to well over four hundred and fifty K. Twenty years ago, that was a lot of money. Today, it's small potatoes compared to the new trend of SY "destination" affairs where whole groups of guests are flown off to Paris, Jerusalem, Cancun, or some other exotic place. Rumors flew around that one SY real estate baron spent close to five million for his son's Bar Mitzvah party.

Syrian Jewish tradition in the Sephardic custom (though a bit dissimilar to Sephardic Jews from Spain and Greece) holds the following: a firstborn son is named after the groom's father, whether alive or deceased; firstborn daughter named after the groom's mother. The second son and daughter are then named after the bride's father and mother. All children after that may be given any name, usually those of biblical heroes or other relatives, alive or dead.

Of course, Jewish males must be circumcised, but there is another quaint ceremony called a *Pidyon haben* that is considered a *Mitzvah*. It calls for the redemption of the first natural born (not by Cesarean) son of a father not belonging to the tribe of *Levites* or *Kohanim*. This Mitzvah is derived from the tenth plague on the Egyptians where every first born son was to be slaughtered. God then commanded that the first born sons of the Hebrews be given over to the Kohanim, the priests. The infant must be redeemed from a known *Kohen*, a descendant of the priestly tribe of Aaron, thirty days after the birth by paying five silver coins.

At the Pidyon there are many singing and prayer recitals, and there is a spread of food. I went through this ritual with my son, Ezra, forty-nine years ago, when I was just twenty-six years old. Now Ezra is much older than I was when we celebrated his *Pidyon*. He went through the same ritual with his first-born son, Daniel (my name), who is now eighteen and heading off to college.

The night of my son Ezra's Pidyon celebration is one of the few memories that are still vividly clear in my mind. I can see the faces of the guests. I can hear the singing of the *pizmonim*, those loud and joyful songs of the celebration.

Forty-nine years ago! The world has gone through so much change during that time, All of my heroes are dead: JFK and MLK; Sinatra, Johnny Carson, Rita Hayworth, Mickey Mantle, Ronald Reagan (yeah, I voted for him in his second election). Mrs. Greenhouse, my sixth grade teacher, is gone, too, though she lived past one hundred.

The war in Vietnam ended, and Nixon resigned. There was genocide in Bosnia and Rwanda; the collapse of the Berlin wall; the stealing of a Presidential election; 9/11; the Middle East wars and the fall of despots in Nigeria, Iraq and Libya. The first Black President in American history was elected into office twice and the hometown of my SY ancestors, Aleppo, Syria, has been destroyed; and now, of course, Donald J. Trump. But, to paraphrase King Solomon, the world goes on.

Lately, I have wondered how difficult it might be for movie stars with long careers to look back on their existence. Not only do they have their memories, but there is film footage of the different periods of their lives. Take Sinatra, for instance. What do you think it felt like for him to see himself as a successful singer in his twenties, a movie star in his thirties, or relive his romance with Ava Gardner? On film, he was able to see himself alive at the instant the camera was rolling, each frame a fleeting moment in his life. I am left mostly with my faded memories and a few bunches of photos.

You go through stages in life's passage that are problematic at the very least and often unmanageable. There are pleasant moments, of course, but they quickly fade into that netherworld of memories where, if you are stricken with Alzheimer's, you lose even those.

So much worldly change has occurred, yet so little modification in the SY culture. In fact, many aspects of the community have regressed. Today, I consider myself a good person, an honorable man, but not without faults. The values instilled in me in childhood have had to be re-examined, and looked at honestly. Having gone through dramatic changes in my life, my standards had to be re-measured for me alone to see if the needle had been pushed closer to a fuller understanding of who and what I am. One thing for sure: I am not the same man I was thirty-two years ago.

And now, as I am in the bottom of the ninth inning, my one major regret is that I have not been able to effectuate progress in the growth of the community I have always loved. My efforts always seem to have fallen short, leaving me to wonder what could have been done differently by me to change that world. I have no Messianic illusions, just a simple recognition that each person on the planet can change his or her world if even in a miniscule way. I have failed to do that. Each time I watch the movie *Schindler's List*, I burst into tears during the scene where Schindler cries out, "I have not done enough. I could have done more."

For the first half of my existence, I did nothing but worship money as my God, gaining riches, but losing bits and pieces of my spirituality along the way. So, today, I am not only seventy-five years old, but left alone to rue the failures of my life.

Despite any fears or misgivings, life does go on — until it stops without any consultation or negotiation, whether one likes it or not. There is no choice, even though religion teaches us that God has given us "free will." If we truly had that, which of us would not "will" to live on forever along with the people we love. Unfortunately, reality is always present, whether we believe it or not, or even when we attempt to create a false realism. This is the path of life to death, and whoever created this difficult and unexplainable trail had to be irrational, or at best a sadist.

2

FAT BOY FINDS BOMB

December 7, 1941, a *"date that will live in infamy"* was not just the day Japan bombed Pearl Harbor. Two hours before the sneak attack, I emerged into the world and for years, while growing up, my siblings and friends taunted me that my birth was the cause of World War II.

Mom was thirty-eight years old when she had me, and due to complications, which ended up with a hysterectomy, she would no longer be able to have children. After six kids, she was fine with that. Pop? Not so happy.

My father told me years later that I cried and wailed for a good forty-five minutes after having my penis sliced with a surgical tool by a *Mohel*, a religious man trained in the mutilation of infants. I have no recollection of this, being but eight days old at the time. Circumcision dates back to the days of our Old Testament forefather, Abraham, who entered a covenant commanded by the Lord. Abraham was truly a brave man because, as a ninety-nine year old male, he performed the ritual on himself, not to mention all members of his household, including his slaves. That took balls the size of watermelons. I often wonder why Jewish male infants must be bound to a law created by a promise made by a man we never even met.

Recollections of my early years are minimal; my memories are vague. I enjoyed banging on pots with spoons as a pastime. I did so smiling, until Mom took off her shoe and hit me to stop the noise. I was a chubby little boy eating all the Syrian dishes and desserts my mother made without doing much in the way of exercise. A photo of me at seven years old, shows about ten pounds too much.

Once, as an adult, when I visited my sixth grade teacher, Mrs. Green-house, at her nursing home on her 90th birthday, she related the time she came to my family's apartment to see if my mother could find better clothes for my sister Esther, instead of the torn and dirty garments she had been wearing to school. During that visit, the teacher saw me walking in a half-pinned diaper with feces about to fall out. She picked me up, she said, and changed the diaper on the spot.

We lived in a cramped apartment, six children and two adults sharing three bedrooms, a kitchen, and one bathroom that had a stall shower with a light bulb. One Friday after school, my brother Michael got undressed and entered the shower room. It was dark, and when he looked up at the socket he noticed the bulb was not lit, so he unscrewed it and stuck his finger in the socket. Smart ten year old. The shock knocked him across the stall, and the entire house went black.

My brothers and I shared a bed in one room, my sisters slept together in another, and Mom and Pop had the third. Mom was short-tempered, with little patience for unruly kids. I can recall her often meting out punishment for bad behavior, and simply removing her shoe was enough for us kids to quiet down. At times, she got my oldest brother, Jacob, who we called Jakey, to inflict further penalties on us by lashing us with his belt. Jakey seemed to enjoy in-flicting pain on his younger siblings.

There were moments when Mom could be loving and compassionate. She had a pleasant singing voice and would sometimes lull me to sleep singing, of all songs, "Silent Night." She was an orthodox Syrian Jew who spoke broken English and probably had no clue the song was about baby Jesus. Sometimes she would sing the Muslim call to prayer, which, of course, she had grown up with in Aleppo. On occasion, she told funny tales about how, when it was rain-ing, little chickens had to wear galoshes to get to school. Her preferred stories came from the Bible, re-telling tales of the forefathers' and mothers' heroic battles against sin.

Mom's favorite tale was of Jacob, son of Isaac and grandson of Abraham, wanting to marry Rachel, the daughter of Laban, Jacob's uncle (complicated, no?). Jacob was smitten by Rachel and offered to labor for Laban for seven years to get her hand in marriage. After Jacob completed the seven years, and when the time came for the betrothal, Laban put the wedding veil on his older daughter, Leah, to trick Jacob into marrying her. That is where the tradition of lifting the bride's veil at the wedding ceremony is derived, to reveal to the groom, he is getting the woman for which he bargained. Jacob had to work another seven years for the hand of Rachel, whom he loved more than her sister.

My mother was a kind-hearted woman in the presence of strangers, fawning over her friends and acquaintances. But her demeanor changed radically on the rare occasions she was in the company of rich people, the *zengeneem*. She spoke of them with awe and respect, as if God had anointed them. She truly believed wealthy people new secrets about life that poor people could never learn.

Mom's compassion didn't surface too often, but one winter's day during a snow storm, when I was about six, she let me play with the other children who were romping in the white powder. Mom sent me out wearing cotton socks on my hands because we did not have the money to buy gloves. We were neighborhood kids building an igloo in front of our building's backyard. Periodically, when my "gloves" became soaking wet, I'd scramble back into the house, and Mom would exchange them for a pair of warm socks that had been sitting on the radiator.

Mom gave more attention towards playing cards with her friends than taking care of her children. There were few boundaries in our chaotic home; we kids could come and go as we pleased. There was no set time for meals as a family; Mom just cooked and left the food on the stove from which each of us could feed ourselves.

Hygiene was not a big priority in my house: no one ever taught me how to brush my teeth. That would end up costing me tens of thousands in dental fees later on in life. We kids showered once a week, on Fridays, in preparation for Shabbat.

Often, when he had no hot water at home, my sister Esther would take us to the school lockers across the street and showered us there.

Sometimes, as a five or six year old, I would look out the window next to my bed and stare at the sky. On clear nights the stars would sparkle and I would lose myself in the vastness of the universe. The longer I stared the more fearful and small I felt. What was a little boy's worth compared to the infinite heavens? I asked my mother if that was where God lived.

"Yes, Rohi," she said. "And when we die we will meet Hashem in *Olam Ha Ba*. All the people you know and love in this life will be there in the afterlife."

When we "die?" The "afterlife?" What did that mean? That scared the hell out of me even more. I clung tightly to my mother for comfort.

Pop was passive. He seldom raised his voice, and pretty much looked past any misbehaving. What I remember most of those early years was that Esther pretty much took care of me, and blocked the wrath of Jakey's attacks. However, she was unable to stop the taunting and abuse inflicted on me by my brother, Al.

Another memory that stands out in my childhood was when while digging a hole to China in our backyard, the shovel struck something hard. Probing a little deeper, I saw a metal object that looked like a bomb and mined it out of the ground. I picked it up and studied it for a moment before trying to twist the top. It wouldn't budge. In the house, I found a hammer and banged the head several times attempting to loosen it. Mom was annoyed by the noise, and before she could remove her shoe, I ran out into the street with the hammer and the bomb.

There I was, a seven year old, walking on 20th Avenue with a bomb in my hand and hammering away at it. Shelly, the mailman, whom everyone in the neighborhood loved for his singing Yiddish songs and his happy go lucky manner, saw me and stopped dead in his tracks. He used to call SYs 'Yachabebes,' a poor pronunciation of the Syrian word for sweetheart.

"Hey, Yachabebe," he said quietly, though there was a terror in his voice. "What is that?"

"It's a bomb, Shelly. Found it in my backyard. Gonna take it apart." And with that, I continued to bang the head.

Shelly put down his mailbag and approached me slowly. "Listen carefully, kid, and do what Uncle Shelly tells you. Put it down, very slowly." I glanced up at this man who always had a smile on his face, but now saw how pale his skin was, with droplets of perspiration beading on his forehead.

"Put it down, Danny, and walk away. That thing can blow up and hurt somebody."

I liked Shelly; everyone in the neighborhood liked him, so I did as he asked. A few people had gathered around, and Shelly shouted out to them. "Call the bomb squad!"

The bomb squad did arrive and disarmed what apparently was a dud. A reporter from the Brooklyn Eagle questioned me about what had happened, and, hoping to get my name in the newspaper, I repeated it three times. "Daniel

Dweck," I said clearly, but when the neighborhood daily came out the next day, there was just a small article on an inside page with the heading, "Fat Boy Finds Bomb," with no mention of my name.

From that day forward, I never trusted the press.

3

NEW YORK 1892

History tells us Jews lived in Syria since the time of King David, including Palestinian Jews that escaped from the high taxes of the Crusaders. Most of the Sephardi arrived in Syria after the Alhambra Decree of March 1492 issued by the Catholic Monarchs Isabella and Ferdinand of Spain. That decree ordered the departure of practicing Jews from the Kingdoms of Castile and Aragon for fear they might encourage the Jewish converts to change their minds and return to the fold. These immigrants settled in Aleppo, Syria, which was then part of the Mameluke Sultanate of Egypt.

SY's first immigrated to New York in 1892. The earliest to arrive were Jacob Abraham Dwek and Ezra Abraham Sitt. They, along with other men, came to America to earn some money and return to Syria. When they saw the freedom and opportunities America offered, they decided to stay and send for their families.

In the early 20th Century, Syrian Jews immigrated to America and established themselves in New York. They initially lived on the Lower East Side of Manhattan; some went to the Bronx, but most moved to Bensonhurst in Brooklyn. As they prospered, they settled along Ocean Parkway in Gravesend, Brooklyn, which now boasts the largest population of Syrian Jews in the world. There are similar, but smaller, groups living across the United States and in Latin America. Most of these SY immigrants became peddlers, selling merchandise provided by other Syrians.

A division existed between those with roots in Aleppo, Halabi Jews, and Damascus, Shami Jews, the two main centers of Jewish life in Syria. This divide persists to present-day, with each community maintaining some separate cultural institutions and organizations.

Congregation Magen David Synagogue, on 67th Street between 20th and 21st Avenues in Brooklyn, was erected in 1921. It is still in continual use for daily and Shabbat prayers and funeral services. In 2001, the building was declared a landmark by the New York City Landmarks Preservation Commission, and in 2004, was certified and listed with the National Register of Historic Places.

Congregation Sha'are Zion, on Ocean Parkway between Avenue T and Avenue U in Brooklyn, is the largest synagogue of the community. Constructed in 1960, the synagogue generally serves the Aleppo, or Halabi, Syrian community. The synagogue's social hall is a popular venue for weddings. The current Chief Rabbi is Saul J. Kassin, whose father, Rabbi Jacob S. Kassin, was the previous spiritual leader of the Syrian community until his death in 1994 at the age of 94. Another important leader was Rabbi Abraham Hecht, who was forced to resign from his position because of his conflicting political views in the 1990's. He recommended the assassination of the Israeli Prime Minister Yitzhak Rabin and Foreign Minister Shimon Peres for their proposal in Oslo to withdraw from parts of the West Bank and the Gaza Strip.

Congregation Ahi Ezer, also on Ocean Parkway in Brooklyn, is the largest of the ten synagogues serving the Shami Syrians. There are presently more than fifty Syrian synagogues throughout Brooklyn and Manhattan as well as fourteen in Deal, New Jersey and its surrounding towns where many Syrian Jews spend their summers.

Today, there are many SY millionaires – even a few billionaires, like Jeff Sutton, Morris Bailey, Joe Carey, and Joe Sitt – amongst the close to 100,000 members of the community. The richest ones live in Brooklyn and Manhattan (in the spring and fall); Southern Florida (in winter); and Deal, New Jersey (in summer), which is an old town just North of Asbury Park that morphed into an upper class municipality once visited by Mark Twain.

The middle class lives year round in the Gravesend area of Brooklyn and spends part or all of the summer in Deal or its environs. By 1973, more than 100 families had bought property in the town, and by the 1990's, thousands of SYs were flocking to the area during the summers. In the mid-1990s, a synagogue was built on Main Street in Deal causing friction between the Syrian Jews and other townspeople. Now kosher restaurants and grocery stores line the main thoroughfare. Today, there are many synagogues and yeshivas to serve the Sephardic population in Deal and its environs.

SY's have become fully entrenched in the American story, though, as a group, have resisted full assimilation and cling to the orthodoxy of the Jewish religion. SYs are staunch supporters of Israel, the Jewish homeland. Early on, education was not a priority for SYs; earning money was.

My schooling began in the first grade because my parents forgot to enroll me in kindergarten. During class, I would doodle by drawing a grid and entering numbers in a proper sequential direction as if that would put some order in my life. Learning to read and write was a joyful experience. By third grade, reading became a passion for me. It started with comic books, *Tarzan of the Apes; Captain Marvel* and his evil nemesis, *Dr. Sivana; Superman,* and any other hand me down magazine I could lay my hands on.

Third grade was wonderful. It's where I met Sammy Levy, who became my lifelong best friend. At eight years old, notwithstanding the dysfunctionality at home, the whole world was waiting for me. That was until two traumatic events occurred in the winter of 1949.

4

CARD GAMES & KADEESH

After school, I would often come home to find my mother sitting at the kitchen table playing penny poker with a crew of her friends. While some SY's began faring well in the postwar economy, many families were still poor in the late 1940's, only a few years after the annihilation of Hitler and Tojo. The card games helped the mothers escape the reality of feeling underprivileged.

On a bad day, one or two of the ladies might lose thirty-five or forty cents. However, it was an unwritten rule that the winners would chip in to reimburse the losers for half their losses. Of course, before the winners would return any money, there were long, somber, interrogations on how much the losers came into the game with; how many dimes, nickels, and pennies they had taken out of their worn, cotton, change purses. Woe to any player who claimed a greater loss than they had experienced. The errant woman would be banned from any future games until she finally admitted her untruthfulness. Then all would be forgiven, and she would be permitted to return to the tables.

The games went on rain or shine, snow or sleet, Mondays through Thursdays. Fridays were out because these fine religious Syrian Orthodox Jewish mothers had to prepare the *Shabbat* dinner, the one meal during the week our family ate together. Saturday afternoons, it was leftovers re-heated on a stove flame that Mom left on overnight because of the *Shabbat* prohibition of starting a new fire. Saturday nights, after *Havdalah*, the Jewish ceremony that ushers in the new week, Jakey would go the kosher deli on 68th Street and buy cold cuts and rye bread. Every Sunday morning, Esther would go to the bakery across from the deli and return with jelly donuts, Danish and black and white cookies for breakfast. These were expensive meals, but it saved Mom from cooking.

One bitterly cold winter afternoon, a week before my eighth birthday, I came home from school and immediately noticed an abnormal look on my mother's face. She was pale as a ghost, a Pall Mall cigarette glued to the corner of her mouth. Suddenly, she let out a short breath and fainted. One of her friends, a young widow named Becky Shrem, quickly caught Mom before her head hit the table. Becky pulled the cigarette away and shouted to me in Syrian, "Bring water."

My knowledge of the Syrian language was limited, but I understood the word for water. I rushed to the sink, filled a glass, and handed it to Becky. She quickly splashed it on my mother's face. Mom did not stir, and Becky rolled off a few more words in Syrian, none of which I understood except when she said the word "*Am-boo-lance*" in broken English.

Another woman, named Molly, dialed "O" on the telephone and shouted, in a thick accent, "*Am-boo-lance!*" Molly then handed me the phone, nudging me to talk into it. I gave the operator the address of our home and quickly hung up. By then, Becky and two other women had helped place my mother on the floor. She was still out.

I stood there staring at this bizarre scene, this group of women bawling and yelling in Syrian. "*Oolie; Oolie Alena!*" Mollie kept shouting, another Syrian word I recognized because many SYs used it when something terrible was happening, and, in those days, something terrible was always happening. Frozen with fear, I was clueless as to what was going on as the women scurried around Mom, slapping her face, rubbing her hands, all to no avail.

By the time the ambulance arrived, my mother was dead. "Heart attack," I heard one of the male nurses tell Becky. "What's a heart attack?" I asked, but was quieted by Molly. The attendants put Mom on a stretcher and carried her out of the house, her body covered with a clean white sheet

And that was it. My mother, Fortune Dweck, at forty-six years old, was dead. I wasn't even sure what '*dead*' meant. Was Mom sick? Would she have to stay in a hospital until she got better and came home? It wasn't until that night when my brother Jakey explained that Mom would not be coming home ever again that some sense of the finality of this event kicked in. I prayed it was not true, but this was my introduction to the concept of death.

The funeral was a disconsolate affair, held in the Magen David Synagogue on 67th Street, opposite my school, P.S. 205. The "Big Shul," they called it; a brick building built in the 1920's where all the adult SYs would pray on Shabbat and the High Holy Days. The *Talmud Torah* built adjacent to the *shul* could service up to three hundred boys, and in the basement of that building, a *Mikva*, the ritual baths for women, was installed. In a few years, my friends and I would sneak a peek at the SY ladies taking their ceremonial bath.

The SYs are a tightly knit community, and all feel the loss of any one member. Pop was bereft by Mom's death; it was the first time I saw him cry. He loved my mother; that was well known, and everyone wondered how he could go on without her. A man named Jack Arama, a nearsighted Moroccan holy man, conducted the funeral. His job in the community was thankless, and he was seldom invited to people's homes on a social level because of fear he would bring along bad tidings to their household.

There were lots of prayers and the Chief Rabbi of the community, Jacob Kassin, said some very nice words about Fortune Dweck — a woman he barely knew — how she was a devoted wife and mother, an upstanding Jew who upheld the laws of the Torah. What he omitted was that Mom was charitable to a fault. She would give away what little money she had to any charity that asked. Once, I saw what looked like dozens of letters from charitable organizations in a drawer in her bedroom, all pleading for her donations. Mom believed that giving to charity would save her from dying. She got short changed on that one.

I watched as my father and older brothers, Jakey and Michael stood beside the coffin and joined in saying an ominous sounding prayer which I later learned was called *Kadeesh*, sometimes known as the Prayer for the Dead.

Funny, the things you learn as you get older and are exposed to knowledge. The so-called "Prayer for the Dead" has nothing to do with death or dying. It is an Aramaic verse that praises the God Jehovah. Jewish men are obligated to say it during morning, afternoon and evening prayer services for eleven months when mourning the loss of a parent. A Rabbi once explained that a person who loses a loved one might become angry with *Hashem* (a word that literally means 'The Name' and is used by SYs when speaking of the Lord), and, in anguish, might even curse God for their loss. So, the mourners are required to recite *Kadeesh* so as to prevent them from committing blasphemy.

When the eulogies and services were over my mother's casket was carried out to a waiting hearse. More prayers were said as they rolled the pine box into the long Cadillac, and the chauffeur slammed the door shut. The driver drove the vehicle slowly up the street while the crowd of sympathizers and mourners walked listlessly behind, chanting even more prayers. Finally, several men got into their cars and followed the hearse to the Syrian burial grounds in Staten Island.

In those days, females were not permitted to go to the cemetery, so my sisters, Esther and Marilyn took me and Al home and fed us as we awaited the return of my father and two older brothers from the burial. I had not cried throughout the entire service, but as soon as I entered the house and saw the empty kitchen table, tears flooded my eyes. Momma was gone, and she was not coming back. Esther held me tightly and comforted me as I sobbed uncontrollably.

The Syrian Jewish orthodox laws of mourning are extensive. When a parent dies, the children must mourn in three stages. First, by sitting *Shiva* for seven days, days in which the bereaved may not go to work, drive a car, or bathe. Men cannot shave, and sex is not permitted, but other forms of intimacy and affection are allowed. All mirrors in the home are covered, and upon the return from the burial services, the surviving spouse and all of the deceased person's children have their shirt or blouse torn by a rabbi as they each recite the prayer ending with the words *Dayan ha emet*, referring to Hashem as being the 'true judge'.

The family then sits on the floor, cushioned by pillows, and is usually given a hard boiled egg and pita bread, the "meal of condolence," so they may say a prayer over the food. During these three mourning periods, all prayers are believed to help elevate the deceased closer to *Olam Ha Ba*, otherwise known as "the world to come." Soon after these initial rituals, a steady flow of guests arrives to offer condolences. Daily prayer services are held in the home of the deceased, and members of the community come to participate.

For the mourners, nothing pleasurable is permissible, including the study of Torah. The only book permitted to be read is the *Book of Job* because it is a tale of woe and sorrow. *Shiva* is not permitted on the Sabbath when family members attend the synagogue for prayers.

The second stage is thirty days. Bathing is allowed, but shaving and cutting of hair are prohibited. After the first seven days, intercourse with a spouse is permitted. Mourners may return to work, but must continue to say the Kadeesh at daily prayers that have a *minyan*, a quorum of at least ten males thirteen years of age or older. Entertainment of any kind is forbidden. The surviving spouse's mourning obligations end when the thirty days have passed, and may even re-marry on the 31st day.

The third stage for the children is eleven months, during which time life pretty much returns to normal, except parties or celebrations from which the mourners are still restricted and the recital of Kadeesh continues. I learned all these laws when Pop died. By then, I was a grown adult, married, with two children, but at eight years old I was exempt from all the rules.

As tragic as my mom's death was (an event I could barely understand), it would be overshadowed by what would happen just one week later; an incident that would alter my life forever, though I was unaware of that at the time it happened.

5

A COLORFUL ROBE

My father was a religious man, not fanatically so, but he kept the Sabbath and all holidays, ate only kosher food, and prayed three times a day, sometimes with a *minyan*. As a kid preparing to go to school in the morning, I watched as Pop put on his phylacteries and prayer shawl, and then say the prayers silently. I could see his lips mouthing the words. Whenever he left or entered the house he would kiss the Mezuzah.

Pop worked hard, came home from work tired, and the first thing he would do, when sitting at the table waiting for my mother to serve him his meal, was to play a little game with Al and me. "Who will get me a cold, cold glass of water?" He'd ask out loud. "Albert? Good boy; Daniel? Bad boy." My brother and I would stand behind Pop awaiting his choice, even though we knew that one night it would be Al and the next, me. Still, we always felt the tension in the moment before he called out the lucky water bearer's name.

Pop was a quiet person, but when he did speak it was with conviction, no matter the subject being discussed. He related biblical stories about Abraham, Isaac and Jacob, the sacred fathers of Judaism. I found the story of Joseph and his brethren most fascinating – and scary.

Joseph was born when Jacob was in his later years, and his brothers were jealous of him because their father had given Joseph a colorful robe to show that he was his favorite son. One day, while they were all tending to their flock, Joseph's brothers, out of jealously, plotted to kill him. Reuben, the eldest, tried to protect Joseph, suggesting they put him in a dry well and let the wild animals kill him. Reuben planned to come back and rescue his sibling. So, the brothers pulled off the fancy robe and threw Joseph into a dry well to die.

While Reuben tended to the flock, another son of Jacob, Judah, saw a caravan heading for Egypt and convinced his brothers that they not kill Joseph, but sell him to the caravan. They sold Joseph to the Midianites for twenty pieces of silver.

When Reuben returned to the well to rescue Joseph, the boy was gone. Reuben tore his clothes in mourning. "The boy is gone!" he cried. "What am I going to do?"

Joseph's brothers killed a goat and dipped Joseph's fancy robe in its blood. They took the robe and showed it to their father and said, "We found this. Look at it carefully, and see if it belongs to your son."

Jacob knew the coat belonged to Joseph. "It is my son's coat! He has been torn to pieces and eaten by some wild animal."

Jacob mourned for Joseph a long time, and to show his sorrow he tore his clothes and wore sackcloth. He was inconsolable despite the attempts of all his children to comfort him. "I will go to my grave mourning for my son," he said. So Jacob kept on grieving.

My father told me this part of the story when I was nine, and it scared the hell out of me. After all, I was Pop's youngest son and fancied he thought of me as his favorite. I didn't learn the rest of Joseph's story until I was eleven. About how Joseph went on to interpret the dreams of the Egyptian Pharaoh and became a member of his court. And how he got his brothers to bring their father, Jacob, to Egypt, and in the end all was forgiven.

The sibling rivalry between my brothers and me was rampant in our house with no one to keep us kids in check. Jakie and Michael were always fighting and/or arguing over nonsense. Al picked on me, constantly teasing and pulling annoying pranks. Esther did her best to instill a sense of family, but after Mom died each of us vied for the attention of our father, who mostly favored me, his youngest child. To this day, I wonder whether my brothers were jealous of my successes and whether they held me in contempt for becoming a renegade of the SY community.

6

A WELCOME FART

Trump's rhetoric was mind-boggling. He says one thing one day and then denies having said it the next. He has lied, according to reliable fact checkers, 67% of the time. He has shown ignorance of foreign affairs and no clue about the Constitution. He is completely ignorant of the process of governing yet he will be the 45th President of the United States of America. My friend Sammy voted for him and we had many arguments about Trump and Hillary. Today, however, I would avoid any discussion of politics when I visited him in the hospital.

"Sammy," I shouted into my iPhone. "How the hell are you, pal?"

His response was long in coming, and when Sammy finally did speak, his voice was weak and raspy, "Dying, is how I am, you idiot."

"Bullshit," I answered. "You're just using that as an excuse to screw the nurses."

"Yeah, jackass, they're all over me. Are you coming today?"

"Wouldn't miss it for the world, pal. Can I bring you something?"

"Yeah. How about a cure for lung cancer?" He barely finished that sentence and coughed for a full minute. "I need a big favor, Danny," he said catching his breath.

I waited until he was calm again before saying, "See you at noon."

My best friend, Sammy Levy, whom I have known since third grade, sixty-seven years ago (my God, the passage of time is mind boggling), will be dead in no more than a month or two. How I pleaded with him to stop smoking, as I did thirty-two years ago. He insisted the "rumor" that cigarettes caused cancer was a government conspiracy to control people. Even after they discovered his malignancy, Sammy continued to smoke. "Doesn't matter anymore," he would say, mordantly.

Sammy was a lot smarter than me in school. He got A's in everything while I struggled to get a passing grade, not because I wasn't smart, but rather because it was difficult for me to sit still in class. Teachers loved Sammy. He was always polite, did all his homework, and even volunteered to run errands for the teaching staff. Me? I was a troublemaker, always cutting up in class, seldom submitting my homework on time. More than once my brother, Jakey, had to come and get me from the principal's office.

I made the short walk from my apartment to the Sloan Kettering on 64th. As I entered his hospital room, Sammy was being turned over by a nurse to get his ass wiped. He heard me come in, raised his head, and let out a resounding fart that made the plump nurse jump back a step.

"Nice welcome for your guest," she offered.

"He deserves the best. Danny, it's good to see you."

The nurse finished her duty and rolled him back. She covered Sammy then adjusted the bed upwards. "What'd you' bring me?" he asked with mild anticipation.

"Feast on these," I answered, handing him a package of chocolate chip cookies. He ripped the bag open and grabbed a handful. "Help yourself," Sammy said, as he tossed the cookies back at me. He shoved two of them whole into his mouth and chomped away. "It's great that no one tells me what to eat. Everyone knows it's the end."

"Stop that," I countered. "You need to have a more positive attitude."

"I do. One sorry thing is I won't be around when Trump's inaugurated."

"You gonna' start that again?"

"Your girlfriend, Hillary, never had a chance, Danny boy. No better con man on the planet than Donald, but he's still my guy. Look at all the money you're going to save when he slashes taxes."

He grabbed the bag back and stuffed two more cookies in his mouth, and then his face turned sullen. "Fuck politics." He put the bag down and chewed rapidly as if his end were seconds away. "Listen to me," he said almost in a whisper. "I need you to do something. No one knows what I'm about to tell you, but you're my best friend, and I trust you more than my brothers." He waved for me to move closer. "I have two million in *nedi* in a Swiss Bank."

That came as a surprise to me that he still had that much money since everyone thought he was broke after he filed bankruptcy seven months ago. "Which bank?"

"The one we all used. Danny, you gotta' swear to me, on my dying bed, you'll do what I ask."

I pulled a chair closer to the bed and leaned in. "What are you asking?"

"You need to go to Geneva, get the *flooce*, and give each of my three kids half a million. The rest goes to Martha."

Martha was the Latina woman Sammy was spending time with after his wife, Sarah, died three years ago. In truth, he started sleeping with Martha during the two years Sarah was sick.

"Promise me." he pleaded, as he reached into the drawer of the nightstand, removed a small piece of paper and handed it to me. "There's the account number and pass code."

I studied the paper for a moment and then looked up at him. "How the hell did you pull this one off?"

"Don't ask; a lot of creative bookkeeping regarding invoices and skimming the cash. It took me two years. Never thought it would lead to going *BK*, but here we are. All that cash in a Swiss bank and me about to kick off." He grabbed my shirt and pulled me in close. "Swear to me, Danny. Swear you'll take care of this."

I pulled back slowly and stood. "Don't be a *schmuck*. You know I'll do it. You're my *buckee*; my best friend," and as I said the word friend, tears gushed from my eyes. I turned away for him not to see, but he joined me in crying; then, just as suddenly, we both laughed out loud.

"Look at us," I said, wiping the tears. "If we cried like this in the school-yard when we were kids, we would have had the shit kicked out of us."

"Remember the time we were at Coney Island and we each had a dime for the subway home?"

"Do I!"

"How old were we," he asked. "Twelve? On our way to the train, we passed that freak show with that guy, what's his name, the half man and half woman?"

"Albert, Alberta," I recalled. "Ten cents to get in. Every one of us, except Eddie, said we had to see who this weird person was. So we decided to walk home and paid the dime to get in."

"Looking back," Sammy said, "it was like a mild porno show. Remember how the guy, or whatever he was, looked around to see if there were any cops then showed one breast like a man and the other as a woman's?" We both laughed.

"Then he offered to sell us postcards showing his one female teat," I added, and we both laughed.

"What happened after that was a pisser."

On our walk home along Cropsey Avenue, we passed a large golf-driving field. There was a hole in the fence, so we all went in and began collecting golf balls and stuffing them in our shirts. What we would do with them, we had no idea. Suddenly a jeep comes barreling towards us with a bearded guy standing in the passenger's seat pointing a shotgun at us and yelling, "Stop in your tracks, or I shoot." We thought the guy was crazy enough to do that, so we raised our hands, our shirts bursting with golf balls.

The guy held us there while his friend went to the office to call the cops, who then took us to the station house. One of our Italian friends that were with us, Kenny Traventino, called his father, a lawyer, who came to the station house with a case of Scotch, and we were all sent home.

We both laughed again at the story, until Sammy turned serious. "It's over for us, kid," he said "But we had a nice run, eh? Sixty-seven years of friendship. How many people can say that?"

I smiled at him, and then said, "Yeah, we did have a great run."

On my walk home, I thought about what Sammy had asked me to do. I would be committing an illegal act by sneaking the money back into the country, and I was uncomfortable with that. But how could I refuse the request of my dying best friend? Getting a cashier's check from the bank in Switzerland would not be the problem. The danger would be bringing it back to the U.S. without declaring it and not getting caught by customs. This was not a plausible solution. I contemplated an alternative plan to get the money to his kids and to Martha and finally settled on an idea.

7

MR. PEABODY & THE MERMAID

The first seven days of mourning for my mother went so slow it felt like seven years. When you're eight years old, time crawls by at the same pace as your horse running last in a race. When you get older, as my sister Esther often told me, the passage of time is faster than the speed of light.

It was the last day of that first period of bereavement, a Wednesday, as I remember, when they held the *Arayat*, which consists of a group of men sitting around a table to read *Teheleem*, the Book of Psalms, after which the male mourners recite Kadeesh. Mom's friends, Becky and Molly, were at the house serving the men nuts, dried apricots, cookies, and cold drinks. I sat fidgeting in a chair, bored out of my head.

Becky came to me and smiled. "You not happy *Rohi*," she said softly in her thick accent, and handed me a quarter. "Here. Go to movie."

"Who with?" I asked.

"You' 'self. You' big boy now." My eighth birthday had just passed, and I *was* feeling big about myself. I took the quarter, kissed her hand, a sign of re-spect for our elders taught to all kids when very young, put on a coat and walked out of the house. No one noticed me leaving.

It was still light out as I walked the three blocks to the Metro Theatre, an old vaudeville venue on 20th Avenue and 64th Street the owners had converted into a movie house. On special occasions, the Metro ran Egyptian films for the SYs who loved the overly dramatic scenarios and the Middle Eastern music. Mostly, the house played second run films, and that day "Mister Peabody and the Mermaid," with Ann Blyth and William Powell, was being featured. I paid the fifteen cents admission and walked in. No one asked my age or why I was alone.

An elderly woman stood behind the candy counter. "Can I help you, sonny?" That's what older people called us boys, "sonny." Girls, they called "girlee." I didn't answer, but stared at the selection of treats in the glass case for a moment. It was a critical decision for me: two candy bars at a nickel each or a bag of popcorn for a dime. I opted for the Baby Ruth and Peanut Chews, wishing I had the additional money to buy the popcorn and a Coca Cola.

The theatre was sparsely populated with less than a dozen people scattered in different rows. A burly man sitting on the opposite isle seat of my row looked at me and smiled, then turned his attention to the screen which was just coming alive. A newsreel came on first, showing a plane flying over the destroyed city of Berlin, the Nazi capital, which stunned the hell out of me. I was terrified by the sight of young boys and girls strolling the bombed out streets while adults cleared the rubble from the destroyed buildings. An endless flow of cartoons followed, mostly with Bugs Bunny, who I loved. Finally, the main feature began, just as I felt the need to pee.

I had finished the Baby Ruth and was saving the Peanut Chews for later, then got up and walked to the bathroom, not noticing that the man at the end of my row got up too. It was just a few steps from the rear of the theatre to the rest room, and when I entered, it was empty. I stood close to the urinal and peed, but it wasn't until I nearly finished that I noticed the man from my row standing next to me.

"Hey kid," he said in a friendly voice. "How'd you like them cartoons? Funny, right?"

I smiled and nodded my head.

He had very curly hair and bushy eyebrows that moved up and down as he spoke. "Say, how'd you like to make a quarter?"

The bag of popcorn and the Coca Cola suddenly appeared before me. "How?" I asked.

"Easy. We sit next to each other and enjoy the movie together." He approached me as I zipped up my pants and put his hand on my shoulder. "Okay? We'll have some fun."

"Can I have the quarter now?" I said wisely, after all, I was a smart eight year old.

"Sure, sure, kid." He reached into his pocket and pulled out a coin.

"I want to buy popcorn and a soda. Will that be all right?"

"Yeah, Go ahead and meet me at the seat." He walked out first, and I followed, heading straight for the refreshment stand.

While walking to my row, I was careful not to spill the soft drink or the popcorn. The man was sitting in the middle seat and beckoned me to sit next to him. I noticed his pants zipper was open and something quite long seemed to be standing at attention. "What's that?" I asked.

"It's my *thing*," he responded. He reached over, took the soda from me and put it on the floor in front of the seat. As I sat, he grabbed my hand and put it on his *thing*, jerking it rapidly. "What are you doing?" I asked, not frightened, just curious.

"I have a problem with this *thing*. It's too big and doesn't fit in my pants. You have to help me make it small again."

"How?"

"Shhh," he whispered. "I'll teach you."

After a short period of his jerking his *thing* with my hand, I saw white stuff spurting upwards, some of which landed on my arm; sure enough, the *thing* became smaller. He wiped himself with a napkin and cleaned my arm as well before putting the *thing* back into his pants. He stood, turned towards the opposite end of the aisle, and walked away. I had no clue about what had just happened, thinking only of the soda and popcorn, and what a great deal I had made. That was the first transaction in my long business career, but one experience I never shared with anyone until many years later.

8

EDDIE FISHER

My brother Michael was five years older than me and my hero. He was an independent soul and a brilliant kid who knew everything about everything. He loved books on any subject: novels, biographies, politics, and history, despite his rabbis' admonitions against reading the secular material. He taught me how to play *Ringo Levio*, a game where kids chased each other around the block trying to tag each other. I also learned triangle, a ball game with three bases instead of four and played in the gutter that was constantly interrupted by passing autos. Kids were always playing stickball in the streets, and on weekends, there was a softball game going on in the schoolyard with large bets placed. In the playground, serious handball tournaments were played. Again with big money involved.

One Sunday morning, when I was six years old, the local handyman picked me up and was carrying me towards the subway station. His name was Lavon, a tall, black man with bright green eyes and only one tooth in his mouth. Apparently, he had been drinking because he reeked of alcohol. When Lavon passed Michael, who was involved in a stickball game, my brother said, "Hey, *ahbud*, what are you doing?"

"I'm takin' the kid to Coney Island, to bury his head in the sand."

Michael, who was eleven at the time, did not hesitate one second before punching Lavon squarely in the face. The man dropped me and fell to the ground. "Stay away from my kid brother!" Lavon laid there, drops of blood seeping from his nose. I felt bad for him, even though he had been planning my murder.

Michael was a student of the Torah having gone to a yeshiva until his Bar Mitzvah. He truly believed in and observed all the laws given by Hashem. That was until he was fifteen when he began reading accounts about the Holocaust. Those stories shook Michael's profound belief that God was this omniscient being who protected the world from harm. The tales of the survivors led him to read books relating the horrors the Nazi regime perpetrated against Jews and other minorities, and he began to wonder why *Hashem* had not interceded in the destruction of six million of His people. How had He allowed the evil Hitler to nearly bring about the ruination of the world at the cost of tens of millions of lives, and the suffering of many millions more?

My brother sought answers to these questions by re-reading the *Talmud*, the *Gemaras*, commentaries on the Torah, and the *Nevi'im*, which are the books of the prophets, as well as the works of Jewish philosophers, but he could find no satisfactory explanations. Once, Michael told me, he asked his rabbi a question that got him a reprimand.

"Rabbi," he inquired, "is there anything your son would do that you would personally kill him for?"

The Rabbi pondered the question for a moment, and then reluctantly answered, "No."

"Then how could *Hashem* allow the killing of *His* children?" His rabbi grew irritated and advised Michael never to bring up this subject again.

So Michael went to another rabbi and posed the same question. The second rabbi responded with an answer that shook my brother to his core. "The Holocaust occurred because the Jews had turned away from Hashem." Michael couldn't believe what he had just heard: the victims of Hitler's master race were to blame for what had been done to them.

"What you say is sick, rabbi. All that was needed was for the finger of God to be pointed at the death camps, and poof! God's awesome power would have destroyed them. All those lives, those *children*, would have been saved."

"Hashem works in mysterious ways, Michael. We cannot grasp his master plan."

"Well, here's *my* master plan, rabbi. You won't see me in *shul* again."

So, my brother turned to even more secular readings, including Karl Marx's "Communist Manifesto" and came to agree that, indeed, "religion was the opiate of the masses." His faith had diminished until he abandoned religion completely. Pop was not too thrilled that Michael no longer went to the synagogue on Saturdays and blew his top when he learned my brother was not keeping kosher and espousing ideas that were anathema to the SY community.

To Michael, all the Orthodox Jewish laws now seemed antiquated and obsolete. He came to believe the Jewish religion, as practiced by SYs, was unfair towards women, treating them as 'baby carriers' and 'cleaning women,' known as *khadamehs*, who, when their monthly menstrual period came, were considered "unclean." How they could be unclean, he wondered, if God created menstruation to prepare a woman for pregnancy? And how come men were allowed multiple wives, but women, only one husband?

His rabbis had taught him there was not one superfluous word in the Five Books of Moses, yet there was no mention of the world being round. Surely, when God wrote the Books he could see that in the future slavery would be abolished, so does that now make the laws of bondage unnecessary? My brother's questions had planted a seed of doubt about my own faith that would plague me throughout my life. Observing my brother Michael up close was a valuable lesson since he taught me how to think.

Michael loved the movies. Most Sunday afternoons he would take me with him to either the Metro to see an old one or to the Marboro Theatre, on Bay Parkway and 69th Street, to see one of the latest releases. Once, in 1953, when I was twelve, he even took me on the subway to Manhattan to see Eddie Fisher. Eddie had just gotten out of the army and was performing at the New York Paramount with Hugo Winterhalter and his orchestra. Can't remember the movie, but watching my brother become mesmerized by Fisher's voice was something I would never forget.

When we left the theatre, we went to the Horn and Hardart automat on Broadway, a place where you put coins into a slot and got your food. At that time, I was kosher, so I ate spaghetti, mashed potato, and creamed spinach. Michael, free of the laws of *kashrut*, had turkey with stuffing and a sweet potato. This meal was the big time for me: lunch in a restaurant.

We talked more about Eddie Fisher than the movie, and Michael declared, "You know what Danny? One day I'm gonna' be a big star. Go to Hollywood, make movies, and become famous. What do you think?"

"Why not? You're smart, very handsome, and you know how to sing."

"Yeah, but I need to study acting. Maybe join a summer stock group."

By the time Michael started college he had become an atheist, but none of this detracted him from his passion for being in show business. He had a great singing voice, somewhat in the tone and style of Eddie Fisher, who was his idol. He managed to get an audition on the Ted Mack Amateur Hour and won the first night out, singing Fisher's big hit, "Lady of Spain." The second week he was beaten by a group of young, white, rock and roll singers from Brooklyn.

College did not last long for Michael. At the end of the first semester, he quit and enrolled in an acting class at the New School and another class at NYU to learn about filmmaking. During this time he met a strong willed woman named Nancy Moen, and they fell in love. They moved into a small walk-up apartment together in the West Village, which only infuriated my father more since Nancy was not Jewish, and they were living in "sin." My father insisted his children never mention Michael's name again. But we did.

That summer, Michael and Nancy joined a summer-stock theatre group in New Hampshire and invited me to go with them. It was at this time when I began smoking cigarettes and saw myself as a grownup. We lived in a trailer which, while being crowded, was something I had become used to after having shared a bed with two of my brothers. To this day, even though I own a king size bed, I sleep near the edge.

My first chore when we arrived at the theatre was to mow the lawn of the huge field surrounding it. My salary was ten bucks a week, but this task alone, which took three days using a hand mower, was worth at least a hundred. My main responsibility was to sell cold drinks out of a tub filled with ice during the intermission of the evening shows, which that week was "Finnian's Rainbow," starring Gloria Vanderbilt. She was a real beauty; very nice and polite to me in those few moments we made contact.

Selling soda brought in fifteen or twenty dollars each night, but I only turned in 75% of the gross to make up for what was an unfair wage

After three weeks I grew completely bored out of my head. Michael sensed I wanted to leave and it was clear he was disappointed in me.

"Why are you quitting?"

"It's boring and I'm being underpaid."

"It's not a good habit, quitting."

I thought a moment, then countered, "Are you saying I should put up with an unpleasant situation so I won't be called a 'quitter?'"

"No," Michael said. "I'm saying when you make a commitment you need to abide by it, whether or not you like it. You give your word, you keep it."

On the eight hour bus ride back to New York City, what resonated with me from Michael's words was the idea that once you gave your word to someone, you had to keep it. Although this was the first time in my life I went against my brother's wishes, his message was not lost to me.

I took the Sea Beach subway to Brooklyn and by the time I arrived home it was nearly ten p.m. As hectic as things were in my house, it was good to be back in the neighborhood. But the short time away from home was an important learning experience for me. It showed me I could handle my own life by making my own decisions.

9

CHANEL

Three days after Sammy asked me for the favor I booked a first class seat on Delta to Geneva, using one hundred twenty thousand Amex points, leaving me with more than two million (I charge everything, personal or business, with the Amex Black Card). Immediately after passing through Swiss customs, a taxi carried me to the bank where I, and at least a dozen other SYs, held an account, so the manager, Mr. Arner, knew who I was.

"I wish to close this account," I said, handing him the paper with the account information.

"Sorry to hear that, Mr. Dweck. How shall we handle the withdrawal?"

"I would like you to wire the money to the American Cancer Society as a donation in honor of my friend, Mr. Samuel Levy."

"Of course," the banker said. "That is most generous of you."

After signing a few documents, the bank arranged for the wire transfer, and then closed the account.

There would be a four hour wait for my return flight, so I headed for the First Class lounge, and sat in a far corner of the room hoping to catch a few z's. Just as my lids closed a middle-aged woman stood before me and said, "Of all the seats in this place you had to pick mine?"

I opened my eyes and saw this rather attractive lady, in her late forties or early fifties, dressed to the nines in Chanel and wearing an eighteen karat rose gold Cartier watch on her left hand and an intense yellow diamond bracelet on her right. Her hair was cut short, and her eyes were bright blue with just a slight twinkle in them. "Sorry?" I said, shaking off the grogginess.

"That's my bag next to the seat. I just went for some coffee."

"Oh, I didn't…"

"That's okay," she said in a soft voice. "Stay. I'll just scoot over here." She stepped over my carry-on bag and sat perpendicular to me. "Heading for New York?"

I nodded.

"The four o'clock plane?"

I nodded again.

"Me, too. My name's Claudia Gemal. You look familiar. Do I know you?"

"I dunno," I answered, but hearing her name led me to ask the next question. "You're SY?"

Her eyes brightened. "Why, yes. You?"

I nodded once more. "Danny Dweck."

"Danny Dweck? Marilyn's your sister?"

"Yeah, I…"

"She's my Aunt Sylvia's best friend. What a coincidence to meet another SY here in Geneva, and on the same flight, no less. Here on business?" I nodded, and she continued. "I just finished with the banks myself. You see, my husband, Manny, passed away four months ago, pancreatic cancer."

"I remember hearing about it." The death of any SY spreads quickly throughout the community within hours.

"*Hazeet*, he suffered, but, *Baruch Hashem*, he went quickly; but not before preparing my kids and me for his end. He and his lawyers wrote down everything to do; like clockwork. What a *haborb*. Did you know him?"

"Casually," I lied.

"Ah," she said as she took a sip from her coffee. "SYs all know each other." She took another sip. "Danny Dweck," she murmured, as though she were thinking out loud. "You were involved with the Suttons, no?" And without waiting for my answer she went on. "Yes, Jackie Sutton, right?"

"We split up two years ago."

"Nice fellow, Jackie," she said. Claudia finished her coffee and set the empty cup down on the small table beside her. "I'm hyper from all this coffee," she continued. "Are you in first class?"

I nodded, which was the easiest way to respond.

"On the flight here two days ago, there was an ahbud sitting next to me all the way from Paris."

"You had a *slave* sitting next to you*?*"

She looked at me quizzically.

"You know the word *ahbud* is Hebrew for a slave," I explained.

She was genuinely surprised. "No, I didn't. Always thought it meant '*black*.'"

"Many SYs think that way. Now that you know, don't you think you should stop using that word?"

She pondered that a moment. "I will do my best not use the word anymore," she said, and my esteem for her rose a bit.

"What were you doing in Paris? It's a dangerous place these days."

"*Lu-uv* Paris! Never mind all the craziness. One has to shop, no matter what's going on there. But here I go blabbing again." My eyelids were getting heavier by the moment, and I was afraid I'd doze off while she was still talking. "*Any-hoo*," she said finally, "I'll let you rest."

"See you on the plane," I said, sinking into my seat and falling right to sleep.

The flight home seemed to last forever; they always do when flying east to west. We left on time, and to my good fortune, Claudia was sitting two rows behind me, so there was minimal conversation between us. She did come by after dinner was served and chatted about this and that, none of which registered in my brain. When she went back to her seat, I conked out, but awoke quickly moments later, thinking about Sammy. I could not fall asleep again and watched movies or read magazines. I actually wished Claudia was talking to me, but she was out cold for the rest of the ride to JFK.

So I closed my eyes again, thinking about my best friend and my thoughts went back to a card game he and I were in with a few other fellas from the park; we were about fifteen years old. The game was a version of Texas Hold 'Em except that it had two columns instead of one. My two hidden down cards were a pair of fives. I bet five dollars and two people called. Sammy folded.

The flop showed two fives in column one and one six in column two, which gave me four fives. I slow played them and bet ten dollars. The same two people called. When the next card didn't change anything I pushed "all in," about ninety dollars. Player two goes out and the dealer calls. The river cards flop and the final first board doesn't change, but now there are two sixes in the second column. I turn over my pocket fives, showing my quads. The dealer smiles, hesitates for just a moment, and then turns over his hole cards:

two sixes, giving him four sixes! As he reached for the pot money, Sammy grabbed his arm. "I saw what you did," he said calmly.

"Did what?" the dealer said, raking in the cash.

"You stacked the deck."

"You're crazy."

"You set it up for Danny to get the four fives and for you to get the four sixes. I saw you." Danny pulled the dealer's hand away from the money. "My friend wins the pot."

"Says who?"

"Says me!" And with that Sammy rockets a jab to the guy's nose. "This is a friendly game. We don't like cheats. Don't come back."

The dealer put a soiled rag to his bloody nose and stood up. "I *will* be back, you bastard. You'll pay for this." Despite his threat, the guy never showed up in the park again.

When I awoke as we were landing there was a broad smile on my face in recalling Sammy looking out for me. That's how it always was; we looked out for each other.

I passed through immigration and customs quickly. Claudia had offered me a ride to the city, but I politely excused myself. I took an Uber and by the time I arrived home, it was nearly 7:00 p.m., New York time. At that moment, a text came in from Sammy. "Hey, pal, you back yet? Call me."

I speed dialed him, and he picked up at once. "Is it done?" he asked with a slight tremor in his voice.

"Done," I assured him, withholding the fact that the money was sent to the Cancer Society. "I'll call your kids tonight, but I'll need Martha's number."

"Check your texts in a minute. Look," he said softly, "don't call anybody just yet. Wait 'til…" I could hear the choking in his voice. "I can't thank you enough, Danny. This means the whole world to me."

"Forget it. I'll stop by in the morning."

"Goodbye, Pal, he said softly, and there was a morbid quality in his voice that frightened me.

I checked in with my daughter Tuni to see how she was and how the kids were doing. Everything was okay; same story with my sons. Good to hear this. I felt exhausted from this whirlwind trip, so it was a quick hot shower and a cheese sandwich for dinner. The TV in my bedroom lulled me to sleep instantly.

In the morning, I phoned my office to check in. Fran, my secretary for the past thirty-five years, assured me the ship was still afloat and reminded me there was a meeting scheduled with Citi Bank at three p.m. I stayed in bed a few minutes longer to grab some extra winks, then got up, showered and dressed. As usual, I stopped at the Juice Press store on the corner and picked up a banana smoothie.

It was a beautiful winter day in New York City, sunny, not too cold, with an unusually bright blue sky. I walked to the Sloan Kettering on 64th off 3rd. The lobby was busy, but I squeezed into an elevator and went to the third floor. When I got to Sammy's room, it was empty. I stopped a nurse and asked where he was, and she pointed me to the main desk.

A young woman was sitting at her station punching keys into her computer at such a rapid rate; I wondered how many mistakes she had made. I stood there silently a moment. "Excuse me, Ma'am. Can you tell me where Sammy Levy is?"

She stopped her typing and looked up. "Are you a family member?"

"I'm his best friend, Danny Dweck."

She searched her desk a moment, and found an envelope with my name on it. "This is for you, Mr. Dweck. It was lying next to him in his bed. We have notified the family, and I believe they are on the way."

My eyes did a quick spin. "Notified the family? What about?"

She stood up and walked around the counter to stand beside me. "I am so sorry Mr. Dweck, but Mr. Levy passed less than an hour ago."

"Passed? What the hell does that mean? He's dead?" My eyes began to roll again, and I felt a bit woozy. "I spoke to him just last night." My balance faltered, so I pressed against the counter top for support.

The nurse steadied me. "Would you care to sit, sir?"

"No!" I shouted. "I would care to see my friend, Sammy!" I was about to run back to his room when I noticed his two daughters and his son rushing towards us, their spouses not far behind.

Isaac, his eldest, ran up to me and stared straight into my eyes. They must have looked empty because the first thing he said was, "Uncle Danny, are you all right?"

I just shook my head and finally sat on a nearby bench. Isaac's wife, Laura, sat beside me and made an attempt to console me. "It's best for him, Uncle. No more suffering. He's in a better place."

What trite bullshit, I thought. My best friend is dead! There is no better place for him than with me! Did they even know who he was? His daughter Lynn burst into tears, and so did her sister Renee. I watched them cry, and without thinking, shouted "*Oolie! Oolie Alena!*"

I went home after spending the whole afternoon and night at Sammy's house with his family, devastated by the loss of my dear friend. It felt as though I was floating through some unknown cosmos, drifting aimlessly through a black-clouded sky. A warm shower soothed me a bit, and, when hanging up my clothes, I remembered the envelope the nurse had given me. I opened it and after reading the first line of the handwritten note, my eyes clouded with more tears that I thought they possessed.

> "My dear friend, Danny,
>
> My love for you is the greatest gift *Hashem* has sent me. All the years we spent together growing up, the stupid things we did as kids, the trips we made around the world with our wives, the sharing of celebrations, the comforting of one another during tragedies and losses of loved ones; the arguments we had over politics, all this I hopefully take with me to *Olam Ha Ba.*
>
> When you read this, my life will have ended. I hoarded a bunch of painkillers until there were enough to take at one time that would end this agony. I needed to know you had done that last great favor for me by going to Geneva, and I trust you completely to follow the rest of my instructions. Please forgive me for committing the cardinal sin of taking my life, but I pray *Hashem* will absolve me under these circumstances. I had to do this, Danny, to avoid any investigations about the money that would deprive me giving it to the people I love.
>
> For sure, we'll meet again in heaven, Pal, but hopefully not for many years.
>
> Your Buckie, Sammy"

I put the letter in my drawer and sat on the edge of my bed, processing the loss. There were no tears left by the time I finished reading his final note to me; they had already been spent. But I will miss this son of a bitch until the end of my life.

10

THE IRISH

Tommy O'Malley was a quiet, but tough, kid. He never started trouble, but when pushed he shoved back hard. He lifted weights and had a tight, strong, body for a twelve year old. He was tall, with dark golden hair, and a personality that was a bit subdued. He never made a sound when he laughed, usually covering his lips after hearing something funny.

Tommy was a member of the Irish community that mixed in with the SY's in the neighborhood. His father, Brian, was a printer and a nasty drinker. Brian always had a scowl on his face, and he never laughed. Every word out of his mouth blamed one group of people or another for the problems of the world. He beat his two sons ferociously for the slightest misbehavior and Tommy would often come to school or the schoolyard with bruises on his face or body.

I liked Tommy; envied his strength and toughness. He was a great handball player and played alone against me and my friend Eddie Mansour, one of my "Pack of Four" best friends. He ripped us apart, twenty-one to nine. That same Saturday morning a kid from another neighborhood, Sonny was his name, came around the P.S. 205 schoolyard and talked his way into a handball game with Tommy. Sonny was taller than Tommy and equally buff, but Tommy moved around the court faster.

Eddie and I were amazed at the grueling pace of the twenty-one point game, which Tommy won by three. Sonny was pissed and threw the ball on the low roof atop the handball court.

"Why'd you do that?" Tommy asked. "We need the ball for the next game."

"Go get it then," Sonny made the mistake of saying.

"No," Tommy answered. "You threw it, you get it."

"Fuck you!"

"You can say 'fuck you' all you want," Tommy said calmly, "but you have to get that ball."

Eddie looked at me with a half grin on his face anticipating the fight that was about to come. Sonny brushed Tommy aside and turned towards the gate.

"You ain't leaving 'till you climb that roof," Tommy insisted.

"Who's gonna' make me?"

And without another word, Tommy lifted Sonny over his head and threw him to the ground. He sat on top of the kid and pounded his face with six quick blows. He got off Sonny and without losing a breath, asked, "Who's gonna' get the ball?"

Sonny arose slowly, made his way to the drainpipe running alongside the building and shimmied up to the low roof. He disappeared from view for a moment, and then let loose a torrent of Spalding rubber balls he had found up there. Everyone laughed at the sight.

When Sonny came down, Tommy handed him a bunch of the balls to take away with him. "I enjoyed the game, Sonny. Come by again for a rematch"

Sonny backed away slowly and left the schoolyard. I was in awe at the strength and power of Tommy, all while he still remained calm.

"How'd you do that?" Eddie asked.

"Wasn't anything. He just had to get the ball. That's all."

Just then, Tommy's father, Brian, entered the schoolyard and approached his son menacingly. "I told you to clean out the garage before you left," he shouted at him.

"I did, Dad."

"You left all the shit near the backyard." He gave Tommy a swat on the back of his head. "Get the fuck home and finish the job."

Tommy's face turned red from embarrassment. His jaw tightened and I was afraid he might punch his father the way he did that kid, Sonny. Instead, he sulked away and left.

Brian turned towards me and scowled, "Hey, *kike*, pick up those balls and give them to me."

I dared not look at him or respond, but just scooted around the court, picked up the balls, and handed them to him. Without another word, he turned and walked away.

"Thank you," I whispered.

Brian stopped and turned back. "What?"

I stared at him defiantly. "You could've said thank you."

"Fuck off, *Yid*," he said and left.

Eddie looked at me in high esteem for having stood up to Brian.

Eddie's biggest wish in life was to be a dentist. He'd say it was his destiny and took it very seriously. He was a real wise guy, though, always testing the boundaries. Eddie was shrewd, constantly looking for an edge, and he knew how to get himself out of trouble.

One summer evening, when we were twelve years old, Eddie noticed a candy truck parked by P.S. 205 on 67th Street. He talked me, Sammy, and our fourth friend, Louie Shamah, plus a few other neighborhood kids, into breaking into the truck to steal the candies and nuts inside. Where he got the crowbar to break the lock I never found out, but within minutes the rear of the truck was opened and we all jumped inside, stuffing our pockets with goodies.

Suddenly, we heard a police siren so we all scattered into the street running away from the cop car. Eddie, with his infinite wisdom, walked slowly and quietly *towards* the police car, thereby getting away as the vehicle sped past him. The police rounded the rest of us up and took us to the luncheonette on the corner of 67th Street and 20th Avenue, but Eddie had escaped.

The police questioned us about the burglary, and a crowd of neighbors gathered around to see what was happening. Eddie watched this from a distance and couldn't stand not being part of the group; so he walked up to a cop and confessed that he was involved in the peanut truck robbery. As the officer walked him into the store, Eddie shouted, "My career as a dentist is over!"

11

MATTIE'S HOT DOG

Seth Low Junior High School, located on West 12th Street between Bay Parkway and Avenue P, was a wonderment to me, so grown up compared to P.S. 205, the grade school on 20th Avenue from where Sammy and I had just graduated. In 6th grade, Mrs. Greenhouse had us sew an apron out of denim to use in the 7th grade shop class.

The third day after we arrived, they gave all the new students a test to see how smart we were. Sammy and I passed with flying colors, so they put us into this rapid advance class called SP. Kids in that group got to skip the 8th grade and go directly from 7th to the 9th.

Our friend, Hymie Ades, one of the highest scorers, refused to take advantage of this opportunity because he wanted to play basketball with kids his age. He said if he skipped that year he would have to play with older kids. This was nonsense. Being in the SP did not preclude you from playing with anyone you chose. We all thought Hymie was afraid he might not live up to the challenges of that special group. Sammy and I were anxious to skip a grade and spend less time in school and more time in the park.

Seth Low Park, across the street from the school, was a remarkable place. It was huge, with handball, basketball, and two softball fields; a wading pool; swings, sliding ponds, and dozens of benches, all lined with beautiful trees. And then there was Mattie's, a hot dog stand right in the middle of the grounds that became our hangout during lunch and at night. The frankfurters looked and smelled delicious, and I was tempted to eat one. When I mentioned it to my brother Michael, he said, "Go for it, kid. It'll be a new adventure."

"Pop will kill me. I…"

"He doesn't have to know. Danny," he interrupted. "You're old enough now to keep secrets." With my hero's support, I wasted no time in devouring my first un-kosher meat. It was better than imagined.

No matter what we ate for lunch, one had to have one of Mattie's knishes. He would cut them in half, put them on a grill for a few minutes, then paint them with deli mustard and stuff them with sauerkraut. What a flavor! It was not too long after this break from eating only kosher food that I was consuming ham and cheese sandwiches and no longer observing the Sabbath. Michael was my inspiration and mentor into a world without religion which brought with it a great sense of freedom, though I still believed in God.

In the evenings, after dinner with each of our families, boys and girls would gather at Mattie's and listen to the various *A Capella* groups in the park singing the top ten Rock and Roll songs. One group, the Kings Highway Boys, sang jazz songs in four part harmonies. Dumb name for a group, but they sounded terrific.

Saturday afternoon was movie day at the Marboro theatre on Bay Parkway. Some of us would attempt to sneak in to save the twenty-five cent entrance fee, but invariably we were caught by the manager, Mr. Alper, or one of his elderly matrons hired to see that customers smoked only in designated areas and kept their feet off the seat in front of them. Mr. Alper was always nattily dressed and drove a new Cadillac Coupe Deville.

The usual routine was that the boys would go to the theatre together, and the girls went with the girls. During the newsreel and coming attractions, two boys would stroll up and down the aisles looking for two girls. A ritual was followed wherein the boys would pass a row with two girls sitting together, stop for a moment to check them out, and be looked over by the girls. The boys would continue walking down the aisle, and as they turned to walk back, they would stop at the row with the two girls they had encountered. If the girls were still sitting next to each other, the boys knew to move on. If the girls had separated, it meant the boys were welcome to sit with them. Many 'steady' relationships began that way.

One Saturday, a very handsome kid named Charlie Adeo was my aisle partner. We strolled up and down a few times until we stopped by a couple of pretty girls who had separated their seats. Charlie sat next to a girl named Melanie, and I sat next to a cute blonde named Judy. After only a few minutes of chatter, all four of us were "making out" heavily.

Charlie's romances usually lasted the length of the movie. In the two years he had been attending junior high he had gone steady with at least forty different girls. Once I heard him say to one, "I don't know your name, but would you like to go steady with me?" Because Charlie was more handsome than most other boys, the girl responded with a resounding "Yes!"

Charlie was a wild kid with a great sense of humor. On July 4th of that year, he was in the park playing with firecrackers and other explosives. He was trying to combine a cherry bomb with a rocket launcher. The experiment failed and blew up in his hand, causing him to lose the tip of his right pinky and singeing his eyebrows and hair. When the smoke cleared, we saw him standing there smiling. "Lucky me," he said, "I won't need a haircut for a while."

Monday to Thursday, all the SY pre-teen boys had to go to yeshiva after school from 3:30 pm to 6:00, where we were taught to read Hebrew in preparation of our Bar Mitzvah. The classes were held in the Talmud Torah building next to the Big shul, which was opposite P.S. 205. We'd rush there after school to get a knish from Uncle Miltie's truck before going into class. Milt was a rotund individual who loved kids. His knishes, which hardly rivaled Mattie's, were fifteen cents, but if a kid were short a few pennies, Miltie would cover the difference.

In the classroom, each of us would take turns reciting a passage from the *Chumash*, the printed form of the Torah. I was a pretty fast reader, but no one beats Sammy. He not only mastered the Hebrew words, he also grasped the musical intonations of the passages.

Our Rabbi, Yitzhak Shamula, was a psychopath. The man was in his fifties, a brilliant scholar who knew every Hebrew book and prayer by heart, and had an eagle eye that could spot a boy in the class not paying attention from anywhere in the room. He would fling this long, thin, metal rod he always carried at the culprit with deadly aim, usually hitting the victim on the hand, but on occasion missing the mark and landing on the student's head. It's a wonder he didn't take a kid's eye out.

The classes always started exactly (by the rabbi's watch) at 3:30. He'd enter the room, slam the door shut, and lock it so latecomers could not get in. Then, he would close the lights, casually remove his trousers and appoint one of the students to take it to the dry cleaners for a pressing. Other times, it was his jacket that needed to be tended to, or perhaps his shoes had to be taken for a shine. He would open the door only slightly to let these couriers pass, and after they squeezed their way out, he slammed it and locked it again.

Once, as he stood over me while I searched for the correct passage, the rabbi waved his rod over my head and said, almost in a whisper, "Place." As I continued to search for the right sentence, his voice rose, and he repeated, "Place." You had three "Place" queries to respond with the correct words before he would rap you on the back of the neck with his rod. "Rabbi, I can't see too well. It's too dark," I pleaded.

"Take you' eyes to the shoemaker," he would respond, and then laugh at his joke. If you still couldn't find the place after being whacked on the back of your neck, he would shout out your name and add, "Dweck, *seben-turty*," which meant you would have to stay late after class and run some chores for him.

During class, while the students read, Rabbi Shamula would spend this time sitting at his beat-up desk repairing old prayer books. The ones that were irreparable were set aside to be buried in the coffin of the next deceased community member. Without ever looking up, Rabbi Shamula corrected the mistakes we made while reading.

At 6 p.m., when the bell rang, he would jump out of his seat and rush to the door, blocking any kid from escaping. With his rod pointed at the class, he'd turn and say, in a voice that was low, but with the tonal quality of a mass murderer, "Anybody gonna' make a move, gonna' *kill* 'em." He'd walk slowly back to his desk, sit, and remove the tiniest piece of paper from one of the books he was unable to repair. Then, squinting, he read off the names of the students who could leave. You'd pray your name was on the list.

"Sutton, out," Rabbi Shamula said, and Ralphie Sutton wasted no time running from his seat. "Maslaton, out," he went on, reading the names of the free one by one until he came to end of the list, or what we called the "*guillotine part*," when his voice became elevated. "Bijou, 6:30," which meant Izzy had to stay in class an extra half hour. "Hanono, 7:00 o'clock," and then, finally, "Dweck, gonna' *die*!" And with that he'd slap his rod so hard on his desk it bent. "*Gonna' die*" meant not only that I had to stay late; I would be hit at least five times on my hand with the rod before running his errands.

One night after being kept after class, I arrived home late for the *Eid il Jar* party Becky had every year, a celebration SYs held every winter, usually in February, which most of us kids had no clue about; we just enjoyed the treats that were dispersed by the grownups. I suspect it was a Syrian custom because of the word *Eid*, Arabic for Holiday. My brother Jakey was upset and asked why I was late. I told him: Rabbi Shamula had hit me and made me stay late. Jakey saw the red mark on the back of my neck and grew furious.

"Get your coat back on and come with me."

We rushed back to the yeshiva where Rabbi Shamula was still pasting books together. Jakey stormed into the room dragging me with him. The surprised rabbi looked up at him and smiled. "Hello, boy," he said cheerfully.

Jakey squared off with him and stared menacingly into his eyes. "I'll say this once, Rabbi. You hit my kid brother again, and you'll feel the pain, too."

Without another word, he turned and walked out, pulling me along. On the walk home, a growing admiration for my oldest brother blossomed. "You let me know if he ever hits you again," Jakey said. I could still hear the anger in his voice.

"Thanks," I said, but was confused. "How come *you* can hit me all the time?"

Jakey answered with the utmost sincerity, "I'm your brother, that's why."

12

UNCLE SAM

I was twelve years old, three months before my Bar Mitzvah when my father married Becky Shrem, my mother's friend. Everyone was happy for him. He had been miserable in the first year after mom's death, but rumors began floating around about Pop and Becky, so he finally married her. I never mentioned the incident in the movie theatre to anyone.

Becky had no children of her own and quickly took to Al, Marilyn, and me. Esther acquired the role of surrogate mother

Pop's wedding was a small affair held in the "small" shul on 64th Street off 20th Avenue. It was once a two family house that had been converted to handle the overflow from the "Big" shul. There was a small terrace that overlooked the subway tracks of the Sea Beach line. Rabbi Kassin officiated at the quiet ceremony after which Molly served cake and coffee on the second floor. My brother, Jakey, was best man and handed my father my mother's wedding band to give to Becky, who had no compunction about wearing a dead woman's ring. She was just thrilled to find a man this late in her life.

Becky liked to buy nice (read expensive) things, which drove my father nuts. They had arguments over her shopping habits, and each time they did, she would promise to curtail her spending. Never happened: Becky was a compulsive Shopaholic.

My brother Jakey was not the sharpest kid on the block, but he did have a certain charm about him. Many times he said things that were funny without having a clue as to why. He was not bad looking but did not measure up to the star quality of Michael. Jakey always had a pretty girl on his arm, and everyone, including his friends that were much better looking, wondered how he got them. When I was older, he revealed his secret. "I'd ask a hundred girls for a date, and only ninety-nine refused."

Once, Jakey had made a date with two girls for the same night. He called one of them, Marsha, to cancel, but had erroneously dialed my sister Esther's number. When she picked up the phone, she recognized Jakey's voice when he said, "Hello, Marsha?"

Esther decided to play along. "Yeah," she answered.

"I'm sorry, Marsha, I'm not feeling well tonight so I'll have to cancel our date."

"That's too bad."

"We'll do it another night."

Finally, my sister confessed. "Jakey, it's me, your sister, Esther."

"Esther?" he replied, a bit surprised. "What are you doing in Marsha's house?"

That was my brother, Jakey; a workhorse, and though only 5'7", he was strong, tough, and afraid of no one, not even guys bigger than him.

After Mom had died, my father had Jakey quit school so he could go to work and help support the family. Pop got him a job with his boss, Judah Cohen. In 1953, two weeks after he turned twenty, Jakey received his "Greetings from the President" letter ordering him to report for his army physical. He showed me the message, and we both laughed at the one subway token Scotch-taped to it. "They're in for a surprise," he chuckled, but I had no clue what he meant.

When Jakey went to the downtown Brooklyn draft center on Whitehall Street, accompanied by Pop, he was wearing filthy clothes and reeked of body odor. His hair was disheveled, and his pants had urine stains. He spoke in a mumbled voice and had spittle dribbling from his mouth. His plan, he later told me, was to beat the draft, as many young SY men did during the post WWII and Korean War period. In World War II, SY boys rushed to enlist and fought heroically in Europe and the Pacific. Many were wounded, and nine of these volunteers were killed in action. One Syrian young man, Mark Zhaga, was even awarded a high honor for his act of bravery. Members of the community at home, mostly women, published a magazine called "Victory Bulletin" that related stories of goings on in Brooklyn and tales about the boys fighting overseas.

But this was not wartime and this was a different generation. With the World War long past and the Korean conflict nearly over, a large proportion of the eligible SY draftees had little sense of patriotism. They were needed at home to help support the family.

Pop held Jakey's hand throughout the interview with the psychiatrist, saying his son was slow thinking, needed to be cared for by someone most of the time, and could barely read (all of which was not true). Jakey was deemed 4F and went home to celebrate with his friends who had done similar things to avoid the draft.

Three years later, when my brother Michael was ordered to report for his physical, Jakey instructed him on what to do, but Michael was having none of it. "I am going to enlist," Michael said defiantly "Do my two years. I owe it to my country."

"You're crazy," Jakey answered. "It's a waste of time. You can't make any money in the military. What about your girlfriend?"

"She'll wait for me."

"Ah, you're a fool, kid. How you gonna' live on $85 a month. It gets you nothing.

"What if there was a war?"

"Maybe I'd go in," Jakey answered, and then thought for a second. "But I'd find a way to make some money, maybe selling guns or shit like that. Don't be a fool, Mikey. No SY goes into the army anymore."

"This one will." And sure enough, Michael did enlist. For me, that was one more feather in my hero's cap, and I loved him even more for it.

Michael looked great in his new Class A uniform, his brass belt and shoes sparkling and reflecting the light. After Basic Training at Fort Dix in New Jersey, he was deployed to Germany for the rest of his service. His girlfriend, Nancy, did wait for him. She even flew to Germany on two different occasions, each time spending two weeks of his leave in Vienna, Nuremberg and Berlin. Nancy wanted to be an actress, and they made plans to study together after his discharge. His classes would be financed by the G.I. Bill, and Nancy's tuition to be payed by her father.

The two years went by, and when Michael returned home, he and Nancy enrolled in The New School acting class.

13

DRY HUMPING

Seth Low Junior High was where I got my first hardon. Every Friday afternoon, the one weekday we were free from yeshiva classes, when the bell rang ending the school day, all the kids rushed to the gym for Social Dancing, where boys and girls danced to popular rock and roll songs. Sometimes girls danced together, but as soon as a slow song came on, all the boys would grab the nearest girl and dance very close to their partners, rubbing against their legs. We called it '*dry humping*', and the sexual sensation was amazing. Within seconds, any number of us boys had an erection. One kid, Abie Serure, once got so aroused, he actually reached a climax and had to cover the wet spot on his pants as he rushed to the bathroom.

In November, the school threw a '*Sadie Hawkins Day*' dance, named after the character from the comic strip '*Lil' Abner*' by Al Capp. At this party, the girls invite the boys to dance. One cute teenager, Susan Schwartz, who was in my SP class, shyly approached me. I had seen her in the classroom, but hardly took notice, but that night, when she asked me to dance, I quickly fell in love. She would not permit dry humping, but danced close enough for me to be smitten by her.

Susan was petite, with a cute little pug nose. Her hair was coifed in the style of the day, a ponytail, which swung back and forth as we danced the '*Lindy Hop*' to Bill Haley's '*Rock Around The Clock*'. She had deep-set green eyes that blended well with mine, which were blue. We talked a lot, her in a soft-spoken manner, me a bit louder, and it became immediately apparent to me that Susan was a very smart girl. She knew about politics, supported

President Eisenhower, and spoke intelligently about foreign affairs. I had no clue what she was talking about.

SP students were required to take a foreign language. Coincidentally, Susan and I both chose French, but while I barely understood the meaning of the verb *avoir*, Susan spoke the language almost fluently.

"Mrs. Bagdano says you have a nice accent, Danny." She was our French teacher. "I help her marking test papers and I notice you always fail. Don't you like French?"

'It's hard. Besides, why do I need to know French for? I ain't going there."

"A foreign language broadens your personality. It widens your world."

"Yeah, maybe"

"I saw you in the auditorium the other day and you were disrupting Principal Ross's speech. Why do you do that?"

"Dunno," I shrugged.

"You *were* very funny. I made up my mind that afternoon I would ask you to dance tonight." She leaned towards me and kissed my forehead. "Would you like me to help you with French?"

I did, but was embarrassed to say so. She picked up on it and leaned back.

"Think about it. If you let me help it would mean we could spend more time together."

In between dances, we "made out" on one of the benches lining the gym. She had soft lips that felt good when she pressed them against mine, and she smothered me with heartfelt embraces.

It was the last song of the evening, "Earth Angel" by the Penguins, and Susan and I were dancing very close. "I really like you, Susan," I said, and meant it.

"I like you, too, Danny."

"Let's go steady."

"Isn't this too soon?"

"Nah. I like you, you like me, that's it. What do you say?"

"It's a big commitment. Can I tell you tomorrow?"

I was a bit disappointed and struggled not to show it. "Sure, Susan; let me know; whenever."

As I walked her home, we talked about rock and roll and who our favorite performers were. She loved Elvis Presley, a new young singer, and so did I. I liked Chuck Berry and Little Richard. When we arrived at her house we kissed good night. I walked home on clouds, feeling very confident of myself.

The next day I was on pins and needles waiting to hear Susan's answer about going steady. When we finally met at Mattie's she had a solemn look on her face.

"I talked to my mother about you, Danny, and she thought we were too young to be going steady."

My face turned crimson, preparing for the worst. I turned away from her, but she grabbed my arm and spun me back to face her. This time she was smiling.

"I told my mother I was old enough to make my own decisions and I've decided to go steady with you." She was beaming now, and so was I. We embraced and I kissed her on the lips. The crowd of kids standing around us began applauding. At twelve years old, Susan became my girlfriend for life.

We continued to see each other on Saturdays, going to the movies, and at night, at the park; or attending a party or dance, usually at the JCH on Bay Parkway and 78th Street. On Sunday afternoons, we might go on excursions, like a boat ride to Bear Mountain or horseback riding at Bergen Beach. She did help me with French and to my surprise my grades did improve.

My relationship with Susan was going along fine for the next three months until one day a girl in my math class named Nedra Sheinberg trapped me in the clothes closet of the classroom after everyone had left. Nedra always wore tight skirts to school, used bright red lipstick, and often spoke foul language. She had gained the reputation of being 'trampy'.

"Danny," she said, "I've always had a crush on you. Why don't we see each other?" Taken aback by this revelation, I was unaware how to respond. She put her hand on my crotch and rubbed it. "I can make you happy," she offered.

At first I stepped back, but she moved in closer to me, lowered my zipper, put her hand in my pants, took hold of my erect penis and masturbated me. Where did she learn how to do that at age twelve, I wondered? My thoughts quickly turned to the sensual experience at hand. The feeling was ecstatic, something I had never experienced before, and I wanted it to go on forever. Suddenly, a blast of guilt overcame me. "Nedra," I pleaded, "We shouldn't be doing this. You know I'm going steady with Susan Schwartz."

"Does Susan Schwartz do this for you?" she asked, continuing to stroke me. She sounded like a grown up woman of twenty. Overwhelmed by the sexual sensation, I could not resist and allowed her to continue until the climax — my first ever — was reached. It made me heady, a bit woozy and my knees buckled. She cleaned me with a handkerchief, and then ran off without uttering another word.

That night I went through a tortuous battle with guilt. The encounter with Nedra was not initiated by me, but I didn't resist it. What should I do? Tell Susan? Or hope she never finds out. After a long struggle with these options, I settled on telling Susan what happened and to ask her forgiveness, but Nedra beat me to the punch. The next day, for some inexplicable reason, she boasted about the encounter to her friends and word quickly got back to Susan.

At lunch that afternoon, I approached Susan near Mattie's, but she walked away from me. I followed, pleading for her to allow me to explain. Finally, when she turned and faced me, sadness had filled her eyes. "You broke a sacred vow, Danny," she said softly, with sorrow, not anger, in her voice. "You asked me to go steady. Don't you know what that means?"

Frankly, I had no clue what it meant, but nodded yes anyway. "It happened so fast. I never meant to hurt you."

"Well, you did," she said, with tears in her eyes. "Don't ever speak to me again." She turned and walked away. I felt her pain, and, when it mingled with my own, nearly cried.

Over the next three weeks, I tried calling her at home in the evenings, two, three, times each day, but her mother said she didn't want to speak to me. If she was standing near Mattie's during lunch and I approached, she would walk away. I was beside myself over the crumbling of this relationship, but Susan was adamant. She would never forgive me. I have never forgotten Susan, and to this day, lament that breakup. Over the next three years I made attempts to find her, but without success.

14

AHBED

The "*Great Peanut Truck Robbery*", as it came to be known, was about the same time I became aware of certain deficiencies in our comfortable little Benson-hurst community. The neighborhood was essentially divided into four groups: SYs, J-Dubs, Irish, and Italians. No blacks, no Latinos. They were only allowed in as handymen or housekeepers. Each group had its own term to describe black people. J-Dubs called them *schvartzes*, a Yiddish code word for *nigger*, while the Italians referred to them as *mulignane*, which means eggplant, the skin of which is black. The Irish simply referred to them as *niggers*.

SYs used the word, *ahbud*, a derivative of the Hebrew word "*aved*" which literally means 'slave'. It is true that many in the SY community believed the word *ahbud* meant black, but enough members, especially the rabbis, were aware of the true meaning. They did little, if anything, to enlighten their congregants. All groups referred to Puerto Ricans and Latinos as *spics*.

Epithets were not limited to Blacks and Hispanics. SYs called Italians "*Talyanies*", Italians called SYs "*A-rabs*"; J-Dubs referred to Italians as "*goyim*" and Syrians as *Yachabebes*. The Irish: *Arabs, Wops and Kikes*, respectively. Despite these prejudices, a level of civility was maintained between these groups, until, one particular day, one I'll never forget. On June 13, 1953 I would witness one of the most brutal outpourings of hate on a black kid, no older than myself.

It was exceptionally hot that Saturday, so I went into Charlie's candy store on 69th Street and 20th Avenue, for a cool Cherry Lime Rickey, the ingredients of which consisted of ice, seltzer, a shot of cherry syrup and a quarter slice of lime, squeezed, then rubbed around the rim of the glass. I sat at the front counter sipping it slowly, savoring the flavor.

At the other end sat Tommy O'Malley, and his father, Brian, finishing off their plates of ice cream when in walks this black kid, no more than twelve years old, who sits at the counter two seats away from me. "Can I have a Coke with ice, please?" He asked politely, putting five cents on the counter.

Charlie, who was SY, and was a generally mild mannered man in his forties, but had no great love for anyone who wasn't SY, pulled the lever of the fountain for the Coke, and then added the ice. "Straw?" he asked, as he served the boy his soda.

"No, thank you," the lad responded and began drinking the cola.

"Since when do you let niggers drink from the glass, Charlie?" Brian's voice thundered from the end of the counter.

"Never mind that, Brian," Charlie retorted.

"It ain't right, Charlie. He should be using a straw."

"He paid his nickel. He can drink it any way he likes."

Brian got up and walked towards the boy. "Finish up and get outta' here," he said, in a menacing tone. The boy finished his drink, stepped off the stool, and headed for the door. Brian waved to his son Tommy, and they both followed the boy out. I moved closer towards the front to observe what was happening.

"What are you doing in this neighborhood, boy?"

"Walking home, sir," the boy responded, with just a trace of fear. He started to walk away, but Brian grabbed his arm and spun him around.

"Tommy," he shouted to his son. "Teach this little nigger-baby to keep away from this neighborhood." Tommy looked confused. "Go on, son," his father urged. "Teach him a lesson."

"Come on, Dad," Tommy resisted.

"You beat him, or I beat you. Which will it be?"

Without a moment's hesitation, Tommy lunged at the boy and began bashing him with hard punches. I turned back to Charlie and saw him come running around from behind the counter and run outside. He pulled Tommy off the kid, but Brian interceded and gave Charlie a sharp, right jab to the jaw. As Charlie fell, Brian turned to his on and shouted, "Finish the nigger off."

I ran back inside the store, lifted the pay phone and dialed the operator. "Send the police! Hurry!" I shouted in a trembling voice. "People are being beaten up. 69ᵗʰ and 20ᵗʰ! Hurry!" I hung up and ran outside, screaming at the Irish father and son.

"Stop it! Stop it!" I cried. "They're hurt!"

But Tommy continued beating the kid until his father said, "Enough."

The police arrived about ten minutes later, but Brian and his son were gone. Charlie was standing now, holding a towel with ice against his jaw, but the black kid lay on the ground, bleeding from his face. One cop called for an ambulance while the other questioned Charlie. "You know who did this?" he asked, but Charlie just shook his head.

I stepped up to the cop and blurted out, "It was Brian O'Malley, officer, and his son Tommy. I saw them do this and know where they live."

The officer took down my name and address and when the ambulance came, they took the boy away and the police left. Nothing ever happened to Brian or his son, Tommy.

I was angry, but mostly frightened, by what happened that day and don't know what prompted me to want to help the kid. Maybe it brought up the pain of my mother hitting me with her shoe. Maybe it was because I felt the helplessness of that boy.

I was one of the SYs who thought that the word ahbud meant black. Every Syrian in the community used it when speaking of black people. It was an epithet that would one day be cited by Louis Farrakhan, the head of the Nation of Islam, in a speech railing against Jews. One thing was for sure after what I witnessed that day: I would never again call a black person an ahbud.

15

PARTNERS

Becky Shrem, now Becky Dweck, had great influence over my father. For years, Pop had worked hard for his boss, Mr. Cohen, but now she was prodding Pop to seek some additional form of income to finance her extravagant spending. She worked for a Palestinian importer, a gregarious man named Ahmed Ramallah, who sold damask and linen table clothes and always had a broad smile on his face. She convinced Ahmed to extend her credit of two hundred dollars in merchandise and talked Pop into spending evenings going door-to-door selling the goods to local residents. Many SY men traveled out of town selling carpets and tablecloths. Pop did well, and a new side of my father was emerging as he found he could be a persuasive salesman.

That first week out he managed to sell all the tablecloths. When Becky paid the invoice on Friday, Ahmed offered her more credit, and within a couple months Pop was selling more than six hundred dollars a week at a fifty percent profit. Becky and my father were flourishing in money they had never imagined would be theirs.

From the start of this endeavor Becky had a plan to get my father into his own business. With great effort, she curtailed her own spending and saved every dollar they made. After seven months of Pop's peddling successes, she decided he would have to expand his territory and go into this business full time. She had saved more than seven thousand dollars of the profit my father had earned and convinced him he should quit his job and open a store of his own. Pop was a bit anxious about that and hesitated pulling the trigger.

Ahmed and his spouse, Latifa, a robust lady with a boisterous laugh, had become good friends of my father and Becky and were often invited to dinner at our house. One night, as the Turkish coffee was served, Ahmed cleared his voice and spoke.

"Ezra, my friend, you have become one of my best customers," he exaggerated, "selling my goods so easily. I have been thinking. Why do we not expand the business?" Then, after hesitating for just a split second, added, "Together."

Pop took one quick glance at Becky and was immediately convinced she had induced Ahmed to broach the subject. "I don't know, Ahmed. It would mean quitting my job. I am afraid. My age… Come January, *inshallah*, I will reach fifty years."

"God willing," Ahmed repeated.

"It is a big risk. What if…?"

"Do not be afraid, Ezra. *Allah* will watch over us."

Ahmed, being a Palestinian, and my father, born in Syria, both spoke Arabic. Jews and Muslims of Syria used the word *Allah* when speaking of God.

"How much money will we need?"

"We decided seven thousand each would do it," Becky interjected, which confirmed to my father that she was the instigator of the negotiations. "I found a store on Madison Avenue and 33rd Street. The rent is only eight hundred a month. I have already spoken to the landlord, Mr. Nowak, a very nice gentleman."

Pop smiled at Becky, and then turned to Ahmed. "You two have been plotting against me. How can I fight off such armies?" Everyone laughed, and that was the start of "*Dweck & Ramallah Trading*".

The hard part for my father was telling his boss of more than thirty-five years, Judah Cohen, that he was quitting. Mr. Cohen tried talking him out of it.

"After all, Ezra," the old man said, "you are like a son to me, I sponsored you to come to America."

But Pop resisted. "*Allah attiq ilafia*," my father said.

"Hashem has always given me strength."

"My gratitude to you is enormous Mr. Cohen, but I must do this," my father explained.

The old man shrugged. "Then, go, Ezra. *Allah ma 'ack*. God go with you." And so, Pop took the biggest leap of his life, but the check for five thousand dollars as a parting gift from Mr. Cohen made the landing a little softer.

The lease for the store was signed and the landlord, Mr. Nowak, gave the two partners three months free rent so they could prepare the store for its opening. My father worked twelve to fourteen hours a day painting the store and laying down a carpet. He hired an electrician to add lighting to the dimly lit premises. Since summer was just a month away, the partners took the bold step of spending Two Thousand Dollars of their investment money to install an air conditioning system. When he heard about it, the honorable Mr. Nowak offered to contribute half the cost, and the partners were very pleased.

Opening day was fast approaching and my father, Becky and the Ramallahs were excited, but not without some trepidation.

16

KIBBEH

I waited until the *Shiva* week for Sammy was over before telling his three kids about the money. They were ecstatic at his largess and thanked me profusely. The day after the *Arayat* they came to my apartment to settle the matter. Each received a check from my personal account for half a million dollars. Of course, I never mentioned that Martha would be receiving a similar check.

"This didn't come from me. Your father arranged it. I'm only the messenger."

"Believe me, Danny." his eldest son, Isaac, insisted. "None of us were aware."

"Nobody was. Now listen, your father took a big chance doing this, and that money isn't really his to give away. So be discreet on how you spend it. No large purchases that might raise questions. Understand?" They each nodded, hugged and kissed me, then left. My conscious was clear: I had fulfilled Sammy's request without breaking the law. Cost me Two million, but what's money when it comes to friendship.

The apartment was empty and felt like a huge sinkhole as the death of Sammy suddenly slammed me. I've heard of people dying of a broken heart and this felt something like that. There was no one left for me to hang out with, to call and argue with over politics or some other nonsense, to go to dinner with, and talk about the old days. For me, it felt like the "old days" never really happened because there was no one left to re-live them with. All that was left was today, an empty, lonely, short period of time that was leading me closer to the end of my universe. When we were kids I used to see men carrying signs that read "THE WORLD IS COMING TO AN END." I never understood how anyone would know that, until one day it came to me. They were talking about *their* world coming to an end.

This morose depression hit me so hard it felt like death was just two steps away, ready to drag me along. Yet, there has always been an inexplicable spirit within that stopped me from sinking into the abyss over life's tragedies. Somehow, no matter how terrible things might be something inside my head would lead me to believe that, no matter how bad things got, they would change for the better. Of course, as I learned in AA thirty-two years ago, that was the description of irrationality: No matter how often you got slammed by one activity or another, if you repeated the behavior that was the best definition of insanity. So maybe I *was* off my rocker, but that spirit told me to get up and try again to imagine that life would be good.

That evening, I decided to drive into Brooklyn and eat at an old haunt, *David's Restaurant*, on Kings Highway. It was a small joint with no more than twelve tables, but if you loved chicken kabob on a skewer, this was the place to go. Not only was the chicken out of this world, but his Syrian and Israeli dishes were also incredible. *Kibbeh*, ground wheat stuffed with chopped meat and spices molded into the shape of a torpedo; *Majadra*, a combination of rice and lentils cooked with fried onions on top; *fasoulia*, navy beans in a tomato sauce over rice; *bazergan*, Syrian style salad with ground wheat, dates and spices; and of course, hummus, tahini and pita bread. By the time you finished eating, you needed a crane to lift you from your chair.

When I arrived at David's, I was surprised to see another Rolls Royce parked in front. It was a convertible. Mine was a brand new Wraith, a powerful and sleek two door, given to me three weeks earlier by my children for my 75th birthday. I hesitated to accept it (Lexus had been my brand for the past twenty years), but once driving the Rolls, I was hooked.

As I entered David's and looked for an empty table, I noticed a familiar face standing at the counter ordering takeout. It was Claudia Gemal, the woman on the plane from Geneva. She turned and saw me, smiled, and approached.

"What are you doing here?" she asked, wearing a big grin. "I thought you lived in the city."

"I do," I answered, feeling trapped like a sewer rat caught by a coyote. "Once in a while I come here to stuff my face."

"Oh, I get it: slumming." She giggled, pleased with her own words.

"It's the food," I offered. "It's irresistible."

"You can say that again. I was just ordering takeout. Say, want some company?" I hesitated for a split second and she picked up on it. "If you'd rather eat alone…"

"No, no," I recovered. "Please, join me."

"Love to. Let me first just double check my car is locked. A Rolls Royce Convertible on Brooklyn streets. You know what I mean? I should have brought the Mercedes."

They sat me at a table near the back and, without a glance at the menu, knew exactly what I would order. Claudia returned and slid into the chair opposite me. She really did look terrific for her age. Her hair was dark blonde, probably dyed, contrasting well with her fair skin. Her eyes were brown and seemed to sparkle. Her figure was curvy, and it appeared as though she had not one ounce of fat on her body. For a recent widow, she seemed to be feeling no pain. As irritating as Claudia could be, I was glad to be sitting with her on this night.

"You look sad," she said. Her voice came across as sincere.

"My best friend, Sammy Cohen, just died."

"Yes, I heard. I'm so sorry. You must be terribly upset."

I nodded. 'It's tough to lose a friend you've known all your life. The love mass inside you is reduced in size, as if it were being ripped away. You must know what that feels like, having lost your husband."

"Truth is, I lost Manny years ago. I caught him having an affair with Sharon Maslaton. She'd been cheating on her husband, Max, for years." I was more than a bit surprised by her openness and felt a second twinge of admiration for her candidness.

"I should have sued for divorce, but you know how it is with SYs. Divorce is considered a no-no. Besides, he always took good care of me and the kids. Manny was very generous and prepared us for his end. I'll always bless him for that."

We ordered and worked our way through the appetizers. Claudia's disposition seemed to change as we devoured the food. She wasn't as talkative as she had been earlier or when we were at the Geneva airport. There was pathos in her voice as she poured out her feelings.

"Manny's death put a whole new perspective on my life. You sleep with someone for years, carry his babies, and spend the holiday's together, raise the kids, and suddenly, it's over. We were married thirty-three years. I was a teenager, seventeen; Manny was fifteen years older. My mother pushed me into marrying him. He came from a 'good family,' she said, which, to Syrians, means he was rich. My father didn't care one way or the other, but he did remind me if I didn't marry by the time I was eighteen, the men in the community would consider me an 'Old Maid.'"

"Did you like Manny?"

"He was funny, great sense of humor. Manny was born here, but he could capture the Syrian accent perfectly. Sometimes he would sing popular American songs with the accent, and it was hysterical."

"But did you like him?" I persisted.

"Like my mother said, he came from a "good family.""

After devouring our food I paid the check, and Claudia had the waitress pack the leftovers. "Syrian food always tastes better the next day." As we walked towards the door, she said in a low voice, "Why don't you come to my house for a drink. No one is there, and it's only a few blocks away."

I glanced at my watch. It was only 8:45, so I said okay.

The house on East 5th and Avenue S was in the prime location of the Syrian Jewish community of Brooklyn. The whole neighborhood was flabbergasted upon hearing that Claudia's husband, Manny, had bought the two lots on the corner and tore them down to build this one huge home. The word was he spent twelve million dollars on the project. In addition, they had a huge oceanfront home in Deal, and a four thousand foot Florida condo in Porto Vida. Each residence had a Rolls Royce and a Mercedes, and in Florida there was a Ferrari for their twenty-two year old youngest son, Eli, to play around with.

Manny Gemal had worked in his father Shaya's import business, *Kiddie Kids*, manufacturing and importing a line of children's' wear initially from the Philippines until WWII, when he opened a factory on the lower East Side of Manhattan. After the war, the production moved back to the Philippines, then to Hong Kong and Taiwan where they offered better prices. When those countries' wages rose, *Kiddie Kids*, along with other SY importers, moved their manufacturing to South Korea, Vietnam and Bangladesh. Then, it was on to India and Pakistan. When China opened, they all rushed there because no other place on earth could compete with their prices. The importers seldom, if ever, gave thought to the low wages being paid these foreign workers.

Kiddie Kids' products could be found in every major chain of department stores in the United States; and when Walmart came around, they would devour millions of dollars' worth of goods in just one promotion, making the Gemal family one of the top five wealthiest in the SY community. But this wealth was chicken feed compared to what Manny would accumulate when he re-directed the family business into real estate.

In 1962, Manny convinced his father to fund the purchase of a building on East 23rd Street in Manhattan. The price was $2 million, and Judah put up the deposit of $400 thousand, a huge amount of money at the time. Manny did not renew the leases of existing tenants, and, after doing major renovations to the retail stores and offices above them, which his father also financed, managed to double the rents. Two years later, the building was worth three million. Manny refinanced and borrowed $2 million from CitiBank, repaid his father the $400 thousand deposit, plus the $300 thousand for the renovations, and pocketed the rest. The interest charges were covered by the building's revenue and were tax deductible. He had learned quickly that, because of the laws pertaining to the industry, owning real estate was a license to steal, something many SYs, including me, were eager to learn.

Manny went on to acquire more buildings in Manhattan using the same technique of leveraging, and by the time of his death, owned more than fifty properties, either independently or with partners. Rumor had it that Manny was worth more than three billion dollars.

The tax laws were actually very simple. You buy a building and take depreciation on its value, even though ninety-nine percent of the time the value goes up, unlike an automobile that depreciates over time. When you re-finance the building, the money goes into your pocket tax free, and the interest on the loan is deductible. Should you decide to sell, you can delay paying the tax on any profits virtually forever by doing a 1031 Exchange, a law that allows you to buy a building of like value and avoid paying any tax on your gains from the sold property. Technically, a developer or building owner could do this for years without paying any taxes on the profits. License to steal? I wanted one of those as soon as I found out it existed.

Claudia gave me the grand tour of the house, which took fifteen minutes. Four floors: seven bedrooms, nine baths, an elevator to the upper floors, etched crystal windows. I have seen many beautiful homes, but this one was amazing. The center hall staircase was out of *Gone with the Wind;* the decorations, mostly modern but luxurious and striking, the rooms spacious, and, to my amazement, beneath the house were an indoor swimming pool and Jacuzzi.

We settled in on an Italian white leather sofa that wrapped around the living room. Claudia went to the bar, opened a fridge and removed a half-filled bottle of red wine. She poured some into a Baccarat cut crystal glass, handed it to me, but I refused it. "I don't drink," I said.

"Really? Why not?"

"I'm a recovered alcoholic."

She looked surprised, but made no comment about my revelation. "Mind if I do?" I shook my head and she took a sip of the wine. "What do you think?" She asked, sitting a respectable distance from me.

"This house is something else. Did you have help decorating?"

"Did it all by myself. The only help needed was Manny's checkbook. Did you know Manny?"

"Only casually; mostly from the club. We played gin and poker together. He was a good man." I lied again, not wishing to speak ill of her dead husband.

"Good man, yes. Good husband...?"

What I neglected to say was that the Manny I knew was, on the surface a "good guy," a *haborb*, always trying to make an impression on people. Underneath that surface was a mean spirited racist and a money loving scum bag. He would cheat his mother if she were still alive and competing with him for a property. He did that once with me.

I had been looking at a property on Seventh Avenue and learned one thing the hard way. You don't discuss it with another SY, unless it was someone you knew and trusted and you were trying to partner up with him. I had done a few deals with Jackie Sutton, a guy I thought was a friend, and approached him on this one. The price being asked was Eighty-Nine million, and I wanted to hedge a little. Jackie liked the contract, but thought we should take on a third partner. He called Manny Gemal and, against my advice, proposed the deal to him.

Manny turned down Jackie's offer, saying he did not like the deal. Jackie backed out as well. Three weeks later, I learned Manny bought the building along with Jackie for Ninety-Four million. That was two years ago. I was so pissed at Jackie Sutton and split doing business with him immediately by selling my interest in the three properties we owned together.

A few months after he pulled that crap on me, I ran into Manny at the SY social Club on Ocean Parkway and Avenue J and confronted him.

"Sorry Danny; nothing personal, just business."

"You sound like a member of the Corleone crime family," I snapped. He feigned a smile. "You are a low life, Manny. No honor or scruples." He turned to walk away as I shouted, "You're a scum bag, Manny." He kept walking, giving me the finger without turning around.

Claudia's voice interrupted my thoughts and brought me back to our conversation. "Can I ask a personal question?" She asked.

"Go right ahead."

"Did you ever cheat on your wife?"

I stood up, walked to the bar and decided to pour myself a diet Coke. "The answer is yes and no. During my first marriage to Adele Haddad, which did not go very well from the beginning, I did run around a lot after the first seven years. No question, I was a womanizer, and an active alcoholic. What I learned about the disease is that it goes beyond the abuse of alcohol. It causes a whole mindset of distorted ideas and beliefs. When the alcohol is removed from the equation, you can begin to see things more clearly.

"When I got sober, the concept that women were objects melted away. I came to see them as people first, then as women. Of course, trading addictions will prevent that moment of clarity from occurring, like when a person turns their obsession from alcohol to God."

I sat back down on the couch and continued. "I never cheated on Sonia, though, God knows, I often lusted after other women. When we met, Sonia was in her late thirties and had never been married. We quickly fell in love and promised each other to be open about our feelings for one another. Both of us were aware of the sanctity of our relationship, and that it had to be the most important part of our lives. She became my best friend." I leaned back on the couch and watched as Claudia savored her drink. "You really do enjoy the wine, don't you?"

"The best," she said, holding up the glass. "Manny was a connoisseur. We have more than four thousand bottles in the wine cellar." She went back to the bar, and then quickly asked, "Did you and Sonia fight a lot?"

"We had our moments. Early on in our marriage, we came to understand that respect for one another was vital. If I did something that bothered her, she had to talk about it, so I could try to fix it, and vice versa."

"Grown up stuff," she sighed. "Manny and I never had that."

"I saw what happened with Adele and watched my friends suffer through terrible relationships, their marriages failing because they didn't talk to each other."

Her smile was sad. "If only we had known that."

I glanced at my watch and stood, putting my unfinished diet Coke on the bar. "Did I pass the test?"

She raised her eyebrow. "What test?"

"The test of whether I'm a good enough candidate to fill the void."

She laughed. "Call it curiosity. You seem like a nice guy, Danny. I'd like to know you better."

"I'm sure you will." With that, I walked to the front door.

"Do you want my number?" she asked.

"I can get it from my sister Marilyn." I opened the door and turned to her. "Thanks for the Diet Coke."

"Anytime," she answered and watched me walk to the car.

During the drive back to the city I thought about my conversation with Claudia, having to admit my first impression of her was wrong. Sure, she was into the money, big time, yet there was an openness about her that was intriguing. I promised myself to call my sister in the morning for Claudia's number.

17

HALF YOUR AGE PLUS SEVEN

Despite his fears after the "Great Peanut Truck Robbery" Edie Mansour's career as a dentist was far from over. He became one of the most prominent Orthodontists in New York with offices in Manhattan, Brooklyn and Great Neck. At its peak, Eddie's three offices had more than 18 dentists and 20 staff employees.

Eddie was a very lucky guy. Things always seemed to fall his way. The girls loved him, and he loved them. He bounced from one relationship to another, often going to the Roseland Dance Hall in the city on weekends to meet more women.

He eased his way through college and scored a 23 on the Dental Acceptance Test, where the average was 19, before entering dental school. In 1966, unlike other SY guys his age, Eddie volunteered for Vietnam, honing his dental skills while serving the country and actually walked away without a scratch from an explosion that killed two of his buddies.

Eddie's first office was in Brooklyn, where most of his customers were SYs, all of who were very proud of his being one of the first professionals in the community. I was his first patient, due to the extensive work my mouth needed. He offered his services for free, but I insisted on paying. He had few other patients at the time, so he treated me almost daily for four weeks straight. His reputation grew, due to a little help from me, and the practice flourished. He met his first wife, Sylvia, when she was a patient, and they married six months later. But Eddie still had his eyes on other women. That first marriage lasted eighteen months.

After a few years since beginning his practice, and as his business grew, Eddie developed a passion for automobiles. At one time he had seven cars, including two Cadillacs, two Lincolns, a Mercedes convertible, a Jaguar E Type V12, which gave him nothing but trouble, and a four-year-old Rolls Royce, all garaged in Brooklyn. He met his second wife, Marsha, a *J-Dub*, who had been married to one of his dentists. Marsha divorced her husband to marry Eddie, and they moved to the five towns and his connection to the SY community diminished.

J-Dub, which is derived from the letters JW, which is short for Jewish, refers to a Jew who is not Syrian. (Jerry Seinfeld's mother, an SY, married a J-Dub). While marrying one is permitted, the community often frowns upon it. SYs generally look down on J-Dubs as not being on their level, but then, many believed that, compared to SYs, everyone else was inferior. One incidence, extreme though it may be, tells it all.

One night, it was sometime in January, '78, Eddie, Sammy, Louie, Manny Gemal, and I were in the City sitting in a restaurant called Knickers on 2nd Avenue after coming from the gym. I had never met Manny before, but knew who he was. He and Eddie were friendly, even though Manny was much younger. Manny was in his thirties and single, while the rest of us were married. The Gemal family had money, but hadn't yet reached the enormous wealth Manny would amass.

I had heard Manny was an arrogant, self-centered guy, and now he was bitching about having just written a check to the IRS for high six figures. President Carter had just submitted a proposal that would reduce taxes.

"It's not enough," Manny complained. "They should cut it even more."

"How are we going to pay for all the social services?" Sammy asked.

"Fuck that shit," Manny replied. "Where does that flooce go? To the *ah-beed*, that's where."

"I would be happy to pay the taxes…" Louie started to say, but Manny interrupted.

"Bullshit! You never wrote a large check to the IRS, so you can't know how that feels."

"*I* pay a lot of taxes." Eddie said.

"Not as much as me,' Manny answered. "It is actually very painful to give all that money to the government for nothing."

"What do you mean, for nothing?" Sammy countered, growing a little annoyed with Manny. "There are a lot of programs that help people less fortunate."

"Look, for my money, if you had to kill millions of ahbeed to lower my taxes, I'd be okay with that."

I couldn't sit there any longer and listen to this self-centered prick. I stood up, made excuses, and left.

Eddie's marriage to Marsha fell apart after three years when she caught him, in *their* bed, having sex with the next-door neighbor.

Eddie went through four marriages and had no children, before finally moving, at age sixty-one, to Beverly Hills, California. He had sold his practice for a large sum and parlayed his fortune into twenty million dollars through stock maneuvers and smart real estate investments. He met a woman there, a non-Jew, named Cindy, who was thirty-three. Eddie had developed a formula in which an appropriate girlfriend's age should be no more than half his age plus seven years. So, when Eddie was 61, his girlfriend should be no older than 37. At 36, Cindy met the requirement.

Sammy Levy and I, along with our wives, would fly out west at least twice a year to be with our friend, and he would come to New York at least once. Cindy and Eddie lived together, unmarried, in a four bedroom, 6,000 square foot home on Coldwater Canyon Drive, In Beverly Hills, for which Eddie paid $1.2 million bucks. He redesigned his garage and drive-way to hold his eight cars, by then two Rolls Royce's, two Mercedes, a Porsche, one Bentley, a Ferrari 550 Marinello convertible and a Lamborghini Diablo VT.

The last time we saw Eddie was in January of 2002. Sammy and I, with our wives, were having lunch with him and Cindy at the Ivy restaurant on Robertson Boulevard. The girls couldn't stop *oohing* and *ahhing* over the celebrities: Danny DeVito, Kevin Costner, Demi Moore, Kiefer Sutherland, and too many others to mention. After the meal was over, the women left with Eddie's Rolls to go shopping.

Eddie was sipping a double decaf espresso and eyeing every woman that passed. He stared up and down at each beauty that walked by, rating them from a 1 to a 10. One woman even got an over the top rating of 12. "What a great country America is," he commented, "Especially BH. Look at these broads. Where else are you going to see these many beauties?"

Sammy redirected the conversation. "Cindy seems like a nice woman, Eddie. How's it going there?"

"She's a sweetheart, a great girl. But you know me. I need the variety."

"Why don't you settle down?" I said, digging into my dessert of bread pudding.

"Look, in BH you stop at a red light in one of my cars, and a broad in the car next to you smiles. Five blocks later she pulls over, and within an hour or two you're fucking the shit out of her. Sometimes they might have a friend who would join a threesome. Who can give that up?" He took another sip of his coffee.

Sammy sounded annoyed. "What about Cindy?"

"I limit my fooling around to two nights a week. No more. Cindy's not going anywhere. I bought her a Porsche, let her charge anything to my credit card. I even put half a mil' in an account for her. She's happy." He paused for a second, his eyes looking straight up in the air. "You want eye candy on your arm? You have to pay for it."

I laughed, but Sammy shook his head.

"What's the matter, Sammy?" Eddie asked as he finished his coffee.

Sammy let out a long breath. "You realize these women are only with you for the money. If you didn't have any they wouldn't be with you."

"If I didn't have money *I* wouldn't be with me, either."

Sammy and I laughed. "What kind of life is that?" he asked.

"Look, pal," Eddie responded, using a term we all did when referring to each other. "There are only three things that matter in life: money, cars, and broads, in that order. Money needs to come first to pay for the other two."

That was the last time we saw Eddie. Three months later, Cindy called to tell me Eddie was in an automobile accident while speeding south on the San Diego Freeway with a blonde beauty in the passenger seat. Both were killed instantly when a piggyback truck veered into Eddie's lane. His Ferrari was doing nearly 105 miles an hour and could not stop in time.

18

REVENGE

Pop and Becky opened on Madison Avenue and did well. It was a fairly large store, about fifteen hundred square feet, so they added other kinds of goods besides tablecloths. Using Abdullah's connections they brought in lines of German Dresden plates, dishes, and figurines. Hummel was a big item that drew in tourists. They added Italian porcelains and Chinese figurines from Hong Kong, and that first year grossed more than Three Hundred Fifty thousand in sales. My father was thrilled at the success, having netted more than fifty grand from his share.

My father and Becky, along with a Spanish stock boy, Fernando, worked the store Sundays to Fridays, closing early Friday afternoon for Shabbat. Abdullah and his wife worked Saturdays. The partners had worked out an arrangement, approved by an SY rabbi, whereby Pop would sell his interest in the business to Abdullah on Friday afternoons for an enormous amount of money and buy back his share on Saturday night, when Shabbat ended, for the same amount he had been paid. The purpose of this arrangement was for Pop to circumvent the religious prohibition from earning money from a business operating on the Sabbath.

While my father's business flourished, my school career did not. Seth Lowe's principal, Mr. Lazarus D. Roth, had "had enough of Dweck's wild antics." I was now in the ninth grade SP class and failing all my subjects. They considered putting me back to the eighth grade, but were apprehensive about keeping me in that school for another year. So, they transferred me to a ninth grade "*Boogy*" class, comprised of thirty failing male students, where we were taught and learned nothing. Our teacher, Miss McGee (seems most teachers in those days were Irish) was a staunch anti-communist, forbidding the class from wearing any garment that was red. Each time a plane would fly overhead, she'd rush to the window, look up, and make the sign of the cross while saying, "Thank God, they are ours," even though there was no way she could be sure they were.

1954 was the year of my Bar Mitzvah. Rabbi Shamula had taught me to read Hebrew well, but neglected to teach me the Torah portion of that week. When the day finally came, it was Monday, December 6th, one of the weekdays the Torah can be read. My father accompanied me to the Small shul on 64th Street, where I said the blessings for reading the Torah, and he read my portion. When it was over, we walked back to our apartment where Becky had whipped up a small party which soon turned into a card game. Pop went off to work, and I went to the bedroom to open my presents: Thirty-five in cash and a flannel shirt with a birthday card that read, "Happy Birthday Grandpa", obviously a re-gift. I rushed off to the park and made my own party, treating everyone to hot dogs and knishes from Mattie's.

In June of the following school year, before my fourteenth birthday, I did not graduate from Seth Low. That fall, I was transferred to New Utrecht High School on 16th Avenue and 80th Street. Martha Stewart, Robert Merrill, and actors John Saxon and Arnold Stang were alumni; and, because I lived on the wrong side of 20th Avenue, (Sammy lived on 21st Avenue as did Eddie and Louie), I was the only one of my friends in that school. I lasted one semester, even though I tried my hardest to succeed by joining the football team and, in fact, was written up in the New York Post as "an up and coming" right guard. I signed up for the school band as a drummer, and, at the same time, developed the deadly habit of smoking. A kid my age named Jeremy hooked me early by introducing me to cigarettes and dice. Outside the school, he hustled me into a crap game. I had thirty-five cents on me, and he had $11 dollars in coins that filled his dungaree pockets. He taught me how to play and, with an incredible streak of good luck, I took him broke.

Every afternoon a bunch of us would sneak into the boys' bathroom for a smoke. Once, Jeremy, who was still pissed at me for taking his money, grabbed my pack of cigarettes and threw it out the window to the adjoining rooftop. I climbed out the window to retrieve the pack and heard someone shout from a window across the way, "He's gonna jump!" Minutes later, the Dean of boys rushed into the bathroom, climbed onto the roof, and dragged me back into the bathroom.

"You stupid kid," the Dean admonished. "What on God's earth made you try and kill yourself?"

"I wasn't…"

"Quiet!" He ordered. "The police will arrive soon enough."

"My cigarettes, someone threw them out the window…"

"Enough! We'll see about this."

And he did see about it. They sent me to a child psychologist to find out my reasons for attempting suicide. Luckily, she was an intelligent woman who believed my explanation of why I was on the roof.

"Daniel," she asked, "What is it you want most in your life?"

"To drive a car."

"Why?"

"The freedom it gives you to go anywhere you want at any time."

"Daniel, you are fifteen years old. You'll have to wait three years."

"That's too long to wait," I answered. That was sixty years ago.

I took this opportunity to ask the therapist if she could get me transferred to Lafayette High School on Benson Avenue in the Bath Beach section of Brooklyn, where all my friends were, and this kind woman arranged for my relocation.

Things seemed to go better there, with me actually doing my homework and paying attention in class. But, by the end of the fourth term, I began experiencing great anxiety and restlessness.

It began one day, when I saw the man who gave me the quarter in the Metro theatre strolling along Bay Parkway. I followed him as he entered the park, apparently seeking out another victim. He stopped at Mattie's and ordered a knish, and just as he bit into it, I asked him, "Wanna' make a quarter?" He turned to me and his eyebrows rose up, just as they did in the movie house; but he had no clue who I was.

"What do you want?" He said, biting into the knish.

"You don't remember me, do you?"

"Why, should I?"

"Five years ago, the Metro theatre on 20th Avenue, you gave me a quarter to jerk you off."

"Go away, kid," he said, continuing to eat the knish.

"I was eight years old."

"I don't know what you're talking about," he lied, finishing his meal.

"I'm gonna' call the cops," I threatened.

"What are you gonna' tell 'em, something that happened five years ago? They'll never believe you."

"Then believe this!" I shouted and kicked him squarely in the nuts. He buckled over in agony, and I gave another swift kick to his groin. People stared at me doing this, but dared not interfere. They thought most of the park kids were juvenile delinquents and stayed clear of us.

I leaned over the man and said softly, "That should help your *thing* stay small." I kicked him once more in the ass, and then walked away.

As gratifying as it was to have harmed the man who had harmed me, the incident stirred up an inexplicable emotion. Walking home, I was shivering all the way, and when I got there, went to my bedroom and broke down in tears. My sister, Esther came home from work and found me laying there with reddened eyes. She rushed in to hug me.

"What happened, Danny?" She asked softly, and the tears flowed again. For the first time since it happened, the story was revealed.

Esther fixed me some dinner, and when I was done eating led me into her bedroom. She shut the door behind us and told me to sit on the bed. "Honey," she said firmly, "You cannot tell anyone about this." I looked up at her, surprised by what she had just said. "This could hurt our family. The community will look down upon you, upon all of us, if this gets out."

"Why?" I asked incredulously.

"Because we just don't talk about things like this." She ran her hand through my hair and planted a kiss on my forehead. "You understand this, *Rohi?*" she sighed as she used the SY term of endearment. I nodded, not really understanding.

19

HOWLING DOGS

My sister, Esther was born in April 1937, in the midst of the great depression. Unemployment was rampant and families were evicted from their homes. One such family put out on the street was that of Mr. Baruch Beyda (a man who had lost a leg in his youth) along with his wife, his thirteen children, and his twelve year old brother. They were offered support from the government, but Mr. Beyda refused to accept it. He had given his solemn vow to American immigration authorities in Le Havre, France, to never seek aid since U.S. Immigration had attempted to bar him from entering America for fear he would become a financial burden. "God took my leg," he averred, "but left me my hands. I will never take charity." When his family was evicted, three caring SY neighbors took in the family and fed them. Old man Beyda went on to become a member of the *Ma'oz Levyon*, the charitable group formed by the community to help its indigent members.

There was a great story about Mr. Beyda that circulated in the late forties. By then he, and most of the nation, had recovered from the disastrous financial crisis, thanks to the war economy, but there were still many impoverished SY families. Mr. Beyda had built a manufacturing business that was doing quite well. He had access to canned foods at a wholesale price, so he decided to buy them in bulk and resell them at or below cost to other Syrian families that were still struggling, even giving some away for free to those who were neediest.

His wife soon heard certain members of the community speaking ill about her husband's sale of these goods, saying things such as, "Beyda has so much money, yet he needs to take advantage of the poor."

Mrs. Beyda confronted her spouse with this and pleaded with him to stop selling the canned goods so people would stop talking unkindly about the Beyda's. This wise man responded with an allegorical tale.

"There was a large puddle of water in the courtyard of a building and the full moon was causing a bright reflection of light. Some neighborhood dogs began howling because the moon was so bright. People in the neighborhood, whose sleep was disturbed by the barking dogs, looked up to the Heavens and pleaded with *Hashem* to make the moon go away. God responded by saying, 'For a few howling dogs, you ask me to remove the beauty of the moon?'"

In 1959, Esther was twenty-three and unmarried, considered an old maid by community standards. She was not pretty, but had a face that exuded warmth and sincerity. She loved her family and did everything in her power to nurture us. When Esther was six years old, she bathed and fed me, washed my diapers and clothes, and sang me to sleep. When we started school, she got Marilyn, Al and me our supplies, shopped for our clothes (mostly second hand), and helped with the homework. She did all this, helping Mom, and later Becky, care for the apartment while personally scoring great grades at school.

Most SY girls did not go to college, even dropped out of high school to get married or work and contribute money to the family. They were trained in cooking and housekeeping in preparation for their marriage. Their lives' roles were in the kitchen and the bedroom, to fulfill the family needs for nourishment, raise the children and perform their marital obligations to their husbands. But foremost, they were charged with the obligation of the first biblical commandment, to "be fruitful and multiply."

Esther was the rare SY woman to graduate from Brooklyn College and now, at twenty-three, the only job she could find was selling flowers in a store on Bay Parkway. Pop made several attempts to arrange a *buzrah* for Esther, a negotiated marriage, but he couldn't sell the dowry requirements. She became a *hazeet* case, someone to be pitied.

One day, a plain looking young man with bushy hair walked into the florist shop and inquired about buying a dozen long stem roses. Esther politely showed him the flowers that were kept in a cooler.

"They're beautiful; how much?" He asked.

"Six dollars for the dozen," she answered, avoiding his glance.

"Can you wrap them nicely?" He quickly removed six one dollar bills from his coat pocket and handed them to Esther. He smiled, as he looked her over while she rang up the sale and wrapped the roses. He turned and examined the shop as though taking a survey. "How long have you been working here?"

"Three weeks,' she answered with a slight flutter in her voice.

"Where did you learn about flowers?"

"Reading books. The best roses come from South America; Columbia, in fact." She continued to wrap the flowers, and then said, "Your girlfriend will love these."

The man's smile widened. "They're for my mother's fiftieth birthday."

Esther blushed at his response. "Do you live around here?"

"East 12th, he said, and after the slightest pause, added, "I'm Jewish, twenty-eight years old and I like you." Esther's face turned crimson. "My name is Sol Bernstein, but everyone calls me Bernie."

"J-Dub," she said. "My name is Esther Dweck; I'm a Syrian Jew, and I'm 23 years old." She turned her eyes away from him. "I like you, too."

Bernie courted her for five months, and then came to the apartment to ask my father's permission to marry Esther. He seemed like a nice man, Pop thought, but would he come up with any money?

Bernie thought about it for a minute. "Whatever money I have will be spent on the wedding and setting up an apartment to live in. Or I can bet it all on a horse and see where that takes us."

Pop laughed, and the tension was broken. "God bless you both, and give you much happiness and lots of children."

They were married five months later, had two kids, a boy and a girl, following the J-Dub custom of not naming them after living relatives. The boy, Gerald, named after Bernie's deceased grandfather, was a problem child from the start. Esther had gone through two miscarriages before carrying Gerald successfully to term. They spoiled him rotten. Bernie bought him toys, enough to fill up a nursery, coddled him to no end, and set no boundaries for him. His parents nicknamed him Lucky because he had not been miscarried.

Lucky went to Flatbush Yeshiva, where many SY kids were now attending, but had trouble focusing on the work. He began to feel inadequate because he could not keep up with the other SY kids. Esther found him a tutor who suggested he learn an instrument. Lucky did like music, so Bernie started him on piano lessons when his son was ten years old.

The kid did have talent. Lucky became very good at playing the instrument, and Bernie bought him a baby grand to practice on at home. He played at parties and amazed audiences with his dexterity and expressions. By the time he graduated from the Yeshiva, he could play Mozart, Chopin, and Paderewski as well as any professional artist. His tonal quality had the sound of one who had been playing for many years.

Lucky loved playing twelve bar blues, but most of all, he was taken by Dave Brubeck, whose style ranged from refined to overbearing. Lucky was mesmerized by Brubeck's unusual time signatures and contrasting rhythms and tonalities.

Unfortunately, by the time the boy was seventeen, he was hanging out with musicians who were older than him and he became hooked on drugs, first on marijuana, which soon elevated to heroin. He became a junkie, either constantly high or so low he would get sick until he found his next fix.

One day, he disappeared from home. Esther and Bernie searched frantically for him, but he was nowhere to be found. Two weeks later, Esther received a call from an anonymous stranger in Miami saying her son was in Cedars Sinai hospital after being hit by a truck.

"Lucky suffered a few broken bones," the caller said, "but otherwise survived the accident. Sad to say, the kid was completely in "la la" land. He must have OD'ed on something." The young man would not give his name or number and hung up.

After calling the hospital to verify that Lucky was, in fact, a patient there, Esther and Bernie took the next flight down to Miami; and I went with them. When we landed, we rushed to the hospital and found Lucky in a coma like state, with tubes coming out of and going into every orifice. The doctor told us they had operated on his left arm and right leg, resetting some bones, but they assured us he would pull through, He had indeed OD'ed on a very pure form of heroin that should have killed him, but his name saved him.

Two days later, Lucky awakened and began to cry when he saw me and his parents standing before him. "Uncle Danny... Mommy... Daddy," he said almost in a whisper. "I am so sorry."

"Shhh," Bernie said, leaning over to kiss his son's forehead.

"You just need to get well," Esther added. "Uncle Danny has arranged for you to go to a re-hab center as soon as we get back to New York."

The kid looked towards me. "What can I say, Uncle Danny?"

"Just promise to do the recovery work. I'll help in any way I can." He reached up with his good hand and clasped mine.

"Thank you, Uncle. You have my solemn promise I will get through this thing."

And he did; after ninety days in a rehab center not far from Deal, the kid was back to normal and has been clean and sober since. His family was thrilled, as was I.

Lucky's addiction got me thinking about my own abuse of alcohol, but, typical of one addicted to any substance, it was quickly brushed aside.

Bernie and Esther shared a beautiful union between two wonderful people that lasted 52 years and ended, in the physical world, when Bernie died. But their relationship continued on spiritually in my sister's heart until she passed in 2010 of pneumonia. I loved Esther dearly, and followed her advice to never speak of the "Metro theatre" incident. That is, until much later in my life.

20

HONOR THE CONVERTS

There was something both charming and annoying about Claudia. I did get her number from my sister Marilyn, and we went on our first date two weeks after eating at David's. What was charming about her was a solid sense of humor (she laughed at my jokes) and her straight forwardness. Claudia was an open woman, unafraid to reveal her secrets, unapologetic about her life of fabulous wealth (Manny had left behind an estate of more than two and a half billion dollars) and a willingness to discuss anything. That was very refreshing. What annoyed me about her was her obsession with branded goods: Chanel, Prada, Louis Vuitton, and of course, Christian Louboutin.

"Only the best," she said more than once during dinner at Due, my favorite Italian restaurant on the Upper East Side. "There's no point in wearing knockoffs. Only demeans you."

"What if someone couldn't afford them?"

"I'm talking about women who *can* afford them. Lots of the wealthier SY wives and daughters look for copies or second hand stuff for bargains. Me, I want the originals. Never mind the price. *Baruch Hashem*, I have the means."

Claudia was kosher; I was not. She ordered the grilled whole Branzino, and me, the chicken parm. She finished every last bite, including her sautéed spinach, but I left over half of mine. We shared Tartufo for desert, and, when offered Grappa by the waiter, Claudia declined. She did not have any wine that night and inquired about when I stopped drinking.

"Got sober the first day I walked into an AA meeting thirty-two years ago. What a laugh that was. I went up to the front desk and asked for the application form to join. Even asked how much it costs to be a member. The laughter those questions triggered from some of the old timers relaxed me, and the camaraderie was terrific. I took to it at once and got the message."

"Do you still go to meetings?"

"No, stopped after two years. AA got me sober, but I found the petty squabbling and archaic rules disturbing. Many members treat AA like a religion, and lack the willingness to let it grow and evolve. I went to ACOA meetings instead."

"What's that?"

"Adult Children of Alcoholics, a very enlightened group that focused on the dysfunctional home; taught me a great deal. It was with that group that I was able to confront the sexual abuse I encountered as a child." I noticed her jaw slacken a bit as she took in those last words.

"How old were you?" she asked gently.

"Eight. It happened in a movie theatre."

"My God; did they ever catch the guy?"

"No," I answered, and then related the story about my confrontation with the perpetrator in the park, and the warning from Esther not to speak of it.

I paid the check and helped Claudia on with her coat. An autumn chill had swept in early, but we decided to walk a few blocks anyway. "This is my favorite time of the year," I said as we strolled downtown on Third Avenue. "The air is crisp, the trees are shedding, and the fall foliage is stupendous."

"Manny and I used to fly to Israel for Rosh Hashanah and Yom Kippur when the kids were young. Stayed in Jerusalem, where the weather was still in the 80's, and dry."

"King David Hotel?"

"That's all there was in those days; loved it. Have you been to Israel?"

"Once; I was not overly impressed."

"Oh, my God, Danny, the history of that country, and the stories behind it that is simply amazing. It's our homeland."

"Reminds me of Brooklyn," I said, half-jokingly. She laughed and slipped her arm through mine as we walked. "Say," I suggested, "I've seen yours so why don't you see mine?" Her eyes widened. "You have a dirty mind," I said, mischievously. "I'm talking about my apartment. What did you think I meant?" I laughed. "There's a bottle of fine Merlot handy for guests. It's unopened, never been touched."

She smiled, then, childlike, skipped a few steps, dragging me long. "I'll be the judge of how fine your wine is, Mr. Daniel Dweck."

We walked the entire eighteen blocks back to my building. When we entered the apartment, she was awed by the view of Manhattan from the 44th floor. She perused the furniture and built in closets, all of which were black. "Nice bachelor digs, "she commented.

"Redid the whole place after Sonia died. The decorator said, 'Let's make a statement,' hence the all black. Then she sent me *her* statement which was black and white and in the low six figures."

Claudia laughed. "What about that wine you were bragging about? I got a chill from that walk." I uncorked the bottle and poured her a glass. She took a sip and nodded her approval.

We shared tales about our marriages, and, of course, we discussed our children; how lucky we were they all turned out okay, though she still had her fingers crossed for her youngest son, Steven. "Manny and I spoiled him," she confessed." Luckily, he took a liking to Rabbi Cohen who has been so helpful in redirecting Steven. That man is a blessing to the community. Do you know him?"

"Yes, quite well, actually. We've had many discussions over the past years. He's a good man. Not like that other rabbi in Deal, Rabbi Dwek."

"He *is* a bit of an authoritarian," she agreed.

"That guy has taken the community back to the 12th Century with his strict rules, while his son, Solomon, brought such shame to all SYs with his real estate Ponzi scheme crimes. There are a lot of hypocrites in the community. Take Rabbi Saul Kassin, the Chief Rabbi, who preaches to people to be ethical, then confesses to money laundering for a 10% share of the deal. His father, Jacob, married me to my first wife".

She slid a bit closer to me on the couch and settled in still clutching her glass of the Merlot.

"And what about the rabbis rulings about conversion? You know what I find strange?" I continued, "The book of Deuteronomy says to honor the convert even more than those who were born Jews. Yet, going back to 1935, the SY rabbinate, headed by Chief Rabbi Jacob Kassin, signed an edict that forbids acceptance of those who have made the transition to our faith. They ratified it again in the forties, and once more just a few years ago. What gave these so-called 'scholars' the right to change the will of the God they hold to be infallible?"

"There was too much intermarriage."

"But people convert. Jews believe that if the mother is Jewish, so is the child. So let's say an SY woman marries a non-Jew, doesn't matter. The kid's still Jewish. That child should be allowed to attend the yeshiva, but they won't allow it."

"You have a point."

"The Chief Rabbi's son, Jakie Kassin, told the New York Times a few years ago that the SY's had to remain a pure community and to never accept a convert or a child born of a convert. Why? 'Because we don't want gentile characteristics,' he said."

"He did say that, but many of us objected to his remarks and pushed back at him. He thinks he should have become the Chief Rabbi instead of his father. Did you know his sister ran off and married a non-Jew?"

"I heard that."

"The family didn't talk to her for twenty-five years. They said they'd welcome her back only if she left her husband and kids behind."

"How cruel is that," I remarked.

"It's sad, but it seems it is the only way to keep the community from losing its identity."

"Where did we ever get the idea that anyone is *born* a Jew? Judaism is a *religion*, not a race. There are all kinds of Jews of different races around the world, even blacks and Chinese. This community vets any non-SY Jew carefully, going back three generations and requiring the stamp of approval of an Orthodox rabbi. You know, Hitler called Jews a race. The Nazi's went back three generations to confirm that a German was an Aryan. Judaism is a religion, not a…," but before I could finish the sentence, Claudia leaned in and kissed me. I hadn't expected that, and at first recoiled slightly, but so as not to embarrass her, responded in kind.

As the kiss ended, she pulled back and took another sip of the wine. "I'm sorry," she said coquettishly. "I shouldn't have done that."

"Don't be silly. It was a sweet surprise."

"I really like you, Danny."

"And I like you, too, but let's not rush. '*Nice n' Easy*', as Sinatra sings."

"I'm embarrassed," she said as she moved away.

"Please don't be. It was a spontaneous action and I admire you for that. Besides, you tasted good. I'd like more of it, but at a slower pace."

She laughed. "Sometime in this century, I hope."

21

LOUIE & THE BLOW JOB

The fourth friend in our group growing up was Lou Shamah, or Louie, as we called him. He was tall, good-looking, with a full, curly, head of hair that he pasted down with Wildroot. Louie had a condition called exotropia; his left eye would move slowly from the center to the edge whenever he was excited or mad at something.

Louie was the oldest of our four-man group, by almost a full year. He worshiped Eddie, would kill for him, and did whatever Eddie asked. It all started when Eddie got him his first blowjob. That was a strange story.

Sammy and I were in the 9th grade SP, Eddie and Louie in a regular 9th grade class. We were all 13 or 14 years old when we heard about a girl named Maryanne Bonivito, who was said to be giving guys blowjobs. The rumor was she was a "nympho."

One afternoon, when school was over, Eddie had arranged for her to be taken to the basement of this kid's apartment building on Bay Parkway for a gang bang. There were seven of us, plus Maryanne, walking along Bay Parkway to the building on West 9th. A couple of the guys were teasing Maryanne, grabbing at her breasts and her crotch. At one point, she slipped and fell to the ground. I helped her up and she smiled at me.

"Thank you," she said. "You're a nice guy. What's your name?"

"Danny Dweck," I answered innocently. As I looked in her eyes, I felt sorry for her and decided not to go along with this. "Hey fellas, let the girl go home," I pleaded but no one responded. I turned left on 68th Street and went home.

Well, Louie got his first blow job, but the next day, while sitting in my classroom, the Assistant Principal, Mr. Greenspan, came in with a police officer. Mr. Greenspan whispered something to the teacher, and called my name out. It seemed Maryanne had named me as one of the boys who gang raped her the previous day even though I never laid a hand on her. Mine was the only name she remembered. Eddie, as usual, got away with it, but Louie and I, along with three other kids, were taken to the 62nd Precinct for questioning, and booked for sexual assault.

The detective took each of us, one by one, into a private room where he assured us nothing was going to happen if we followed his instructions. We would have to go to court in about two weeks, stand before a judge, and tell him what had happened.

"Danny," the detective instructed me, "you say, 'Your Honor, I fondled Maryanne's breast,' and that's it. Just say that, and nothing will happen to you." Similar instructions were given to the rest of the boys. I was surprised that the cop was taking this attitude in our favor and ignoring the seriousness of what had happened to that teenage girl.

Court date comes and five of us were lined up before the judge, who turns out to be a woman. Each of our parents was there behind us; Becky stands stiffly erect as a flagpole. First kid makes his plea, so does the second and third, until it comes to Louie.

"What did you do, young man?" The Judge asked.

Louie stared quietly at her, so terrified he was unable to speak. The Judge was looking at him as his eye started drifting. She found it amusing and couldn't help but smile, which immediately relaxed Louie. "Take your time, young man."

He had been instructed to say, "I groped at her vagina," but in his excitement he blurted, "I stuck my finger in her hole, Your Honor." All five of us boys had to hold back our laughter.

"This is not a laughing matter!" the jurist said sternly.

After a moment, I did my allocution as instructed. Becky kicked me in the shin as I said the word 'breast'. The case ended there, with a stern warning from the judge never to do this again. Our records were cleared and we went about our business of growing up. I felt guilty for weeks for not trying harder to stop the boys from abusing Maryanne.

Louie was a hard worker, but struggled with school. He would peddle his bike in the afternoons selling toiletries door to door, and whatever he made went to the family. He quit high school and lied about his age to join the navy.

Louie did four years' service in the Navy and returned home a more mature person. Eddie was in dental school, I was working with my father, and Sammy was a traveling salesman for an SY company importing home electronics from Japan. Louie felt lost, drifting, with no goal in sight.

Eddie convinced him to get a GED diploma, and Louie did. He went on to Night College and graduated with a BA in business. Louie met and married a homely looking SY girl, Milo Swede, the oldest of four daughters of a rich importer of household products, and raised a family of four children with her. Milo was a sweetheart, and what she lacked in looks she more than made up with personality and perseverance, always involved with charitable work and offering to do favors for anyone at any time.

Louie worked for her father and became a partner five years later. Because he had no sons, after Milo's father died, Louie took over the company and made a very comfortable living for himself and his family.

Louie died eighteen months before Sammy, at the age of 73, from a massive heart attack. The loss of this simple, honest, hardworking man who had overcome many difficulties in his lifetime was deeply felt by me and the whole community.

22

TRUMP

I called Sammy's girlfriend, Martha, and asked her to come to my office. When I told her about the money she burst into tears, but a faint smile appeared. "This is why I loved Sammy," she said, stunned by her new fortune. "This was a man who was honorable and loving. I don't know what to say."

"Just be careful how you use this," I warned, and handed her the check. "I'll have my driver take you where you want to go." She gave me a big hug and left.

My secretary, Fran, came into the office and handed me a bunch of phone messages. I skimmed through them quickly, dismissing most, until I came to one from Rabbi Cohen. I speed dialed him and he picked up after the first ring. "Judah, my friend, how are you?"

"Baruch Hashem. Never better. And you?"

"Coping," I answered.

"Good to hear that. Listen, Danny Boy," he continued. "We need your help again."

"How much?"

"I have you down for $10K. It's for *Bikur Holim*. They are short on cash and, well, there are a lot of older community members who need the help."

"Check's in the mail."

"You're a *haborb*. *Skail ha'mitzvot*."

"Funny, you should call today, Judah. Your name came up in a conversation last night?"

"In a nice way, I hope," the rabbi answered.

"Of course."

"How is that going?" he asked.

"How is what going?"

He was coy. "Claudia Gemal. She's a very nice person."

It was not surprising he knew about Claudia and me. Gossip speeds faster through SYs than an Indy 500 race car. "She is," I said, then quickly changed the subject. "Listen, Judah, let's get together at David's one night. There's something we need to discuss again."

"What's the subject?"

"*Ahbud*," I answered, and the phones remained silent for a good fifteen seconds.

"Call me," he said finally. And we hung up.

I'm not sure why I brought up that subject at this time. Maybe it had to do with Trump's winning the election. A large majority of SYs voted for him, despite his racist, sexist, and anti-Semitic positions. The people with whom he has surrounded himself are not much better.

Rabbi Judah Cohen is ten years younger than me, and I remember him being a wild kid, always getting into trouble. At age fifteen, he was arrested for selling marijuana and put on probation. His father put him in the hands of, of all people, Rabbi Shamula. Oddly enough, he and the Rabbi hit it off, and the boy took to the religion. He studied hard, finished Yeshiva, spent four years in Israel for rabbinical study and was ordained a rabbi at the age of twenty-one. When he returned to the community, he focused on helping troubled kids and was overwhelmingly respected by all for his dedication.

Rabbi Judah Cohen developed into a wise man, progressive in his thinking and utilizing any information, no matter its source, to heal the problems of the Community. He did not lead a congregation, but rather worked with groups and individuals to solve their difficulties. The increasing cases of alcoholism and drug abuse were his primary targets, and he did a wonderful job of bringing about solutions.

There were two brothers, whose names shall remain anonymous, who had serious alcohol and drug addictions. They were good people, but had fallen victims to the treacherous diseases. Their family lives were ruined; their children, too, turned to alcohol and drugs, and their wives threatened to divorce them. Judah did an intervention in which I was one of many people who the brothers respected, and to the amazement of everyone, they recovered. After spending sixty days in rehab, both men have been sober and drug free for six years, and their children have joined the road to recovery. Without Rabbi Judah's help, both those troubled families would have been destroyed.

This dedicated, young rabbi has helped many addicts to be restored to sober and productive lives. But the one disease that continues to permeate this otherwise wonderful SY community remains to be a racist streak that just won't go away.

I suppose most communities have some sort of negative views of other societies. I read somewhere it's a tribal thing, going back to cavemen, who lived in small groups, and were constantly in competition with each other for food and survival. The exceptions to this theory are the indigenous peoples of Australia. Aborigines have been known to exist for more than fifty thousand years on that continent. They have an almost reverent respect for the land. Although there were many different groups that spoke as many as 250 different languages, today most Aborigines speak English with the exception of a few words and phrases. The various indigenous groups believed that when a child is born, it is the entire community's responsibility to raise and care for the baby properly.

Racism and hatred of other peoples have been the scourge of mankind. Citizens of one land have allowed their hatred to destroy other lands. Various groups within a country battled each other for supremacy, the stronger groups generally enslaving the weaker. The Bible describes slavery in its most vicious forms. Egyptians subjugated the Jews for four hundred years, and Hebrews, in turn, incarcerated those peoples it overran in wars.

The first clear example of slavery in the Old Testament is in Exodus where the Israelites were made to work ruthlessly as slaves for the Pharaohs. After the Israelites had fled Egypt, they were given the Laws of Moses, which allowed them to make slaves of Hebrews and foreigners. The laws regarding slavery in the Old Testament commanded the Israelites to treat their fellow Hebrews, some who were enslaved because they could not repay a financial debt, as if they were servants and grant them the option of their freedom in the 7th year of their service. These servants could, of course, remain slaves if they chose. There were other laws dealing with physical abuse of slaves, and those who ran away from their masters were to be welcomed and not returned. However, all these laws applied only to the Hebrew slaves.

The Anti-Defamation League describes one important feature of racism, especially toward Blacks and immigrant groups, is in the attitudes regarding slaves and slavery. Jews are seen by anti-Semites as subhuman, but also super-human, devilishly cunning, skilled, and powerful. Blacks and others are seen by racists as merely subhuman, more like beasts as men. If the focus of anti-Semitism is evil, the focus of racism is inferiority.

The incident in front of Charlie's candy store where that black boy was beaten by the Irish kid left an indelible print in my brain and heart and today has given me a clear picture of why Brian had his son beat that boy. It is because *he, Brian*, had a feeling of inferiority and needed to overpower the black kid to puff up his own esteem.

In Hitler's era, the Holocaust was begun with words and pictures. There was a steady stream of vicious attacks by Nazi newspapers, some of which were owned by Hitler, depicting Jews with large noses in photos showing them staring lewdly at young German maidens. The lies about Jewish behavior printed in the articles were repeated often enough by the Nazis and their Leader, and became common beliefs amongst the population.

This is why the continued use of the word ahbud pierces my ears and sets off a flame of anger in my heart. It perpetuates the lie that SYs are superior to blacks, and carries over into a false sense of superiority over others, starting with fellow Jews that happen to be J-Dubs.

I made a mental note to call Judah early next week, and then my thoughts drifted to Claudia.

23

THE FIRST TIME

At fifteen, I was the youngest student expelled from school and jokingly referred to myself as a "high school throw-out." For days after my school life ended, my mind drifted in and out of depression and obsession over being thrown out of school. My self-esteem was shattered, and I felt like a complete failure. One afternoon, I experienced a severe anxiety attack, and Esther had to call in a doctor to give me a sedative.

My father insisted that work would heal me and ordered me to help him at the store. "Pray, Hashem will heal you," he said. Pop was right. Going to work every day with him and Becky took my mind off things, but saying the prayers just didn't appeal to me.

I developed a knack for selling and was soon bringing in serious money for the business, but not sharing in the success. My salary was $35 a week, which included lunch, prepared by Becky. Working for my father taught me a lot about sales. Unfortunately, my rewards were not so great, and after two years my salary never went past $40 a week.

I resumed reading, starting with a book called '30 Days to a Better Vocabulary,' which taught me how to figure out what words meant by recognizing their roots. I learned the meaning of 'ology", which meant 'the study of" that helped define many words. When "ology" is attached to a prefix, such as *psych*, which means, "mind," the combination, "psychology" means the study of the mind.

I bought a pocket dictionary and kept it with me at all times to define words as I read Max Lerner and Murray Kempton in the New York Post and the Op-Ed pages of The New York Times every day. I was drawn to books about World War II, read all six volumes of Winston Churchill's account of that conflict, and was especially fascinated by those histories about Hitler and the Nazis. When Adolf Eichmann was kidnapped by the Israelis, I followed his trial on a daily basis.

Nietzsche, Descartes, and Kafka were a struggle for me, but I thoroughly enjoyed "Madam Bovary" and the full-length version of "The Count of Monte Cristo."

My social life was anything but social. Sammy and I would meet most evenings in the park and usually get into a game of poker with some of the other guys being held under a street lamp. Everyone cheated in those games, and the only chance of winning a hand was the one you dealt.

I had dated a few of the girls in our crowd once or twice, but one night, in the late spring of 1958, at a dance in the Sephardic Center on Avenue P, I hit it off with the hottest girl there, an eighteen year old beauty with a dynamite figure named Cheryl Bookman. Her father owned a Florsheim Shoe franchise on Flatbush Avenue, and Cheryl worked there a couple days a week. She was a bright girl, funny, with a dry sense of humor, and way ahead of her time. She refused to wear a bra, which had all the boys in the neighborhood staring at her ample chest whenever she passed by them.

We dated on and off for about six months and made out heavily most times when we were together. I liked Cheryl a lot. She made me feel good about myself, often telling me how smart I was. Making out with her, which we often did, was great. She loved to watch my expressions while masturbating me and it certainly was a joy as she found ways to increase my pleasure. We never had intercourse until one night, at a Halloween party in the JCH; we slipped off to a small room and began necking. Things got heavy, and I removed her blouse, revealing those marvelous breasts. She removed my shirt and, as the making out got heavier we finally went all the way.

This intercourse was my first time, but apparently not hers. She directed the whole episode, telling me what to do and guiding me inside her. The feeling was exquisitely beyond compare, and I quickly reached a climax. She continued to masturbate herself while holding my now flaccid penis. I was amazed at her dexterity through all this and fell madly in love with her.

Unfortunately, the feelings were not reciprocal. After that evening, for some unfathomable reason, which I never learned, Cheryl would not take my calls. She ignored me completely when we passed by each other in the neighborhood. I was devastated. What had I done? She led me to the intercourse, and both of us, it seemed, wanted it to happen. She was the experienced one, not me. I thought she liked me, but now felt humiliated by her avoidance. I asked Sammy to talk to her, but she refused to speak with him. Louie told me to forget about her and just chalk her up as my first conquest. To this day, I have no clue as to what happened between us, but I vowed to myself never to be shamed again by a woman.

The day after this episode with Cheryl, while having a tuna on rye sandwich at the Sweet Box on Bay Parkway and 71st Street, a darkly tanned and handsome SY guy I knew casually, Cookie Tawil, walked in and approached.

"Danny Dweck, right?" I nodded yes. "Heard you can sell. Can you?"

"I hold my own."

"How much are you making?"

"A $100 a week," I lied.

"How'd you like to make $300?"

"Who do I have to shoot?"

Cookie laughed, and then came straight to the point. "Come work for me in Wildwood, New Jersey, for the summer. You get $125 a week plus pumps. Average week you'll take home $300, off the books and tax-free. "Ten weeks, you make $3,000. You share a house with the rest of us, paid for by me."

"I'm in," I said without hesitation.

"Do you know any other young hotshots who want to make easy money?" I immediately mentioned Sammy and Cookie sealed the deal with him that night. Needless to say, Pop was not pleased with my leaving, but when I told him how much I would be earning, he wished me luck.

Easy money was a gross exaggeration of the job. Our hours were 8 a.m. 'til 1 a.m., seven days a week with no time off for lunch or dinner. Our meals were consumed in the store.

Sometimes, after we closed the shop, we'd go to Junior's, a diner on the main strip for a late meal or, on rare occasions, talk Cookie into driving to Atlantic City to pick up girls (think hookers). Many days we would go to work without having slept and would sneak in a few winks by wearing dark sunglasses and leaning on the showcase.

Cookie and his partner, Jackie Sultan, owned two stores on the boardwalk. Sammy and I worked in one, and two other young SYs, Joey Fallas and Irwin

Krady worked the other. Joey was a strange bird, but funny as all hell. He came up with every dirty joke known to mankind and did the most outlandish things, such as taking a dump in the Junior's bathroom and flinging it to the ceiling. Another time, Sammy, Joey and I were in Cookie's car driving to Junior's when we stopped for a light. Joey dropped his pants, stuck a cigar up his ass then pointed his butt out the rear window at a woman standing at the curb. "Excuse me, Miss," he said. "Can you tell me where the nearest drug store is?"

The woman screamed and jumped backwards and Cookie pulled away fast. A few blocks later a squad car pulled us over. The cop got out and approached us.

"Whose ass was out that window – and don't anyone tell me it was your face!"

Joey was an eater. A typical two a.m. meal at Juniors consisted of a tuna fish salad sandwich with lettuce, tomato and onions on rye; lox and cream cheese on a toasted bagel with tomato and onions; side orders of Coleslaw and potato salad; an order of green peas and a large plate of French fries. He drank four or five glasses of water while devouring the food.

Four salesmen and the two bosses occupied the house we shared. The salespeople slept two to a room, and the bosses each had their own bedrooms. Every Monday, a girl named Theresa would come in to clean and do the laundry. She was a religious Catholic and wore a silver chain and cross around her neck. Theresa was six months pregnant, but the problem was she was not married.

One morning I woke up with a sore throat and begged Cookie to let me sleep in for a few hours. He reluctantly agreed, and I did not awake until 11 a.m. Since it was a Monday, Theresa let herself in to do her work. She noticed I was not feeling well.

"Let me make you some hot tea with honey," she offered.

She was a sweet girl, nineteen, and not too bright. Theresa said she liked to do things for people, took pleasure in providing pleasure to others. She served the tea at the kitchen table. I was wearing only my underwear.

"Is that how you got pregnant?" I asked.

"Kind of. Sal was my boyfriend for eight months, and we never did anything serious in the way of sex. One night," she said as she loaded the washing machine, "we were making out in the back of his truck, and he started licking my ears and that made me nuts."

"Really?" I asked.

"I'm very sensitive there, you know. It got me so turned on. Forget about it." She shook her head back and forth seeming to get excited just recalling the moment.

"Can we try that now, just to see how it works?"

She leaned over the table, brushed her hair to the side and presented her ear to me. I licked it and sure enough, she became aroused. Soon, we were kissing, and we both got heated up. "Do that again," she pleaded, and I continued to work on her ears. Soon, she led me to the bedroom and pushed me onto the mattress.

"God forgive me," she said as she undressed and mounted me.

I had to think of new excuses on the coming Mondays so Theresa and I could continue our little trysts. After Labor Day, I gave her a gold chain with a gold cross. She was thrilled and thanked me profusely.

As oppressive as the job was, when Labor Day arrived, I was Twenty-Eight Hundred dollars richer, having spent only Two Hundred in those few moments when not working. Sammy came home with less, because he lost more than a thousand of his hard earned dollars in card games held every Saturday night amongst the workers. Cookie sometimes joined the competitions and, being a very lucky baccarat player, won back some of the money he had just paid his employees.

With the summer ended, I had no clue about what to do with the *flooce* I had just slaved for, but two things were certain: my work ethic was fully established, and I had become obsessed with making more.

24

CHRISTINA

My father was anxious to get me back to work with him, but even more anxious to get his hands on my cash. Abdullah Ramallah was anxious to sell his interest in the business so he and his wife could move to San Francisco to be near their children, both attending UCSF. He had asked Pop for One Hundred Thousand dollars for his share, was willing to take half down as a deposit, and be paid the balance over two years. The deal was fair, but Pop needed me and my money to make it work.

I agreed to come in, but insisted on being paid Two Hundred dollars a week plus own half the business. Pop approved my terms and assured me, "It will all be yours one day, *Rohi.*"

So, for four years, my father, Becky, and I toiled away at the store, and making good money at it. By November 1962 Ramallah had been paid off and we had $100 K in the bank. My 21st birthday was approaching, and I was feeling my oats. I talked Pop into letting me take Twenty-Two hundred out of the bank to put it down as a deposit on a new 1963 Thunderbird. The automobile was burgundy with beige interior, cost Forty-Two Hundred fully loaded; it was my dream car.

My father turned fifty-six in January of 1963 and looked as if he were one hundred. His face was drawn, his skin sallow, and his gate much slower. Becky forced him to see a doctor, and the prognosis was not too good. He was on the brink of a heart attack and had to take digitalis for congestive heart failure and atrial arrhythmias. They also prescribed nitroglycerin pills to deal with the chest pains. At this time, the order from the President to report for my physical arrived.

I had a girlfriend, a not too devout Catholic named Christina Rowen. We met on a boat ride to Bear Mountain one Sunday three years earlier. Christina was an attractive (if even in a plain sort of way), sweet, person, and honest to a fault, because she always said what was on her mind. There was never a hesitation for her to call me out when I acted like a jerk or said something stupid. She really loved me, but my feelings, though very strong towards her, had to be kept in check because of her religion.

We saw each other in spurts, sometimes three nights a week, and other times, not be together for a month. I really liked her, and she was fun to be with, but looking back, it was clear to me the relationship was doomed. Her sight was on marriage, and there was no shot of me doing that. The boys kept telling me to dump her, but Sammy was the only one who supported me, and with his encouragement, I held on to the connection.

In the early stages of the relationship I would borrow my brother Jakey's station wagon and take Christina out for dinner or a movie, invariably ending up at Plum Beach, a parking spot on the Belt Parkway, for our make out sessions. When I got the T-bird, its bucket seat interior configuration made it impossible to make out so we often took a room in the Golden Gate Motor Inn on Knapp Street, a notorious spot for "short stay" service.

Our sexual relationship had its limits. There's nothing Christina wouldn't do for me, except have intercourse. We performed oral sex on each other, masturbated one another, and kissed nonstop. Christina refused to go all the way until she was married. I respected her position and was more than satisfied with our arrangement.

Christina was a very loyal and caring soul; if she were a J-Dub I would have definitely married her, but the taboos about interfaith marriages had been imbedded in me from childhood. My brother Al was married to an Italian girl, Marie, which had come as a shock to the family.

Christina accompanied me to Whitehall Street for my physical, waiting nearly four hours at a nearby diner. I was not going to do what my brother Jakey and some friends had done, fake my way through the test. When the examination was over, they classified me 1A. While I did not want to avoid the draft, it was not in my plans to spend a couple of years in uniform. By the time my "report for duty" notice arrived, Christina had found an alternative.

"Join the National Guard. Do six months active duty, and five and a half years in the reserves. Go to meetings once a week and, in the summer, spend a couple of weeks training."

"How do you know all this?"

"I called up. They're sending me some literature."

So, she went with me to this reserve unit on 42nd Street, and I signed up. It was a Medical Unit with more than three hundred doctors. The Captain in charge of my section said they would notify me within a couple of months about doing my active duty. Until then, I was ordered to dutifully attend the weekly sessions.

The job of my section, consisting of four other guys and me, was to keep the security clearances of the Officers of the unit updated. That took all of twenty minutes a week. So I made a deal with the other guys that I would do all the work if they would cover for me skipping a couple meetings a month. They agreed.

Now, something had to be worked out with Pop and the store. Since we bought out Abdullah, the shop was closed for the better part of two days a week as well as all Jewish holidays, a total of nearly ninety days a year. At that time, my cousin Joey, my Uncle Moussa's youngest son and a rabbinical student, cornered Sammy and me at a softball game in the park.

"This is the stage of your lives for you bums to turn back to your religion," he said emphatically. Every so often, Joey would pontificate on how we were betraying *Hashem* and our community by ignoring the tenets of our faith. "He is everywhere, watching you, and now, with Passover approaching, you need to return to your faith."

Sammy laughed. "Joey, we're incorrigible. No chance of us guys being saved."

"Quiet!" Joey snapped. "You may be traveling in the world of sin, but it is easy to turn back to the road of *Hashem*. Do it in steps. Keep Shabbat, put on *Tefileen*, and eat kosher."

There was no definite reason as to why Joey's message hit home at that moment. Perhaps, it was my impending induction into the army or my concern for the health of my father, or possibly I recognized a certain emptiness in me that had long been denied. Whatever the reason, I made a promise to Joey and myself to accept his challenge. Sammy, shocked at my decision, promised he would try also.

It dawned on me that same day that it would be better to find a business that worked for me and Pop 24/7 and that would allow me to keep Shabbat. It was then I decided I'd rather be a landlord than a tenant. In a phone call to Mr. Nowak, the building's owner, who was a Holocaust survivor, his interest in selling the building was sparked by my outlandish offer.

"Mr. Nowak, right now you are netting Forty Thousand a year on this building and have to put up with the petty annoyances of the tenants. At a ten cap, the building is worth Four Hundred Thousand. I will pay you *Six* Hundred Thousand for it, with a Hundred Thousand down and you carry the paper, a five-year loan with interest only payments at 6%. That means you earn Thirty Thousand a year doing nothing, have One Hundred Thousand to use at your discretion, and are getting Two Hundred Thousand more than the building is worth."

"Very much interesting," he said with his Polish/Yiddish accent. "I speak with my accountant." Three weeks later, we were in escrow. "You are a smart young man, Daniel," he said at the closing. "I'm like the way you deal."

Now, I had to act fast to make this thing work. The ten-year lease my father had signed for the store had small increases of 3% a year, but the base rent was low. Madison Avenue real estate values were on the rise, and I signed on with a broker to rent my store's space to another tenant, preferably a bank. Miraculously, Chase was looking to open a branch in that area, and we signed a ten year lease at almost five times the rent we had been paying Nowak, with a 3% increase annually and a five year option. The two adjacent store leases were expiring within the year, so there would be big increases in rent for those spaces. Mr. Nowak could never make that deal with Chase because there were still four years left on our lease. The six floors above the stores were occupied by small businesses, and I was sure they could bring in more rents when their leases expired.

In the meantime, I was putting on Tefileen every day and praying. On Shabbat, I attended the services at the Sha'are Zion shul and felt a sense of well-being in sharing the religion of my community and father, who was thrilled with my transition. Listening to the Cantor, whose voice was operatic, caused an emotional and soothing feeling of becoming bonded to God and my people. The level of anxiety I had been experiencing lessened.

So, by the time I reported for active duty the store was closed and the remaining merchandise, about ninety grand, was given to my brother Al, who had a store on 42nd Street, on a consignment basis who would pay for it as it was sold. Pop could live off that for a while.

Chase was in construction, and three months later their rent started coming in. My hope was to break even for the first couple of years, but the results of this purchase would far exceed any expectations.

25

CLIP JOINTS

My brother Al was an exercise freak. He worked out every day, running, lifting weights, and playing basketball. He had a level of energy that amazed me. Al was also a masochist when it came to me, his kid brother. He loved to torture me by pinching my arms, waking me up in the middle of the night, and finding ways to frighten me. Once, on a Saturday night when no one was home (I couldn't have been more than nine or ten years old), I came into the house and headed for the bathroom. No lights were on and unbeknownst to me Al was lurking behind a wall. When I approached, he jumped out and screamed at me. A dreadful chill ran through my body as I panicked and started punching at him. He laughed hysterically as my eyes watered.

Al hung out mostly with the Italian and Irish kids in the neighborhood. He was an excellent bike rider, able to do amazing things with his battered old Schwinn that he had stolen from another neighborhood yard. He would ride hands free while standing on the seat. He and his friend, Johnny Americo, would rush through the schoolyard and streets at breakneck speeds, spitting clams at innocent bystanders.

Al was very smart, did well in school, and even joined the ROTC in Brooklyn College, although he was excused from active military service because of his extremely poor eyesight. He's been wearing coke bottle glasses since he was ten. He dropped out of college after the first year. He and Johnny partnered up in a fruit stand on 18th Avenue. Johnny introduced Al to a friend of his girlfriend, a cute Italian girl named Marie, and they hit it off. Pop and Becky were unaware that Al was seeing Marie and were devastated when they learned he had eloped with her.

The fruit stand did not work out for the partners, so they split up. Johnny became a bookie and Shylock. Al went to work for a "clip" joint on 42nd Street. Clip joints were stores run mostly by SYs although there were a few operated by J-Dubs and Italians. In some rare situations, SYs partnered with the Italians or J-Dubs. These were stores that sold all types of gifts, tablecloths, radios, starter pistols, wrist watches, switchblades, cheap jewelry, pens, and anything else that could be sold to the hayseed tourists trolling along the street, known by the salespeople as "*Zboons* or *G's.*"

The modus operandi of these stores was bait and switch. In the display window, an item was featured at a price below cost. When the customer came in to buy the item, the salesperson or cashier would jack the price up with enormous extra and absurd charges. Say a radio was offered at $9.99, the poor sap ended up paying more than $25.00 after being charged for batteries, case, taxes, and even for the guarantee. Salesmen worked on a commission, which included *pumps*, for charging extra. Pumps are where the salesperson made real money. For every dollar sold over *yuk-yuk*, (the amount equal to twice the cost of an item), the seller received twenty-five cents. Those quarters would quickly add up for any aggressive employee.

There were New York Blue laws in those days that prohibited businesses from opening on Sundays, but the clip storeowners had an arrangement with the policemen in the Times Square area. The stores would open on Sundays, bribe the cop by giving him Thirty-Five dollars, and get a summons from him for which the store paid a fine of Thirty-Five dollars. The owners considered the bribe and the fine as additional rent.

Al was a good salesman, earning a lot of extra money from his pumps. Five years later, he opened his own store with Johnny America's money as his silent partner. Johnny was very successful in his own shylocking business and financed the whole deal with Al. Johnny had moved up the ranks in the Mafia, but he was later killed in a shootout with a rival group of Mafiosi. Al was devastated by the loss of his best friend, but continued to share the profits of the store with Johnny's widow for years after his untimely death.

After twenty years in the business, Al saw the handwriting. New York City officials finally wised up about the clip stores. Laws were passed to stop the bait and switch operations, many of which would run a "Going Out Of Business" sale every so often. Al converted his business into an upper class "G" store, selling "antiques," carpets, lamps, ivory and jade carvings, most of which were reproductions, but sold as antiques and originals. He did better in that venue than with the "clip" store.

Al brought his two sons, Jason and Robert, into the business and began spending more time in his Florida condo than in New York. Al grew to hate cold weather. His boys began transitioning the business in an attempt to operate more legitimately. They took another store on Central Park South that featured higher end jewelry and name brand watches rather than "G" goods. Within two years, they were out of the antique business altogether and were running two legitimate jewelry operations.

At age sixty, Al suffered a mild heart attack and decided to retire. He gave the stores to his sons who would pay him a flat percentage of the profits and split the rest among themselves. The boys also signed an agreement to make the mortgage payments for Johnny Americo's widow's house until she died. His two sons did better than that, for, after one year, they paid off her mortgage entirely.

Al and I fought a lot over sometimes serious and other time's nonsensical issues. He was a right winger, hated liberals with a passion. He always called me a softie when it came to social issues.

"You want to feed these lazy people with money. No wonder they don't work," he'd say, or, "How can you wear blue jeans with a sports jacket? Nobody does that."

When Al heard me say I was an alcoholic, he said I was talking out of my ass. "You like to drink, kid, like I do. You're no more alcoholic than I am."

"Al," I pleaded, "This is serious. I've been going to meetings for the past three months and they have been a great big help."

"You're bullshitting yourself, Danny. You're not an alcoholic. What are you trying to prove?"

"Nothing," I countered. "It's important for my sobriety to find out how I got this disease."

"What disease? This is not an illness. If drinking causes you a problem, make up your mind to stop."

"It's not that simple," I insisted.

"It is, kid. It's that simple. Stop whining and deal with it."

"I thought I was, Al. If you can't support my recovery, there's nothing left for us to talk about."

And that was the last conversation I had with my brother. He moved to Florida with Marie to live out the rest of his life in warm weather. The last time I saw him was when Pop died and he flew in for the funeral. We sat shiva together, but exchanged no more than ten words with one another.

The loss of a connection with a family member is painful, but, as I later learned from ACOA, not unusual. I was told siblings may have difficulty in admitting the dysfunctionality of the family because of the pain associated with that reality. As painful as it was for me to become estranged from Al, I had to maintain that separation for my own survival.

26

LAST NIGHT WHEN WE WERE YOUNG

Claudia and I were seeing each other more often, at least one night during the week, and on Saturday nights after Shabbat. We were growing warmer towards one another, and after our sixth date we began kissing and fondling one another. It was a strange experience for both of us since we were still feeling an attachment to our deceased spouses. Claudia was more open to "making out" (it felt like we were back in our teens) than I was. But I did enjoy it.

We had been keeping our dating secret, as secret as one can in the gossip-ridden SY community. One night, we ran into my 2nd wife Sonia's brother, Abie, at the kosher restaurant Tevere on East 84th Street in the City, and that hit me with a wave of guilt. Abie was cool about it.

"Good to see you getting out, Danny," he said graciously.

"Thanks. How's the family?"

He nodded okay, and we chatted a bit before he and his wife left.

We sat and Claudia ordered a Merlot. When it came, she took a sip and raised her eyebrows.

"Any good?" I asked.

"Not bad for a kosher wine."

The food was so-so, but we were there for Claudia's sake. "Do you mind coming to a kosher restaurant?" she asked.

"Not if it makes you happy."

She smiled. "That's very noble for an atheist," she responded and took another sip of wine. "Tell me, Danny, Why did you give up your religion?"

"It wasn't just Judaism. It was *all* religions because the basic idea of an omnipotent God does not exist."

"You can't prove there is no God."

"One does not have to prove a negative."

"What if someone said there was no moon?"

"The very fact that you could see it would disqualify a statement such as that. Look, Claudia, I don't want to convince you to not believe in God. Your faith comforts you and gives you strength. Unfortunately, there's no benefit in it for me." She stared pensively at her wine glass. "Please don't hold it against me," I continued, "and I won't hold your being religious against you."

Claudia smiled again, this time wider than before. "Fair enough," she said finally.

"So where do we go from here?" I asked.

"How about your place?"

"I meant..."

She smiled. "I am aware of what you meant, Mr. Dweck."

"Seriously, Claudia, we should talk about this; about us."

"Let's not spoil the evening," she said. The check came. Claudia insisted on paying against my protests. "I can afford it, Mr. Dweck. But I do appreciate your gallantry."

We left the restaurant and headed downtown to my apartment. When we arrived, I immediately told Alexa, my amazing little gadget from Amazon, to "Play romantic songs." It played "Last Night When We Were Young" by Sinatra.

"Love that song," we said simultaneously.

"Dance?" I asked and put my hand out to her. She stepped closer and we embraced.

"No 'dry humping here,'" she cautioned, and we both laughed. I had told her about the Social Dancing in Junior High. We continued dancing even after the song ended. Seconds later, Johnny Mathis's "A Lovely Way to Spend an Evening" played, and we continued swaying. This time there *was* a little "dry humping" which neither one of us were aware of as we kissed and fondled each other.

The next song was Englebert Humperdinck's haunting "Too Beautiful to Last" and in the middle of the song Claudia began crying. "Hey, why the tears?"

"Danny, you make me very happy. And that makes me feel guilty."

"I hear you; same here."

"We *should* take it slow, shouldn't we?"

"I suppose so," I responded.

She rested her head against my chest. "One day at a time."

"That cliché comes in handy, doesn't it? Although, when I think of my age; well, you get my meaning."

"You're not going anywhere. You can't, Danny, because… I'm in love with you."

Now there were tears in *my* eyes, which I tried to hide from her. "It's late. Let me take you home." I kissed her, and she wiped away my tears with her hand.

27

IT'S JUST A WORD

Dinner with Rabbi Judah Cohen at David's was as delicious as ever. Judah could eat the food because it was Glatt Kosher, and he was thrilled that I would treat him to such a sumptuous feast. We talked about *Bikur Holim*, the SYs charitable organization that was the offshoot of an earlier foundation, the Ma'oz Levyon. It did remarkable work in the community, helping the elderly widows and widowers get decent living spaces, supplying low income families with extra money for Holiday expenses. They helped find jobs for unemployed SY's and helped failing businesses to recover. Sometimes, a businessman would help a competitor who might be having financial problems to overcome his adversities. The organization worked tirelessly to make sure that every indigent member of the community could get proper and prompt health care. We talked about how another group, *Rodfeh Sedek*, the one that ensured all SYs got a burial spot in the cemetery in Staten Island, was running out of space. SY laws do not permit the burial of anyone with tattoos or those who married outside the religion. On occasion, however, these rules were waived. And, of course, we discussed drug abuse and alcoholism.

"Danny, my good man," he started, calling any person he spoke to 'my good man' or 'my good woman'. "Maybe you should come to the Sephardic Community Center again and speak to a group about your recovery. It might help someone."

"Name the date, Judah. I'll be there."

"Let me see what can be arranged." He took his last forkful of rice and fasoulia, wiped his beard, and then asked, "When are we going to talk about the word *ahbud*?"

"I had to fatten you up a bit so you wouldn't find a good rebuttal."

"I am in complete agreement with you on this issue, Danny. It is a vile word that should never come across the lips of any good Jew. I've discussed it with the leaders of the community and other rabbis. You'd be surprised at some of the responses they gave. I told one woman that *abbud*, in Hebrew, means slave and not black. It's what most of the community, especially the younger generation, believes. She said she could never stop using that word because it was in her 'DNA'. Another gentleman, otherwise a decent person, said, "It's just a word, like SY, or J-Dub; doesn't mean anything."

"These people are bigoted," I offered. "They won't admit it to themselves. It would be too damaging to their egos. I just can't wrap my head around their logic."

"Why does this bother you so much?"

"Because, Rabbi, it's wrong. For this community, in this time in the history of the world, to still hold these prejudices, is an embarrassment to all of us. I was at the Haddad wedding right after President Obama was first elected, and one of the guys in my Yeshiva class called him 'a filthy nigger.' The SYs, and most Republicans, condemned the first African American President from day one, reproving his policies, most of which had not yet even been implemented. We all should have rejoiced in the progress America had made in accepting blacks as equals. My brothers Jakey and Al still insist they are an inferior race. On the plus side, a small token of the people I've spoken to have gotten the message and have committed to making the change.

"I wanted to place a full page ad regarding the subject in the monthly 'Image' magazine, pay for it myself, but they turned me down. Said it was too controversial, that it would disturb too many people."

"We'll see what can be done about this," he said.

"Don't these people see how hatred leads to an empty life? Do they not recall what it has brought about for our own people in past history? And while we are at it, where did the vile loathing of Hillary Clinton coming from if it isn't from a latent misogynistic view held by many SY men and women?"

"They believe the Clintons are corrupt."

"Do you believe that?"

He leaned back in his chair. "I don't know. This was a very contentious election. Trump won and he is to be the president. Let's wish him success."

"I truly wish he succeeds, but with his record of lies? How can anyone believe he will do what he promises to do? He changes his mind continually. Some SYs say they supported him because he will save them money on taxes; but what good is the money if he ruins the country?"

"Daniel, give them some slack. They are learning, gradually."

"You're way off base, Judah. They're slipping backwards."

He shrugged his shoulders, and then pivoted the conversation. "How is it going with Claudia Gemal?"

"Come off it, Judah. You probably know better than I do. She's a sweet lady, but I'm not sure I'm ready for another romance yet. Sonia is still on my mind. Besides, I'm seventy-five years old. As my stepmother Becky used to say, *'Ma' men am birros'*? 'Who are you dancing with?'"

"You come off it, Danny. Seventy-five is the new fifty. You've still got a lot of energy left. Use it."

"We'll see, Judah." I paid the check and got him a to-go bag full of David's goodies. He thanked me profusely when I dropped him off at his house on Coney Island Avenue.

It was still early so I decided to give Claudia a call to see if she was up to going to the City for a movie. "I'd love to, Danny, but my son Eddie's here, and I'm babysitting for my daughter. Why not come for a cup of coffee"

I processed the idea swiftly through my mind and decided mingling with her family at this time would complicate things. "Another time," I said. "Maybe Saturday night, if you're free."

"I'm free," she responded hurriedly as the sound of kids screaming in the background increased in volume. "Call me tomorrow night.

28

HUP, TWO, THREE, FOUR

Army life was worse than expected. Stationed at Fort Dix, New Jersey, and having to live in a barrack with two hundred other men, waking up at 5 a.m. and rushing out in the cold weather to an adjacent building to shower, shave and shit, with no walls separating the toilets, was a total shock. I had gotten a note from Rabbi Hecht, the J-Dub Rabbi, who had been serving the community for years, saying I was an Orthodox Jew and pleading with the Commanding General to allow me the freedom to observe my faith while serving my duty. Rabbi Hecht told me he received a letter back from General Black stating, in essence, "This is what the Military stands for, to protect our rights to practice the religion of our choice."

The Army was more than accommodating. Each morning, I would get up half an hour before roll call to put on my Tefileen and pray. If I was still in the midst of my observances when the rest of the company was awakened, they kept as quiet as possible until I was finished praying. I was very impressed by the respect my fellow soldiers had for my religious rituals.

There was a group of sixteen other Jewish soldiers on the base who were religious. We were known as the KBs, or Kosher Boys, and were allowed to keep canned kosher goods in a section of the refrigerator in the mess hall. We were dismissed from duty Friday nights and all day Saturday. This meant we never had to attend a G.I. party, which involved scrubbing down the barrack in preparation for an inspection to be held on Saturday, an event we were also excused from.

Military life could be described in four words: "Hurry up and wait." We were rushed to indoor orientation classes, hurried through PT, goaded through chow times, and dashed from one place to another, only to be kept waiting to do the things we were brought to do in any one place.

It was difficult for me at first, being a smoker and out of shape, to complete the daily run around the barracks area before breakfast, a distance of about one mile. I found myself winded about half way through. No one chastised me for that; the sergeants were pretty understanding, encouraging me that by the end of basic training, I would be fit enough to make the entire run.

If they were tolerant of me not completing the run, they were more than punishing about other infractions. Once, while sitting on the windowsill of my barrack when a platoon of soldiers came marching by on their way to the mess hall, I foolishly shouted, "Hup, two, three, four!" The training corporal, a black guy named Rockwell, spotted me and ordered me to come outside at once.

I ran out and stood at attention in front of the non-com. He had a sneer on his face that could melt an iceberg. "You like giving orders, Dweck?"

"No, sir."

"I am not an officer. You call me Corporal."

"Yes, sir… Corporal."

"I think you like to give orders. Drop and give me ten"

I rushed through the pushups, but when it came to number eight, he kneeled down beside me, his face inches from mine. "You see those ants coming your way," he asked without waiting for an answer. "Give them the hup, two three four!"

So I did. After a moment, he pointed to one of the ants and said, "That ant is an officer. Salute him as he passes;" and I did.

"Now get your ugly ass back to the barracks. Next time you want to play drill instructor, you *will* be drowning in my shit!"

I ran like the wind back to the barrack where my platoon buddies were rolling in laughter.

There was a lot of yelling and shouting from the noncoms, which, I later learned, was part of the training. The idea was to put the fear of death of the sergeants and corporals in you, so that in actual battle, you will follow their orders from more fear of them than any enemy. It worked.

Night training was brutal. They woke us at three a.m. and, after breakfast, loaded us on deuce-and a-half trucks that took us out to the rifle range. It was raining that morning, but they had us get on our bellies to crawl under barbed wire while real explosions went off around us. We were told not to stand as there was supposed to be live ammunition firing over us from a machine gun. A rumor had been spread that a guy got killed when he stood up, but I didn't believe the army would ever risk such an incident by using live ammo. Still, we could see red tracer bullets flying overhead, and no one dared to test that rumor.

The one part of the training I dreaded was chemical warfare. We were told we would be going into a sealed gas chamber where they'd explode tear gas canisters so we could learn how to respond. Not my cup of tea, but how could I get out of it?

Turns out the Motorized Division of Fort Dix bailed me out. The day before the gas test a non-com came around and asked if anyone knew how to drive a two and a half ton truck. He said they would be testing our driving skills the next day, so I raised my hand.

"Where and what did you drive," he asked as he wrote my name and serial number on a clipboard.

"A fruit truck," I lied, "In Brooklyn."

"Okay, report to the orderly room at 0800 hours tomorrow."

Promptly, at 0800 the next morning, the noncom led me to the deuce-and-a-half. I put the key in the ignition and the engine started humming. "Put it in first gear," the noncom ordered, but I had no idea what he was talking about. I struggled with the stick shift, the transmission growling like a wild dog, and the engine stalled. I tried it again, but the same results occurred. "You never drove a truck, did you?" The corporal said. "Shut the engine and get out." He failed me on the spot, but my battle was won. I missed the gas chamber.

Each Sunday, my brother Michael would bring in a fresh supply of kosher products for me. On the fourth Sunday, he sent the supplies in with Christina, who schlepped by subway from Brooklyn to the city, then rode a bus for an hour and a half to Fort Dix. She smiled at my G.I. haircut, which left me with an almost bald head. I was happy to see her, but it was time to quit leading her on.

"There's something I need to tell you, Christina," I started, but she shushed me.

"Later."

She took me by the hand and led me to a large open field filled with very tall grass. She removed a blanket from her bag, spread it on the ground, and lay upon it. "Come down," she ordered, and I obeyed. We made out for some time, and then she masturbated me. When it was over, she said, "You looked like you needed that. Now, what did you want to tell me?"

I kissed her on her forehead, then her cheek, and finally her mouth. "I am so glad you came here today."

She smiled broadly, when suddenly we heard a gunshot followed by a loud voice shouting, "Everyone up!" I scanned the field and saw dozens of couples stand up. The trainees called this area "Love Field."

Everything was going well during basic until one day the Jewish Chaplin asked to see me. "Danny, we have a problem," the rabbi said. He was an Orthodox Ashkenazic rabbi, a Captain in rank, and was a career soldier. "One of your Syrian landsman is in the hospital refusing to eat, claiming that our food is not kosher. General Black called me in and wants to know what the hell is going on."

I had heard this SY guy, Sammy Gindi, had tried to beat the draft but got caught at it. He was inducted, but refused to eat even our food, causing the Brass to question the KB boys.

"What should we do?" the rabbi asked.

I thought about this for a moment, and then suggested, "Get him discharged. He'll ruin it for the rest of us if he's kept in."

The Chaplain concurred, and Gindi was discharged under medical grounds. He never knew it was I who got him out of the army.

During basic, I became friends with another SY guy from another company, Billy Cohen, who I knew casually from the community. I was more familiar with his brother Michael, a homophobic, pompous prick.

Billy was religious and kosher and was one of the KB's. He was an intelligent guy and we often, on Shabbat, after the services, discussed politics and world affairs. He was a college graduate, far better educated than me, and I struggled to keep up with him in these conversations. I learned a lot about current events from Billy.

Billy's father owned a chain of ladies' clothing stores across the five boroughs, and after his stint in the Army, he was planning to join the firm. We became close friends, and one Shabbat, after lunch, we took a walk around the base. I could sense something was troubling him.

"What's on your mind, Billy?" I inquired.

"Nothing."

I remained silent for the next few moments.

"Danny, I'm gay," he blurted out from nowhere.

I was a bit taken aback, but recovered quickly. "So?"

"So? I finally told my brother and he went ape on me. If my father found out he would disown me. Not to mention I would be treated like a pariah by the whole SY community."

"Who cares what your sexual preferences are?"

"You are naïve, Danny. I respect you for not thinking bad of me, but the truth is we live in such a closed society that anyone who is different is looked down upon."

He stopped walking for a moment and turned towards me. "I don't know why I'm dumping this on you. I have come to respect you over these past few weeks and, well, I guess I needed to vent my fears."

"Look, Billy, you don't have to apologize for who you are. Nobody has to know about this. You have my word I will never repeat what you told me." He put his arms around my shoulders and thanked me.

My passion for reading had never left me, and I devoured the New York Times cover to cover whenever I could get hold of a copy of the paper. I spent Saturday afternoons and Sunday mornings at the Base Library gobbling up any new biography of a historical figure, but my real interest was still Adolf Hitler and Nazi Germany.

The rise and fall of this evil figure fascinated me, how he had amassed such power and personal fortune. When he became Chancellor, he said he would refuse to take the salary of that office, but had gone from sleeping in Vienna flop houses to becoming a billionaire as well as the master of almost all of Europe. He made a fortune by having his WWI sergeant, Max Amann, run a chain of newspapers he owned. His book, "Mein Kamp," was given to newlyweds and Hitler received royalties of more than one million dollars a year. He copyrighted his image and received payments from the sale of postage stamps that had his image. So, giving up his salary as Chancellor was just a ploy to give the image to the German people of what he was sacrificing for them (sound familiar? Trump, too, has refused to take a salary).

He was an expressive demagogue who captured the hearts of the masses by creating big lies, which he repeated over and over until these desperate and gullible people believed them. Hitler got rid of all other political parties; implemented policies that brought prosperity back to Germany; rejected the Treaty of Versailles; and, by 1939, was on his way to conquering the world. In the end, his megalomania caused his downfall and destroyed Germany while causing massive misery from which the world barely had survived.

Graduation from Basic Training was fun, marching in cadence before the Commanding General and other officers. Eight weeks before the ceremony our company consisted of young men who barely knew their right foot from their left, but who now stepped in unison across the training field.

The two days before the ceremony, however, were torturous. We were taken on a three-hour, fifteen-mile, forced march through the woods in full battle gear, combat boots, and rifle, trudging through mud and sand. It was a scorching, late, spring night and all of us were drenched in perspiration. They allowed a five-minute break every hour, when some of us dozed off or grabbed a smoke.

Corporal Rockwell assigned me to the rear guard to keep any stragglers from getting lost. As it turned out, it was I who got lost. We were resting in a clearing when someone shouted "GAS! The procedure was, as I learned after my episode with the truck, to stand, put your weapon between your legs, remove your helmet, place the gas mask on your head, and wait until you heard the words "All Clear".

"All Clear" did not come, or at least I ever heard it, and, after waiting more than ten minutes, I slowly lifted the mask and found I was completely alone in the middle of nowhere. The rest of the company had moved on, leaving me stranded in the middle of the forest with no clue as to which direction to head. So, left with no choice, I leaned against a tall tree and drifted off to sleep. Two hours later, a jeep came by and drove me back to camp.

With basic training over, we were given two weeks of military leave. It was now the middle of June and the SY families were in the process of migrating to Bradley Beach. My sister, Esther, and her husband, Bernie, had rented a house for the summer next door to the Shul on Fifth Avenue, and I spent most of my leave there, just lolling around the beach during the day reading one book or another and listening to classical music. Nights were spent hanging out at the Sand Bar, a place not unlike Mattie's in Seth Low Park, and run by a middle aged Jewish woman named Mrs. Kutner. Located right on the boardwalk at 2nd Avenue, it was a place to congregate with friends. The food was kosher, to accommodate the needs of its customers, although the place stayed open on Shabbat, which meant it could not be called Glatt kosher, and so the stricter Orthodox members of the community would not eat her food.

Saturday nights, after Shabbat was over, we'd jump into anyone's car and drive to a place past long branch whose name escapes me, a dance hall that was a precursor to the "Discos" that spread like wildfire in the '70's.

Back in camp after my leave they sent me to a school to take classes in my Military Occupation Specialty, my MOS, determined by a test given the second day of Basic Training. Mine was listed as "Clerk". The class was overcrowded, and because I had scored high on the MOS test, they assigned me to OJT, On the Job Training, (everything in the Armed Forces was reduced to acronyms) at the camp's Walson Military Hospital.

The first day I reported for duty Master Sergeant Riley O'Keefe, a completely bald-headed twenty-year veteran somewhere in his mid to late forties, drilled me on the routine. "Private Dweck, you *will* do all the work here that is necessary which *will* not amount to much. You *will* report at 0800 sharp (all non-coms emphasized the word *will*, each time they said it) and I *will* not tolerate any tardiness, son. You *will* be dismissed at 1400 hours, and have weekends off. Do you own an automobile?" I nodded yes. "You *will* be given a pass to drive on the Base, and, once a week, usually a Tuesday or Wednesday morning; you *will* drive the CO, Captain Farley, to Trenton and wait while he completes his business. After bringing him back to base, around 1300 hours, you *will* be free to leave; any questions?"

"No, Sergeant," I responded, laughing inwardly.

The Sarge was right: the work was a breeze. I adhered to his demand and arrived at the office a few minutes before 0800 hours. The workload was completed by 13.30, when the lunch break began. That's when I left the base and rushed back to Bradley, about an hour's drive, and was on the beach by 3 p.m. with my folding chair, a book, and my Grundig radio listening to my classical music station.

The trips to Trenton for my CO's business actually turned out to be a visit to a brothel where all the girls happily awaited the arrival of Captain Farley.

29

CASH, *SHMASH*

One Tuesday afternoon, I drove from Fort Dix straight to the city to meet with Mr. Nowak, my old landlord. He had called to tell me there was a property available on 3ʀᴅ Avenue and wanted me to have a look at it. It was a Co-Op building with five stores and the Co-Op Board wanted to sell the 69 years remaining on the land lease to the retail space. It was an excellent location, and the price was right: Three Hundred Thousand, including maintenance and taxes. The current leases for the stores stretched out only one and half years.

"What you think?" Mr. Nowak asked, in his slightly Yiddish accent.

"It's a good deal."

"You want to make partners?"

"I'd love to, Mr. Nowak, but right now my cash is a little dry. I'm still in the army."

"Cash, shmash," he replied. "You are a good boy. I like you. I pay. You manage it. We split sixty-forty. Yes?"

"Yes, Mr. Nowak," I answered excitedly. "Thanks for the opportunity."

The deal was made and we closed on it soon after I graduated from the Armed Forces of the United States, having served 179 days active duty, and deliberately released before day 180 because that would have entitled me to Veteran's benefits.

Army life, as well as the summer, was over and it was back to making a living. The deal Mr. Nowak made was generous and a terrific head start. This man, Julius Nowak, a quiet, gentle person, who recovered from the horrific experiences of the Nazis and World War II, was the person who would lead me to riches. And I, in turn, would aid in increasing both our wealth beyond imagination.

Pop was bored doing nothing, so we took a little office in the 110 building on 33rd Street, and after installing phones and furniture, my father would show up a couple of hours a day to hang out. It made him feel better to have a place to park himself.

Rent from Chase was flowing in, and it helped pay the expenses with a little left over for me to subsist. I was still living at home with Pop and Becky, but the place was growing too small for me. I rented a two bedroom on Quentin Road for $175 a month, painted it myself, and bought some used furniture from the Salvation Army. With my own "pad," I was a happy camper.

Christina and I continued to see each other on an irregular basis during the rest of that year and into the next spring. It was difficult to break the connection, but that soon changed.

At the "Matzah Ball" dance at Sha'are Zion celebrating the end of Passover, I met this very cute girl named Adele Haddad. Her father was a well-to-do wholesaler, who had arrived in America in the early forties and made a quick success of himself. He married another "import", as these latecomers to America were often referred to by first and second generation American born SYs. By this time, Egyptians, Israelis, Iraqis and Lebanese Jews had made their way to the "best country" in the world, though they established their own enclaves and synagogues within the community. A majority of them became the lower echelons of the community, owning and operating the kosher grocery stores and restaurants.

Adele was a beautiful, but hesitant, seventeen year old that had the kind of lips a man could spend his entire life kissing. She was a bit shy, but laughed at my jokes, the main prerequisite for me to like any female. She was a great dancer, but the thing that puzzled me most was her smile. There's something in a smile that tells you a lot about a person. Hers was a bit incomplete, not reaching wide enough, and it exuded an unperturbed sadness. Yet, she showed an eagerness to hear what you had to say. Adele was a good listener, and I am a fast talker.

Sammy met his future wife, Sarah Metrano, a smart, seventeen year-old, black-haired beauty whose father did not have change for a quarter. The Metranos were Sephardic Jews, but not SYs. Their ancestors were from Greece. Sammy fell madly in love with Sarah from the first moment they met and never stopped loving her even after she died. The problem was his mother, who was bent on her son marrying a nice Syrian girl.

We danced all night to "Be My Baby", "It's My Party", the Beach Boys, Skeeter Davis' "The End of the World", "Heat Wave"; The Drifters' "Up on the Roof", and of course, the Beatles, along with other top tunes of the day. Most dances were with Adele, but a few were with another girl I was friendly with.

By the end of the party, Sammy and I were ready to head for our Brooklyn hangout, the Four Seasons diner on Avenue U with our new found "girl-friends," Adele and Sarah.

Adele's father, Isaac, was a tall, intimidating, man who, when I went to pick her up for our first date, grilled me about my family, my work, my friends and my religion.

"You go to shul on Shabbat?"

"Yes, Mr. Haddad. I keep kosher and put on Tefileen every day."

"You make money?"

"I make a nice living," I answered, undaunted by the third degree.

"How much," he insisted on knowing. Adele walked into the room just as he finished the sentence.

"Daddy!" she protested. "We're going to the movies, not to the wedding chapel."

I laughed at that, but her old man's face did not change one iota. He maintained that unbreakable stare, even as he said, with his slight Lebanese accent, "Have good time."

And we did. We went to dinner at Bonaparte's on Avenue M, then caught a late showing of "Seven Days in May," from the book I had read about a planned coup d'état of the United States government. Adele enjoyed it as much as I did and we talked about it over coffee and dessert at Four Seasons diner.

My feelings for Adele began with puppy love, which morphed into a genuine liking, that then led to stronger emotions, and finally to love. We went to parties together, spent time with Sammy and Sarah, even went horseback riding. Once, we went to the Empire room at the Waldorf Astoria with Sammy and Sarah to see if we could get in to see Johnny Mathis. When the maître d' asked if we had a reservation, I said yes.

"Under what name, please," he asked.

"Ulysses S. Grant," I responded as I handed him a fifty dollar bill.

He snapped his fingers and suddenly a table and four chairs appeared right in front of the stage. Mathis, so close up, was absolutely sensational.

Within four months of dating Adele, it became clear she was the girl I was going to marry. Telling Christina was going to be difficult, but she deserved to hear the truth from me. We met one last time at Christina's home, a safe place since her mother's eyes were always focused on us so neither Christina nor I would fall into any sexual engagement.

"So, Danny boy," she said, with a trace of sarcasm, "What's the bad news?"

Mustering up my courage I spewed out the words. "There's a girl…"

"Got it," she interrupted, with sharp disdain. "It's dumping time!"

I moved towards her, but she retreated.

"It just happened. We fell in love. I'm gonna' marry her and wanted you to hear it from me. My feelings for you, Christina, have always been sincere, with nothing but respect. The times we spent together were very special. I will always cherish…"

"Stop the B.S., Danny," she interrupted, "I get it. Things were wonderful, but…""

"Christina…"

"Please don't say you love me, but can't marry me because I'm not Jewish. If you truly loved me, that wouldn't matter." There were tears in her eyes, and she turned away from me. I moved closer to her.

"We should never have let the relationship go this far," I said softly.

She wiped the tears away, and then turned to face me. "It's not the end of the world, Danny. I wish you happiness." She kissed me on the cheek, and then said, quietly, "Go."

On the drive home, my feelings were jumbled. It was a sad ending to a very pleasant relationship, but one that was inevitable. Christina was right. If I truly loved her, the Jewish issue would not matter. At one time, I did entertain the idea. My brother Al had paved the way by marrying Marie, but a lifetime of indoctrination could not be overcome so easily.

30

JOHNNY MATHIS

Claudia and I went to a New York Philharmonic recital that Saturday night at David Geffen Hall. Leonidas Kavakos led, and soloed, a Bach Concerto and Schuman's Symphony Number 2. It was a marvelous performance. Claudia had never been to a concert in her life and was visually impressed by the experience. "The virtuosity of those musicians is remarkable," she said, as we left the hall. Being a drummer, and a poor one at that, my pleasure was watching the timpanists playing their kettles.

We shared a salad and a pizza at Café Fiorello on 63rd and Broadway and spoke about our children again. "It's funny," I said, "how having children always makes for good conversation when you're older. No matter what age they are, they're still our 'kids."

Throughout the conversation, I noticed what appeared to be a sparkle in Claudia's eyes, almost like crystal teardrops. She had a half grin on her face as we chatted and occasionally rested her chin on the back of her hand with her elbow on the table. I found that look most endearing. I paid the check, and as I handed the waiter my Amex, she looked straight at me and said, "I'm ready."

"Yes," I answered. "Let's go."

"No, Danny. I mean I'm ready to sleep with you."

I'm sure there was a dumbfounded expression on my face when I heard that. She stood up and kissed my cheek, took me by the arm, and led me out of the restaurant.

When we arrived at my apartment the initiation of our engagement was slow and a bit awkward. I had Alexa play "Johnny Mathis' Greatest Hits," the best music to have sex by: "Chances Are," "It's Not for Me to Say," "Wonderful, Wonderful:" greatest make out music ever.

We began with light kissing at first, but quickly built to a more passionate level. We fondled each other until Claudia pulled back a moment to remove her clothes and bra. I paused just a second before removing all of my garments, except for my underwear where the bulge in the crotch area was embarrassingly obvious. Claudia removed her panties and stood there stark naked, exposing a beautifully proportioned figure, and waiting patiently for me to remove my jockey shorts. I hesitated for just another moment.

"You're going to have to remove that thing if we are to get to the equipment," she quipped. We both laughed.

The tension was relieved, and we continued with our passionate but intimate assignation. It felt awkward for both of us, but the desire was there as well as the intimacy. We stopped for a moment, just looking into each other's eyes, smiling, and then resumed the kissing. Her body felt good so close to mine, and, as our arousal increased, she urged me to enter her. We experimented with each other, and she taught me how to delay the climax, which only heightened the experience. The sensation was as powerful and enjoyable as my first sexual encounter with that girl, Cheryl. I felt like a teenager once again, and, for those brief moments, I was.

It was the most adoring and intense lovemaking, we both agreed, that each of us had experienced in a long time. My last sexual activity was more than two and a half years ago and Claudia's, more than a year. Neither of us thought we had it in us after such a long lapse. But, like riding a bike (though this was more fun), it all came back. I was more than pleased to learn my equipment still worked, and that the plumbing was still in order.

When we awoke Sunday morning we stared at each other and just laughed. "This is crazy. I'm a seventy-five year old man. What am I doing having sex with you?"

"My husband Manny never put a hand on me until we were married. He needed a lot of sex, but I rarely enjoyed it. After three months of dating you, Danny Dweck, I get four orgasms in one night. This *is* insane!"

"Sorry, if I disappointed you," I laughed. "Wanna' try for five?"

She rolled over on top of me and gazed into my eyes. No answer was necessary.

In the early afternoon, I drove Claudia to her daughter's house in Brooklyn and went in with her. She introduced me to Terri, an attractive twenty-eight year old mother of twin seven-year-old boys, Harry and Manny, and her husband Eli, a nondescript though jovial looking fellow. It was a warm and comfortable environment, as most SY homes are. Terri immediately made me feel welcome by putting out a spread of bagels, cream cheese, lox, and thinly sliced tomatoes. One thing was common in the SY community. Walk into any Syrian home, at any time, invited or not, and you will immediately be flooded with food and drink. Rabbi Judah says the tradition comes from the bible when it tells how Abraham had entrances to his home on all four sides to welcome strangers.

About a half hour later her thirty-two year old son, David, arrived with his wife, Sara, and their two children, Manny, twelve and Claudia, nine. It was a wonderful afternoon spent with her family, and we made plans for Claudia to meet my children and grandchildren the following weekend.

Despite my apprehension about engaging in a new relationship with a new woman, I had to admit to myself the sense of happiness that enveloped me during the times spent with Claudia. She was great fun to be with, but there were still doubts that gnawed at me. It felt like a betrayal of Sonya, the great love of my life. My brain told me to slow down, don't get too involved, but my heart delivered a different message: enjoy the moment.

31

SUCCESS AND IMPLOSION

Although I put on Tefileen every day, there were times the prayers were skipped, especially if I was in a hurry to get to an early business meeting. *Kashrut* and Shabbat were observed, but something was missing; there was a sense of confusion. I called my brother Michael, who was working in a summer stock theatre in New Orleans and expressed to him the growing doubts about my faith. To my surprise, he suggested I speak to a rabbi. After meeting with Rabbi Hecht, he insisted the study of Gemara would answer all questions.

So, I began attending classes given by an Ashkenazi rabbi, a rather young *Hasid*, maybe in his early thirties, a very well learned scholar of Judaic and secular ideas and who understood worldly things in a way the SY rabbis did not. Mostly, the classes were about Jewish philosophy. We would read a passage from the Gemara, and he would define it in modern terms. He even discussed the plot of a popular novel at the time, the "Spy Who Came in from the Cold."

"The laws that were given to us by Hashem," he explained during one study class, "do not require justification. They are, simply, the laws. One can debate their meaning or try to attach a reason, but that is not why we follow them. Take the prohibition against eating any animal that does not have cloven hooves and chew its cud. Many people over the millennia have tried to explain that law by saying not eating pig prevents trichinosis. If that were the reason for that law, then one day, if someone finds a way to avoid the disease when eating *chazer*, then that law would become unnecessary. That would make Hashem wrong, which is impossible. Therefore, we follow the laws because He commands us to; period."

I liked this Rabbi, appreciated his reasoning, and looked forward to the weekly classes. Rabbi Elihu Pinchik jump-started my education in Judaism, and my faith did deepen.

In March of 1967, Adele and I were married in an Ashkenazi shul on Ocean Parkway and Avenue I, followed by a small reception in the SY Social Club, also on Ocean Parkway. Two days before the wedding I went to the Mikva for a spiritual cleansing. On the Shabbat before the ceremony, I went to shul and was given an *Aliyah*, the honor to go up to the Tebah for the Torah reading.

At the reception there were less than one hundred guests, and Adele's father had arranged a *Nobeh*, a musical reception, by hiring a Middle Eastern vocalist named Hanan, along with her six piece band, to perform. Though not Jewish, Hanan was very popular with the community, singing the songs from the hometown of Aleppo and the Middle East. In later years, she would be banned from performing at SY affairs by the newly appointed stricter rabbis who prohibited a man from listening to a female singer for fear the woman's voice might arouse him.

It was a fun party and we danced all night. When Adele and I left in the limo for our hotel near JFK, she suddenly became withdrawn and turned away from me.

"What is it, sweetheart?"

She did not respond; so I did a little more prodding. "Anything you want to say, honey?"

"Promise you won't hate me if I tell you?" she pleaded.

I smiled. "Of course I won't hate you. What is it, Adele?"

She kept her eyes on the window and revealed, in a low voice, "I'm not a virgin."

I was a bit surprised by this revelation, but not shocked.

"I was fifteen and was dating this J-Dub guy. You may know him…"

"Doesn't matter who he is," I interrupted.

"Anyway, we were making out in his house one night, and he… he forced himself on me. I resisted but he wouldn't stop. Danny, I'm sorry."

I put my arm around her and kissed her cheek. "Not being a virgin doesn't matter to me, sweetie."

"What about the bloody sheet?"

It was the custom for the groom to provide a bloody sheet to the parents proving the bride was a virgin.

"Not to worry. I'll cut myself shaving and put my blood on the sheet. No one will know." She cried, and I put my arm around her. "No big deal. Are you okay now with what happened that night?'

"Of course not; but there's nothing that can be done about it."

When we went to bed, I was very slow in approaching her, asking every few minutes if she was okay. When we finally had sex she was physically uneasy and was complaining that the penetration was hurting her so I stopped. We did not consummate our marriage that night.

We left for our honeymoon the next day, paid for by the more than $3,000 in wedding gifts we'd received. We stayed at a kosher hotel on Collins Avenue in Miami Beach, just one block from Lincoln Road. The rates were $45 per day, including two kosher meals. The first night in Florida, Adele was more relaxed and the sex was easier for her. She had purchased a lubricant from the drug store which seemed to help.

It rained constantly, but despite the poor weather, we were having fun. We strolled along South Beach in between thunderstorms. We went to Hialeah racetrack, and the movies. Each night, Adele was more relaxed and the intercourse was easier and more passionate. The morning before our last day she even initiated the sex. That did surprise me, but it was wonderful.

That afternoon, my brother Jakey came into town on a business trip, and we invited him for dinner. We were scheduled to leave for home the next morning. Later that evening, we went to the Jai Li Fronton in Dania to watch and bet on the games. Jakey said the meets were all fixed, but he got lucky and picked a few winners and I won $200. That allowed Adele and me to stay three extra nights, during which, I believe, our first son, Ezra, was conceived.

Two weeks after we returned, Sammy and Sarah were married, but not without some drama. Sammy's mother, Grace, had done everything in her power to stop her son from marrying this beautiful Sephardic, but not Syrian, girl, but she did not succeed. In the night of the wedding, Grace even approached our friend Eddie.

"I'll give you five thousand dollars if you marry this girl," Grace offered him. She could not bring herself to say Sarah's name.

"Mrs. Levy, I would love to marry Sarah, but she won't have me."

Frustrated, Mrs. Levy gave up trying and Sammy and Sarah were wed. Three weeks after that affair Eddie Mansour wed his first wife, Cheryl.

Sarah learned of Mrs. Levy's offer to Eddie, and when she returned from their honeymoon, she called Grace. "Hello, mom," she said with more than a touch of sarcasm in the way she said the word 'mom'.

"How was the honeymoon?" Grace asked, not really interested in the answer.

"We had a nice time, '*mom*'. By the way I heard about your offer to Eddie Mansour to marry me instead of your son, Sammy."

"Oh, it was just joking."

"You should have offered *me* the money, and I would have walked away. And that's *not* joking!" Sarah slammed the phone down. From then on, Grace couldn't be nicer to her new daughter–in–law. When Sarah told me this story, I laughed and hugged her.

A lifelong relationship with my best friend Sammy and his new wife began. Adele and Sarah got along like sisters, and we saw the Levy's at least twice a week for dinner, sometimes at a restaurant with other young marrieds, or at either of our apartments for home cooked meals.

Sunday mornings, Sammy and I joined a crew of SY men and women at the Kings Highway tennis courts. Adele and Sarah were content learning bridge, both becoming passionate and proficient players. In fact, Sarah became quite an expert at the game, winning a few amateur tournaments.

Sammy developed into a pretty good tennis player, but I never improved much. Sports were not my strong suit. The tennis court, however, became the location of a big community scandal when it was revealed that more than a few married SY women of the "jet set" crowd, the wives of rich husbands, had affairs with the handsome, young, instructor.

The "Jet Set" crowd was made up of kids from the wealthy SY families. Their privileged childhoods were quite different than mine. They went to Flatbush Yeshiva, a J-Dub institution that the richer SYs sent their children to for a formal religious education. They lived mostly in the Ocean Parkway area, and grew up in large, expensive homes that surrounded the Sha'are Zion synagogue.

The sex with Adele left much to be desired, but I loved her, and that made up for the deficiency. She never really enjoyed it, and it became obvious she engaged in sex to accommodate me. Outside the bedroom we had fun socializing with our friends, and taking annual vacations to the Caribe Hilton in San Juan, Puerto Rico. It was there Adele actually reached climax for the first time and she glowed for the next few days. Sadly, this intimacy would have too short a life span. When we returned home, Adele once again became distant and detached from the relationship. I overlooked her frustrating behavior for the sake of our marriage, but it was taking its toll on me.

During the nine months before baby Ezra arrived, an eight and a half pound pudgy newborn with more wrinkles than an un-ironed shirt, the leases on the stores on the Madison Avenue property began to expire, and new tenants gladly jumped at the chance to pay five times the previous rents. In addition, a drama school negotiated a lease with me for the entire six floors above the stores at the same rent increases. At a ten cap, the value of the building had increased to $2,000,000. I refinanced with my tenant, Chase, a $1.2 million five-year loan at 4.5%, with interest payments only.

Two weeks after Ezra's birth I bought Pop a house on Quentin Road and East Fourth Street for Forty Thousand Dollars; and one for Adele, me and our infant son four blocks away, on East 4th and Avenue T, for One Hundred Thirty Thousand, paying cash for both units. That still left me with more than a million dollars in working capital.

The property I partnered with Mr. Nowak was also doing well. The leases on those retail stores expired and we were able to quadruple the rents. We refinanced and each pocketed half a million dollars.

After the birth of Ezra, Adele fell into a depression and suffered from a severe case of hemorrhoids. She endured frequent panic attacks, feeling overwhelmed and even hostile towards the baby. Forget about sex: what little desire she may have once had, had completely disappeared. A sense of helplessness engulfed me, for nothing I could offer seemed to comfort or alleviate her agony.

We consulted our pediatrician, Dr. Green, who was great with kids, although he treated them while a cigarette was either dangling from his mouth or resting in a nearby ashtray. He said post-partum disorder was not uncommon with new mothers and recommended she speak with her gynecologist.

Adele saw her doctor and she prescribed medication to deal with it. The drugs did improve her disposition to some degree, although at times she would flare up with frustration and anger at petty things. The sexual drive never revived. If we co-habited once a month, it was a lot. Still, we acted as a happy young pair, going on winter vacations to the Caribbean with Sammy and Sarah and other young SY couples.

Adele enrolled in a photography course at the 92nd Street Y and that helped her disposition. She became a bit more outgoing and less depressed.

Her skills in photography were pretty good and she even sold some photos to various magazines.

We both wanted another child, but Adele could not get pregnant. We saw a fertility doctor who gave both of us a series of tests and she determined that Adele should be put on a regimen of relaxation and medication, but it didn't work. Six years after the birth of Ezra, after Adele had long given up the prescribed fertility therapy, we resolved ourselves to the fact that we would have no more children. We decided on a European vacation to celebrate our seventh anniversary. Adele's mother watched our son, Ezra, and we booked the trip to Europe with Sammy and his wife.

Adele was more relaxed, and we got along okay. The romance of Paris, our suite at the Plaza Athene, and the dinner at the first class restaurant, *"Le Pre Catalan,"* in the *Bois de Boulogne*, (not to mention the bottle of Chateau Latour), sparked Adele's sex drive, and those rare moments of sexual intimacy were extremely pleasurable. Surprisingly, my bullets worked and Adele got pregnant.

After our return from vacation, our relationship deteriorated rapidly, possibly as a result of the unplanned pregnancy. We argued over nonsense, fought about which restaurant or movie to go to. Adele's patience with our son, Ezra, became almost non-existent and she grew even more anxious when we discovered she was carrying twins, a boy and a girl. The failure of the relationship was wearing on the two of us and, while we both were saddened by that, it seemed we had neither the drive nor the will to save it.

The birth of the twins was a difficult affair. Adele was in labor for more than twenty hours when the doctors decided to do a Caesarian. The babies arrived into this world safely and in good health on May 27, 1975, the boy, Joseph, named for Adele's father, came first, and the girl, Fortune, who we called Tuni, named for my mother.

These precious infants proved to be too much for Adele to handle, even with the help of a full time nurse. Adele fell into the post-partum nightmare once again. This time she refused to take the medication saying it caused her to feel tired and lethargic. Her depression deepened, and her physician prescribed Prozac, which somewhat improved her condition. She soon lost her passion for photography.

The experience of diminishing love is emotionally crippling. Adele had no desire to communicate on a civil level with me anymore and my patience with her had worn thin. I spent more and more time away from home, coming late from work, going to more Gemara classes and donating time to outside charitable work. My feelings for Adele were imploding, and I contemplated divorce. After consulting with Rabbi Pinchik, he suggested we go to marriage counseling, but Adele refused. Part of the pain of this disintegration of a marriage is the reflection on why we were together in the first place. The initial love, which had grown more and more intense as it deepened was now reversing itself and developing into contempt for one another.

32

JACK DANIELS

Soon after the first birthday of the twins a woman real estate broker, Heidi Gorman, approached me with a deal in SoHo, but I had something else in mind. We went to lunch at Lou G. Segal's kosher restaurant and my flirting began. This turned into the first of my many extra-marital affairs. There were nights when I didn't go home, sleeping in a hotel with one woman or another.

I was never a heavy drinker, only one or two Jack Daniels at most when out to dinner and only because Sinatra drank it. Later, it was Glen Fiddich single malt scotch, simply because it went down smoothly. I found myself getting drunk more often than I cared to admit.

In the meantime, with the backing of Julius Nowak, we acquired more property in the city. Heidi had found a deal to buy the land lease of a co-op in the West Village before anyone heard about it. We gobbled that one up quickly, and then she brought us two properties on lower Broadway, near Canal Street. Mr. Nowak (I never called him Julius) insisted we buy both, but even he was running out of cash.

"Daniel," he said, "You have become like a son to me. I trust you a lot. There are two buildings I own with no mortgage. Maybe you get the bank to lend money on those?" One property was on Fordham Road in the Bronx, and the other was on 57th and Third. "You take over the running of them, the leases they are coming up soon. We go fifty-fifty."

"I'm happy with the 60-40 arrangement," I said.

"No more. Now we are equal partners."

"God bless you, Mr. Nowak," I gushed, and meant it with all my heart.

"God has nothing to do with this; is between you and me." He put his hand out for me to shake. "Mazel Tov!"

Getting the loans was a no brainer. My tenant on Madison, Chase, was all too eager to arrange the advances on the two edifices belonging to my partner, and that money was used to buy the Broadway buildings. I threw my Madison Avenue property into the mix and within three years, our combined holdings were worth nearly Fifty Million dollars with an outstanding debt of Twelve point Five million. Mr. Nowak and I were drawing close to one million each out of the business. The old man was thrilled, and so was I. My father could only muster up a half smile at the success of his son. He was content owning his own home and was supremely happy with Becky. He felt like the richest man in the world when I gave him a brand new 1975 Cadillac for his 68th birthday. Becky was not so happy when she told me his health was failing.

During my eighth year of marriage, my drinking increased dramatically and had become a serious problem. My studies with Rabbi Pinchik led me to more questions than answers about my religion.

"Rabbi," I confessed, "once more, my faith is fading. I talked with my brother Michael, who has turned away from God and all religions, and he makes more sense to me than the books we are studying. I ask myself, 'Why would anyone want to follow the words that were written three thousand years ago?' It makes no sense. There are questions that cannot be answered. Why did God allow slavery, even with the laws governing the way slaves should be treated? Why do we focus on rituals about animal sacrifices? In America and many other countries, that is illegal."

"All the laws of the Torah" the Rabbi answered, "will resume being practiced when the Temple is rebuilt."

"But they are in effect now! Mankind has evolved, *Judaism* has evolved. The Torah says that gay men should be stoned to death, and that adulterers face the same punishment. There are even laws that condemn someone who leaves the religion or breaks the Sabbath, but we don't abide by these laws anymore. Those laws are as antiquated as the Koran, whose commandments on these subjects are pretty much the same. We, as Jews, have advanced, Muslims will, too. So why are we still studying these words when they have become obsolete and irrelevant?"

"They are not irrelevant. They are there to teach us how to live in service to God. Look at the American Constitution. Whenever the Supreme Court gets a case, they look back at what the Framers had in mind."

"I don't agree with that either," I exclaimed. "Who cares what the Framers had in mind? The constitution has to be interpreted to meet today's problems. Those brilliant and brave men who formed this country had no idea about what would exist today. They didn't even have TV!"

The rabbi chuckled.

"That's why there are amendments," I continued. "So it should be with the Torah." I stood up and lowered my voice. "And here's the worst part, Rabbi: I was not there when the Bible was written. None of my thoughts and ideas, nor yours, or, for that matter, anyone alive today has added one word to our Holy Books."

The Rabbi stood up, removed his Black hat, and adjusted his skullcap. "Daniel, my boy, you need to keep studying. The answers will come to you."

"Rabbi," I responded, "I have come to the conclusion that none of us are truly free if we are bound by laws, whether religious or civil, that do not allow us to change them."

Rabbi Pinchik threw up his hands. "Hear me, Danny. Faith is something that must be fed and nurtured. If you fail to do that, it will die."

I lowered my head, and then raised it to face him. "Rabbi," I said, in almost a whisper, "I believe I'm no longer capable of doing that."

"Try. And if you should leave us the door will always be open for your return." With that, he rested his hand on my shoulder for a few seconds and left.

33

THE BOY'S MASHUGA

By the fall of 1975, my marriage had imploded. We were at each other's throats, threatening all sorts of lawsuits. We struggled along for another three years, hoping things might be worked out, but it was a futile effort. I continued to cheat on Adele, but, what was worse, there was no longer any guilt about it.

"The time has come," I said finally to Adele, in June of 1978 "for this suffering to end."

She remained silent for a moment, then nodded.

"We have to be civil about this, for the sake of our kids."

Adele nodded once again. "Whatever you say." She whispered, completely crushed by the battles between us.

The parting had to be done intelligently and fairly. I had watched a friend of mine leave his wife and hole up in a hotel room. Four weeks later, he was back with her, fighting between them growing even more vicious. Another friend hid his money from his wife, and his kids wouldn't speak to him for years. I truly believed this marriage could not be saved, so I thought out the end very carefully. First, I would get a place in the City, furnish it, and then leave home. The lease I signed for an apartment, on 40th Street and Second Avenue, drove in the last nail. We filed for divorce two weeks later.

We went to Rabbi Kassin for Adele to receive a "*get*," the Hebrew document of divorce Adele would need if she were to re-marry. The financial settlement was quick and simple: Adele got the house in Brooklyn, now worth over a million and with no mortgage. I agreed to pay the annual real estate taxes and wrote her a check for $500,000 in cash. We agreed on alimony of

$15 thousand a month and to pay her taxes for seven years or until she re-married, whichever came first. Health insurance, of course, would be provided for her and the kids, plus any additional child support needed. I bought a Two Million Dollar insurance policy with her as the owner.

Adele seemed more relaxed by the settlement, and we began speaking more civil to one another. After a short time, she came to see that the divorce would serve her better as well, and we got along, mostly for the sake of our children. Of course, the most important part of the deal was I got the kids on the weekends and could visit them any reasonable time at Adele's house during the week.

Sammy and Sarah were very distressed by the divorce, particularly Sarah. She was afraid she would lose my friendship by remaining close to Adele. I assured her I loved her and Sammy, and our connection would not be severed. Over the years, Sarah and I had developed a special friendship, without sex; the only one, up until that point in my life, that I had with a woman other than my sisters.

One year later, Adele married an acquaintance of mine named Bobby Sitt. Now, at thirty-six years old, I was a bachelor. The day the divorce was final was liberating; in fact, so liberating I got piss drunk in a strange bar I'd never been to before.

Pop had stopped coming to the office. His heart was giving him problems, and he was in and out of hospitals and doctors' offices. Finally, one day in October of 1978, when I came to visit him at Maimonides Hospital in Brooklyn, I heard the Code Blue alarm blaring through the speakers in the hall and saw a team of doctors rush into Pop's room. Through the slightly ajar door, I watched as one medic was compressing my father's chest attempting to revive him. After several minutes, the doctor stopped the compressions and said, "Call it," and another physician said, "Six fifty-two." That was the moment: six fifty-two p.m., October 13, 1978, that Ezra Dweck, just a few months before his seventy-second birthday, drifted out of his worldly existence and entered the upper reaches of the universe to join his first wife, Fortune, in Olam Abba for eternity.

Becky made sure that all the customs of our SY burial rituals took place perfectly and in good taste. She catered the food for the Shiva week and handed me the bill, which I was more than glad to pay. The multitude of people at the funeral surprised me. I had not realized how popular my father was. A huge bouquet of flowers arrived from Abdullah Ramallah, Pop's old partner. Becky said he broke into tears when she phoned him with the news. There were no less than eight rabbis in attendance, and the morning and evening prayers at his house were overcrowded.

By this time, I had evolved from an agnostic into a full-fledged, card-carrying atheist, but I dutifully sat Shiva and said the Kadeesh for my father. Al even came in from Florida, without his wife, and even he recited Kadeesh. Al and I remained distant from one another during the week of Shiva. My sisters and brother Jakey chided me for my lack of religion and a couple of rabbis attempted to bring me back into the fold. One such rabbi, a black hat Hasid probably in his late 60's, approached me after the morning services. He placed his hand on my head and mumbled some prayers.

"He was a good man, your father." I nodded, and after a short moment he said, "So, they tell me you are not a believer." I shrugged. "Have you ever studied a leaf; a simple, small, green, leaf that falls from any tree? Have you ever looked at it carefully to see the wonder in that tiny leaf?"

"Never had the desire, Rabbi, but I'll take your word for it."

"The beauty of the universe, Daniel, is in that tiny creation. Hashem has formed even that single leaf, which one might think insignificant, to perfection. That tiny leaf is solid proof of the existence of Hashem."

"Or, it could be proof of evolution, Rabbi."

"What would it take for you to come back to believe in Hashem?"

"I have a list I've repeated time and again. Let's start with Hashem abolishing war, hurricanes, tsunamis, and tornadoes. Throw in His preventing babies from being deformed or born with an illness. Continue with His purging of diseases and starvation. Then, we can move on to eliminating all religions from the planet. That would be a good start."

The Rabbi stared at me increuloudly and walked away shaking his head. He looked at my brother Jakey. "The boy's *mashuga*," he said only half-jokingly and moved on.

I followed all the Shiva rituals, and when they were over, ensured my brothers and sisters that Pop died a fulfilled man having seen all his children married with plenty of grandchildren, which he loved to spoil with candy and spare coins. Of course, Pop had been saddened by my divorce since he had genuine feelings for Adele.

During *Shiva*, Becky was beside herself with grief. I guaranteed her, she would want for nothing, and she would be taken care of by me for the rest of her life. "I give all the money away for Ezra to be alive," she said sadly.

34

LILY

It took many months to recover from the loss of Pop, but time is the great separator from pain. There was no let up from drinking, but my disease was peculiar; sometimes it would let me go months without touching a drop, and at other times I would drink myself to sleep. During the day, I was completely functional. In fact, some of my best deals were made during these alcoholic years as the enterprise with Mr. Nowak continued to flourish.

By 1980, at the end of that long dark period after Pop's death, Mr. Nowak and I had seventeen great properties valued at nearly Four Hundred Million. We were each drawing out six million a year and had refinanced and pulled out Sixty Million tax-free dollars. We could have gotten more, but wanted to avoid putting ourselves in a position of being over-leveraged if the market should crash. Mr. Nowak was no longer active in the business, and my secretary, Fran, along with two other women, acted as agents and building managers handling the paperwork, rent collections, bank deposits, and working with brokers.

At the same time alcoholism, in its full blown state, had taken over my existence, making me not only addicted to booze, but to women and sex, sleeping with any lady I was able to seduce. My only requirement was they are breathing at the time. One-night stands were the routine, and my behavior grew more and more volatile with very high highs and very low lows.

My kids, bless their hearts, suffered terribly from the disorder which caused me to be a poor parent, one who was not there for them, unaware of their needs and unable, or perhaps unwilling, to fulfill my parenting obligations. I failed these innocents terribly, spoiling them with money and "things," but was shut down to the important emotional ties that would promote self-esteem within them. One cannot give what one does not possess.

There were many incidents in which I acted reprehensibly, but there was one episode, in particular, something that, to this day, shames me.

I was at a restaurant in L.A. with a broker after looking at a property, and the waitress who was serving us was an adorable young redhead with an ample figure. I had to have her and after three or four drinks started flirting. For some dumb reason, I lied and told her I was a film producer and that she would be perfect for a part in a movie I was making.

The young girl, Lily, (I'll never forget her name) accepted my invitation to come to my suite at the Beverly Hills Hotel for an "audition" and she showed up after her shift. I poured us both a glass of champagne and asked, "How old are you, Lily?"

"Twenty-one," she answered, with a hint of apprehension.

She showed me her ID. "You know, in this film, you would have to appear nude. Is that okay with you?"

"I... Guess so," she responded as she drank down the whole glass of champagne. "May I have some more, please?" I quickly poured her another glass, and she swallowed that, too, in one gulp.

"Would you mind undressing to give me a peek at your figure?" She shook her head and quickly removed her clothes and underwear. "You have a beautiful body, Lily."

"I work very hard to keep in shape."

I moved closer to her. "There are also some sex scenes in this story. Are you okay with that?" Lily thought a moment, and then nodded yes. "Would you like to audition for that now?" I asked and without waiting for an answer, put my arms around her and kissed her. She started to undress me without any prompting.

When the sex was over, Lily got dressed and asked, "How'd I do?"

"Terrific, I answered, still feeling tipsy from the champagne. I handed her five one hundred dollar bills, but she hesitated to take them. "Think of this as an advance," I urged. She finally accepted the money, and I took her phone number.

After she'd left, I asked myself, "What have I done?" Manipulating this innocent girl and seducing her – no, more like *raping* her. How low had I sunk in my life to resort to this? Was I any better than the pervert in the movie theatre when I was eight years old?

I finished the bottle of champagne and passed out.

When I awoke a few hours later, it was nearly four a.m. I had an early flight back to New York at seven thirty. I took a shower and, while drying myself, stared into the mirror for a good five minutes. Who was I? What have I become?

There were many nights when I drank myself into oblivion, thinking about that young girl, Lily. I told Sammy about the incident, and he said it was no big deal. She was probably a hooker, anyway. I lashed back at him, saying, "It doesn't matter if she was a prostitute or not. I lied to her and conned that innocent girl."

My life had entered that dark hole hidden somewhere in the universe that only those who have been condemned to it can know what it was like. It would take the wise words of my partner, Julius Nowak, and a trip he insisted I join him on, for me to see daylight once more.

35

LET'S NOT SPOIL A GOOD THING

Claudia had become a very important person in my life. We traveled together to the Hotel Christopher in St. Bart telling our families we had separate rooms (we had one large ocean view suite). We had a marvelous time, plenty of laughs and great meals. Much to my surprise, the sex was even more incredible, and that triggered a terrible sense of guilt. It felt as if I was betraying Sonia, and the love we had shared for so long. My sister Marilyn, thank goodness, saw things in their right perspective and guided me through this.

"How can I be with Claudia when I still feel love for Sonia?"

"You can love two women at the same time," Marilyn answered. "Sonia was a part of your past. Claudia is your future. You do not have to stop loving Sonia to fall in love with Claudia."

More than several late night calls to my sister were needed to reassure me Claudia and I were entitled to this happiness. The day we left St. Bart, Claudia was a bit depressed. She too was experiencing guilt. "I don't know what's come over me," she cried. "I have never been happier in my life. Danny, darling, you have brought a new kind of love to me that I have never before experienced." She paused to wipe her tears. "My kids will hate me."

"I hear you," I said embracing her. "I'm going through the same situation. It's about giving up the past for the present, which is really all we have. The thing is, I'm learning we don't have to lose the past to enjoy this moment. We hold onto the good parts of our earlier lives in our hearts and let the new times come in alongside." We embraced each other as the bellman removed our luggage.

We continued to fall deeper in love as the months went by; Rabbi Judah told us we should not continue 'living in sin,' as he called it, and Claudia followed up with the subject of marriage.

"Let's not spoil a good thing, Claudia."

"We can make it better," she countered.

"Look, sweetheart, I'm too old for you. You should find another man, someone with more life ahead of him."

"With my money, I could get any young man to kiss my ass. Danny, darling, I love *you*. If we shared only one more day together, it would be a blessing. Besides, who can predict how long anyone will last?"

"Let's see what happens."

That night I cried myself to sleep after having a long one-way conversation with Sonia. "This is crazy, my love," I said, staring at a picture of Sonia and me on our wedding night. "What's happening to me is irrational. I loved you with all my heart. You gave me your love and devotion, brought me joy and contentment, and now I am thinking about betraying everything we valued so much."

My brain ranted and raved, swearing at myself for the duplicity of being in love with Claudia. It was two o'clock in the morning when I could take it no longer and called my sister Marilyn.

"*Rohi*," she offered. "Sonia is dead, gone from this world. You and Claudia are still here. Don't let this winner slip past. If you do, you should crawl into a hole and wait for the Reaper to come."

"What will my kids think? I've damaged them severely once when I split with their mother."

"They survived that. They'll welcome this. Look, Daniel. Your children have their own kids to worry about. If you marry Claudia, they'll have one less burden to be concerned with. Now, go to sleep. Call Claudia in the morning and ask her to marry you. I love you," Marilyn said tenderly, then abruptly hung up.

Marilyn's words rolled around my head and kept me up all night. The struggle with making this decision weighed heavily on me, and, despite my sister's assurances, the answer as to what to do still plagued me.

Contrary to mine and Claudia's fears, our families were happy for both of us. Our children got along with each other, and a strong bond developed between the Dweck's and the Gemals.

For the next few weeks, Claudia wisely avoided the subject until one day my daughter, Tuni, and Claudia's daughter, Teri, invited us to lunch at Le Circe. The girls had planned a joint attack on us, speaking as if reading from a script.

"Daddy," Tuni started, "Teri and I have come to a conclusion. We all agree that marriage would be the appropriate move for you two."

"Yeah, Momma," Teri joined in. "This affair of yours; well, it's an embarrassment to both our families." The pitch of Teri's voice sounded a bit hostile. "*Ayb*," she continued, using the SY word for 'shameful.' "We love you both and wish you only the best," Teri said, "but you have to think of how this looks. People are talking about you, beginning to say nasty things."

"You are not children," Tuni added. "Do the right thing, *ba'ah*."

The comments of our children hit home for both Claudia and me. We discussed marriage, but I still felt it was too soon to take that step, notwithstanding the gossip that was floating around the community. We decided to postpone any decision for a while.

The next morning Rabbi Judah called and got on my case, too. "Danny," he started, and then paused a few seconds before continuing. "My wife and I were talking last night. You need to marry this woman."

"Who called you?"

"Your son, Ezra, phoned last evening," he admitted. "All the children, hers and yours, want you should marry. Do you love this woman, Daniel?"

"I do Rabbi," I answered and felt the love of Claudia rush over me as I said it. "But we need to think about it."

"So? What's to think about? Marry the woman. Make us all happy."

"Thanks for your consideration, Judah," I replied and hung up.

Rabbi Judah was right. What's to think about? Yet, making the move was not that easy and required more thought and reflection. The situation rattled my brain, and an unusual pain filled my heart; not physically, but emotionally. For the first time in my sobriety, I had the urge to drink. I thought back to the last days of my being a practicing alcoholic and recalled the way Mr. Nowak had directed me to take certain steps to address the issues, his voice still ringing in my thoughts.

36

JULIUS NOWAK

Julius Nowak was born in 1918 in the city of Plock, just north of Warsaw, one of the oldest Jewish communities in Poland, a city where Jews had settled in 1237. In 1555, King Sigismund II Augustus granted the Jews economic rights equal to those of other citizens, and in 1576 King Stephen Báthory prohibited city authorities from hindering Jews in their business pursuits. As the centuries flew by, Jewish rights became more limited. In 1754 their situation deteriorated even further when a "blood libel," the accusation that Jews kidnapped and murdered the children of Christians in order to use their blood as part of their religious rituals during Jewish holidays, caused an uproar in the city.

From 1865 to 1871, the town contained a school where Jewish children were taught in Hebrew and Russian, and, in 1872, the first Jewish hospital was built. In the *Talmud Torah*, secular studies were introduced at the end of 1880, and in 1888, a Jewish school, sponsored by the government, was founded. In 1912, a *yeshiva* was opened, and, in 1916, a Jewish high school was founded.

Over the centuries the freedoms of Jew deteriorated, and by the time Julius was born, anti-Semitism was rampant throughout Poland.

When his father died, Julius dropped out of school at age twelve and began peddling piece goods to nearby farmers and laborers. He was not a religious Jew, but was proud of his heritage. He attended synagogue in his neighborhood on High Holy Days, and, on occasion, when he was not traveling, on the Sabbath. He did not have a Jewish "look," and his family name was the equivalent of "Smith," so there was little trouble dealing with his Christian customers. He developed a skill at tailoring and began traveling to far away towns and cities in Poland to ply his skills.

Julius adored his mother, Simcha, and supported her as lavishly as he could with his monthly earnings of nearly Two Thousand Zlotys, the equivalent of approximately Four Hundred US dollars.

Young Julius enjoyed his lifestyle and had increased his income when he bought a horse and carriage, which allowed him to take greater quantities of piece goods bales on his road trips. By the time he was twenty-one, he was earning more than Ten Thousand Zlotys a month. By local standards, he was a rich man.

In May of 1939, Julius moved his mother into a small house he had purchased near the edge of the Jewish quarter, where the wealthier Jewish residents lived. Simcha was in heaven. She lived in a house with a terrace, a symbol of the upper class. Julius furnished it with pieces bought from the *Rynek*, the town market. He sewed the drapes himself using some of his finest materials and installed them one afternoon while Simcha was visiting a friend. When she came home and saw the surprise her son had crafted, she nearly fainted from joy.

Julius was a bit of a ladies man, meeting and sleeping with mostly Christian girls in the towns he had visited. Life was wonderful, and he could not be more grateful for his good fortune.

In early August of 1939, he set out on a road trip that would take him to Warsaw and Lodz, then to Kielce and Krakow, then north to Lublin and finally back to his hometown. He had accumulated a fortune of Forty Thousand Zlotys and used it all to buy a large quantity of closeout piece goods from a manufacturer in Warsaw. With his wagon fully loaded, and after receiving a blessing from his mother, Julius set out for what he expected to be a hugely profitable venture. And then it happened.

On the morning of September 1st, German bombers began their decimation of Warsaw and other parts of Poland. The famous Pomorska Brigade, an antiquated, but courageous and fearless, cavalry of horse soldiers, proved no match against Nazi Panzers. Within days, refugees were heading east towards Russia, many of them killed along the roads by the Luftwaffe's diving Stukas.

Julius escaped the bombardment of Lodz by turning his wagon towards the outlying forest. It was raining as he came to a clearing where he dismounted, staring at the heavens as wave after wave of Luftwaffe bombers and fighters flew over. He sat on a big rock and contemplated what had happened to shatter his world. Julius's reverie was shattered when he heard a Polish voice shouting at him.

"This is your wagon?" a military officer asked, and Julius just nodded.

"I am Captain Wozniak from the Polish Infantry. We need your cart to carry wounded soldiers."

Soon, half dozen men carrying stretchers with their wounded fellow combatants appeared in the clearing.

"I am heading for Warsaw," Julius offered.

"You may be heading for Warsaw, sir, but this wagon is going to a field hospital in Kielce." The Captain turned to his men and signaled for them to unload the wagon. As the warriors began throwing the bales of piece goods from the cart, Julius scrambled to protect his fortune, but to no avail. Julius' years of hard work, his *whole life*, lay on the muddied ground.

The soldiers loaded the wagon with the wounded, and as the cart moved away, the Officer shouted back. "You had better stay in the woods as you make your way back."

"Back? To what?" Julius cried.

At the outbreak of World War II, Plock had nearly 10,000 Jews, around one-third of the total population. When the Germans entered on Sept. 9, 1939, the majority of Jews had fled to nearby Gabin, but they gradually returned. As they did, the Germans hunted down men for forced labor.

Julius had abided by the Polish Captain's admonition and had used the back roads to reach the outskirts of Plock. It had taken nearly a month to complete the trip, sporadically hitching rides with Polish truck drivers, but mostly by walking. By the time he arrived at Plock, towards the end of September, the Germans were all over his city.

Julius waited until dark, then snuck into town and found his way to his mother's house. Simcha burst into tears when he entered, relieved that her son was still alive. They embraced, and Julius was anxious to learn about the situation.

"The German police carry out night raids," Simcha began. "They search houses and businesses, plundering, beating; they even kill people. They are brutal beasts who show no mercy.

"After one of the night raids," she continued, "some Jews lodged a complaint before the German authorities. In retaliation, the Germans arrested and executed 180 Jews. Doctor Karsch from the hospital was ordered to supply a list of the old and sick people. Three days later, all those on the list were rounded up and deported."

Simcha became terrified they might take her. She was shaking as she related the events that had happened. Julius put his arms around her as reassurance. "Not to worry, Momma. Everything will be fine. We will find a way to get free from here."

"Julius," she sobbed, "Plock is my home. I know no other place."

"Not to worry, Momma," he repeated. "I will handle it."

In the following days, Julius made contact with a Catholic farmer he had known for years and arranged for him to take in his mother. He sold the furnishings of the house to a Polish customer of his and gave the money to the farmer.

The Germans ordered all Jews to wear the Star of David on their garments, but Julius resisted. He sneaked out of the Jewish Quarter almost every day until, in November, the Germans created a ghetto, which Jews could not leave without permission, but Poles could enter without difficulty and supplied food at high prices.

In December, a *Judenrat*, or Jewish Council, was established. It created a Labor Bureau to supply the Germans with manpower. It also maintained a clinic and a soup kitchen subsidized by the American Jewish Joint Distribution Committee.

Julius refused to wear the armband and managed to avoid reporting for a labor force until a Polish woman, a neighbor who had known him since childhood, reported Julius to the Nazis. He was arrested and taken to Gestapo headquarters where two men beat him within an inch of his life. One of the Nazi officers was about to shoot him when the other one said, "Don't waste the bullet. This one won't last a week in Sachsenhausen." They were wrong.

On the train to Germany, Julius had promised himself he would endure whatever the Germans threw at him. He vowed to himself that if Hitler and the entire German nation had to collapse, he would see his mother again.

Not only did Julius spend twenty-five months in Sachsenhausen, a concentration camp north of Berlin, but survived through an additional thirty months at the notorious Auschwitz death camp near Krakow, Poland. Hitler had decided in 1942 that Germany should be *Juden Frei*, and, after SS Leader, Heinrich Himmler, effectuated the evacuation, Josef Goebbels, the propaganda minister declared, "My Fuhrer, Berlin is free of Jews!"_

Once Julius arrived at the Polish camp outside of Krakow, he was chosen as a laborer. Soon, he made contact with a Jewish *Capo*, a Block leader, Chaim Pinske, who he knew from his home town. Chaim arranged for Julius to work in the camp bakery where it would be warm during the brutal Polish winters and would allow him access to more food.

Julius quickly found ways to survive the unthinkable conditions of this concentration camp by taking on extra work as a tailor, mending the garments and socks of political prisoners who were still receiving packages of food from their families. Julius sewed extra pockets into his trousers which allowed him to leave his workplace at the end of the day with four extra loaves of bread hidden in them: one for him, one to share with friends, and two to trade with other inmates. Life in Auschwitz, for Julius, was a great deal easier than the brutality he had experienced in the German camp because the tide of war was turning against the Nazis and they had become a bit more lenient.

In the early part of 1944, with the Russian armies closing in on Poland, there was a plan organized for prisoners to escape. Julius chose not to go, but supplied as much bread as he could steal from the bakery. He also sewed civilian outfits for the escapees, but unfortunately, the plan had to be aborted when Himmler ordered the shutdown of the death factory that had taken one million Jewish lives. Himmler also ordered the mass graves with thousands of bodies that were outside the camp to be dug up and burned.

In mid-January 1945, Soviet forces approached the Auschwitz concentration camp complex, and the Nazis began evacuating its prisoners and those in its sub camps. SS units forced nearly 60,000 prisoners to march west from the Polish camp, shooting anyone who fell behind or could not continue. Julius trudged on, urging others not to give up. As many as 15,000 prisoners died during the evacuation marches. And then, suddenly, it was over. Somewhere near Gleiwitz, the SS halted the death march, and the guards disappeared. At last, the prisoners were free.

Many headed back east and met up with the Russian liberators. Julius turned north and began the long trek home to Plock. Arriving there two months later, he learned of the devastating news that the Nazis had liquidated the Plock community in two deportations on Feb. 20 and 28, 1941.

During the first deportation, the Germans had surrounded the main street, and all the Jews were driven outdoors. More than half of the residents had been sent to the concentration camp in Dzialdowo. During the next deportation, the remaining Jews had been sent to the same camp, where they were tortured and sent on to the Radom District. During February and March of 1941, six transports of Jews from Plock arrived in the Radom District. They were dispersed in small localities – barefoot, in rags, and exhausted. Most of the deportees died in these camps. Less than 100 of the 10,000 Jews of Plock had survived the war. Julius's mother, Simcha, was not one of them.

Julius sat Shiva for his mother in one of the few Jewish homes that were still standing. It was the house belonging to the wealthiest member of the community that had been taken by the SS to be used as headquarters. All the remaining Jews of the community paid respects, including a pert black haired girl named Rivka Liebowitz, who had survived the women's camp at Auschwitz. Because of their common experience, she and Julius took to each other immediately. Within weeks, they were married. Since the community synagogue had been destroyed by the Nazis, the ceremony was held in the same house where Julius had mourned his mother.

Two years later, Julius and Rivka immigrated to New York, where he opened a small factory in the garment center on 7th Avenue, funded with the help of a number of Jewish organizations. As his business flourished, he soon began acquiring small properties around the City and was living a comfortable life in a large house in Cedarhurst, Long Island. Though they tried everything, Rivka was barren, and, to their misfortune, they remained childless.

Mr. Nowak had never talked about his experiences in Germany until the day he decided revealing it may be of some help to me. It was the first opening for me of the door of recovery.

37

ANOTHER GENERATION

It was the spring of 1983. The trees were blossoming in Manhattan and the weather had turned quite warm. The beauty of the season was lost to me as my hole to hell grew deeper. I latched on to the one hope, a slippery one at best, I had found after hearing Mr. Nowak's tale of his dreadful time in the concentration camps. If someone could survive that horror and later flourish, then perhaps there might be some prospect for me.

We were standing in front of our 3rd Avenue building discussing how we were going to renovate the front of the stores when he suddenly pulled my arm and forced me to face him. "Daniel," the old man stated. "You cannot continue this way. The drinking has to stop. You must seek help, straighten out. Stop hurting yourself. Think of your children."

"Mr. Nowak, I don't know what to do."

"I will tell you what to do. You are like the son Rivka and I never had. She loves you. *I* love you.

"I love you, too, Mr. Nowak."

"We are going to Berlin in two weeks. Believe it or not, the German government has sent us first class airplane tickets and is putting us up in a swanky-panky hotel. They want I should testify in the trial of a Gestapo agent, the one who beat me up in Plock in 1939; Forty-One years later, retribution.

"Daniel, you come with us. We stay in Germany four days, and then go to Poland to see Auschwitz. There you will see how we lived, and how we survived. That will be your inspiration to help yourself."

We flew on Lufthansa, first class, to Berlin, Mr. Novak's and Rivka's ticket paid for by the German government. We stayed at a hotel near the Tiergarten which the Germans had not fully renovated after a Russian soldier started a fire in the basement. Still, the suite was plush, and the History of Hitler and his henchmen, especially Hermann Goering, lunching here held some fascination for me.

That first night we had box seats at the State Opera House in East Berlin, again, compliments of the German people. The next day, a young government official who spoke little English picked us up in a limousine that took us to the courthouse. Once settled in the chauffeur driven car, Mr. Nowak asked the young man, in German, "Why didn't Germany treat me this nice back then?

The young man leaned forward and said, in German, "*Das war eine andere Generation.*" I looked to Mr. Nowak, and he translated. "He said, 'That was another generation.'"

That morning, Mr. Nowak testified in court describing the brutality inflicted upon him by the defendant, a non-descript seventy-two year old man named Otto Krauss. During the war, Otto had gone on to greater heights of glory, becoming an assistant to the commandant at the infamous concentration camp at Buchenwald. On April 11, 1945, starved and emaciated prisoners stormed the watchtowers, and seized control of the camp. Later that afternoon, American soldiers from the 6th Armored Division, liberated the camp, but Krauss had escaped and made his way back to his home town of Hamburg. He slipped back into the civilian population awaiting help from the Vatican to move him to South America, but the help never came.

The Nazi lived quietly amongst the people of Hamburg for the next thirty-six years, until eight months ago when an anti-Nazi citizen visiting from Berlin recognized him. The man informed the German Police, and Krauss was quickly arrested. Otto was convicted of Crimes against Humanity and Sentenced to life in prison, a judgment that was later commuted to three years.

Friday afternoon, we flew to Warsaw and visited the site of the Warsaw Ghetto, where a handful of Jewish fighters with few arms and ammunition fought off a Nazi regiment under the command of SS General Juergen Stroop, for nearly a month. All that remained now was a plaque noting that this was the location where brave Polish partisans fought the Nazis. No mention of any Jews doing the fighting in this battle, alone, and with help from no one.

The next day a single engine plane carried us to Krakow where we hired a driver to take us to Auschwitz. When we arrived at the gate, which still bore the disdainful sign *"Arbeit Macht Frei,"* "Work Sets You Free," the first thing Mr. Nowak did was spit on the ground.

"Promised myself to do that if I ever came back," he said triumphantly.

There were many people crowded about, mostly students waiting for a guide to enter the camp. "I know this place like it was yesterday," Mr. Nowak said, and walked through the gate, holding the hand of his Rivka. As we walked the streets past the brick buildings, Mr. Nowak pointed to each one and described what went on in there. When we came to Block 10, he stopped and stared at the structure for a long while.

"This is where they did their terrible experiments on innocent people, mostly *der kinder*. Oy! The screams! I worked nearby in the bakery. *Mayn Got*, the sounds are still in my ears. And that building next to it is Block 11, where the Gestapo held trials of the political prisoners. I watched as many of them were executed by the Germans against that back wall. This building is also the place where a Polish Priest, Father Kolbe, a courageous man, was left by the bastards to die of starvation after he volunteered to take the place of a condemned Polish political prisoner."

We continued to walk until we came to the prisoners' barracks, wooden structures with three-tier sleeping quarters lining both sides of the interior. Mr. Nowak pointed out the bunk he shared with three other men. The conditions were deplorable, dampness, leaky roofs, and the fouling of the straw mattresses by prisoners suffering from diarrhea. The inadequate sanitary facilities made matters even worse.

We left the main camp and walked a little over a kilometer to Auschwitz II, called Birkenau, where female prisoners were held, and the gas chambers and crematoria were located. This was the camp Rivka had been quartered in during the war. As we walked along the railroad tracks leading into the camp, she showed us where the selections were made by SS doctors, physicians who placed little value, if any, in the Hippocratic Oath to "do no harm." Instead, they decided who lived and died and *did* do much harm to their fellow humans.

Suddenly, we heard a train whistle, and Rivka was startled by the sound. She put her hand to her mouth and tears covered her cheeks. "That was the sound we heard when a transport was arriving," she sobbed. She directed us to her bunk and the inhumanity of this dwelling still filled the air.

I looked out at the pastoral fields surrounding the camp, tall blades of green grass that belied the horrors of this evil place. My problems paled and quickly melded into a small package of determination. My good friend, Mr. Nowak, was right. This place is where I needed to be, at this moment, at this time in my life. If he and Rivka could live through this tragedy and survive, I could walk through my traumas and come out the other end a better man.

38

THE HONEYMOON PERIOD

The day after my return from Poland, I sought out the nearest AA meeting, located in a church on Park Ave and 78th Street. I listened intently to what different speakers were saying and identified with all of them. My alcohol and sex addictions had consumed me. Cigarettes, too, were a sorry part of my life, despite my belief smoking was a filthy habit.

Things that people spoke of at the meeting resonated, like the feelings of emptiness that had been with me since childhood. I was consumed by a sense of unworthiness, despite my amazing success at an early age. I lacked the ability to form a lasting, intimate relationship with a woman. Depression and anxiety flowed in and out of my daily existence. It felt as though my life was being retold by each of the people who spoke. The message was clear, and the path to sobriety and sanity lay before me to choose.

Embarking on the road to being sober was frightening at first, sort of like giving up an old friend that was always there for me when things got rough. The first week of being dry brought on a terrible case of diarrhea and headaches, but that soon passed. It felt as though my brain had been liberated from the darkness and a clear path into illumination was directing me. Old timers call it the "honeymoon" period.

A month later they handed me a thirty day chip, and the honeymoon ended. Painful feelings of anxiety gripped me, and a deep depression followed. Those were the days when I needed three meetings to keep me on track. I took on a sponsor, an Italian guy named Nicky, with two years of sobriety who was fully committed to his recovery and, as an extension, to mine.

One night, as I began my second year of recovery, I was at home watching TV and drinking Pellegrino, my new drink of choice, when the phone rang; it was my daughter Tuni, crying and terribly upset.

"Daddy," she whimpered. "I'm in trouble."

"What is it, Tuni? Talk to me."

After a moment her words came out slowly and in a very low tone. "After watching you get sober and listening to the things you learned in AA, I had to admit to myself that I had a problem." She paused, then finally confessed, "Daddy, I am addicted to cocaine," and she was bawling now. "I don't know what to do."

"Does your husband know?"

"Mark is aware."

"Is he there with you?"

"Yes," she answered. "He told me to call you. Oh Daddy, I'm so sorry. Please help me."

Her heart-rending plea caused a chilling pain in my guts. I was filled with anxiety and unable to think straight. "Relax, sweetie. I'm coming over."

"Hurry, daddy!"

I hung up from Tuni and immediately speed dialed my AA sponsor, Nicky, more for myself than for her. He agreed to meet me at Tuni's.

How did this beautiful sweet child who never asked for anything, did her school work diligently, listened, as a child, to me and Adele and volunteered for charitable work, become this addict? My divorce had to have some play in this, but it was more than that. My absence from home and my blindness of her emotional needs brought this about. I had to own this, no matter how much pain it caused.

I did not bother taking the Rolls into Brooklyn for fear I might get into an accident caused by my anxiety, and instead, took a taxi. Mark let me in the house, and Tuni was lying on the couch wrapped in a heavy blanket. She sat up, wrapped her arms around me, and bawled again.

"Easy, sweetie," I comforted her. "Everything will be okay." The doorbell rang, and it was my sponsor, Nicky. He quickly took charge of the situation and assured Tuni that she could get through this crisis in one piece if she listened to him.

"Are you ready to surrender to this disease?"

She nodded her head.

"Okay. Your Dad is going to get you into a re-hab." He turned to look at me and I nodded. "You will have to go through a transition, but your husband, Mark, your Dad and I will help you through it."

"What about my kids?"

"Leave them to me, honey," Mark said.

"Oh, Mark, I am so sorry."

"You are going to stop saying that," Nicky interjected. "You have a disease. Would you be apologizing if you had cancer?" She looked up at him. "I think not."

Tuni's recovery began at that moment, and we went to her first CA meeting the next day together with Mark and Nicky.

Tuni's rehab took immediate effect. She experienced no slips or setback and attended CA meetings religiously. I sat in on one meeting where she shared how her father (me) was not present for her, even when he *was* present. She described the emptiness she felt through her teenage years, an emptiness that could not be filled with material things. Her sincere words brought me to tears, but I smiled through them because I was aware her verbalizing the pain would help to heal it.

39

CHUMSEH

The months of abstinence glided by, and I attended at least two AA meeting a day, sometimes three. Gradually, as the clarity increased, the concepts that had guided my life until then began shifting. I recalled my step-mother Becky constantly warning us about weird superstitions. Opening an umbrella in the house brought bad luck. If the postman whistles when delivering the mail, it meant bad news. And if one shoe lands on top of the other, it meant you will be traveling. Dozens of other nonsensical things were embedded in me as a child, but were still with me at the age of forty-three.

The most significant of these was the *chumseh*, which, in Arabic means 'five', yes the *number* five that seems to have a diabolical power over SYs. It brought to mind the Nazi routine I had read about in the death camps, where people were lined up in groups of five and counted by fives. The SY fear of the chumseh gripped the community, so much so that a small, gold, five-fingered hand on a chain is placed on a newborn infant to ward off the evil eye and to send the *chumseh* back to anyone wishing ill upon the infant.

The use of the word had to be avoided at all costs by SYs so as not to give the impression one wished evil on another person. I have heard Becky say in private to a friend about one woman or another she might be angry at, "*Chumseh fee ehna,*" wishing the *chumseh* would strike at a particular enemy's eyes.

Once, I asked a mother in the community how many children she had, and she answered, "Three girls and two boys," rather than say the number five for fear I would think she wished me bad luck or that bad luck would befall her. If one could not avoid using the number five, the word had to be preceded by a Syrian phrase, which broadly translated from Syrian to "The chumseh is on me." Another part of the superstition was the belief that a *shebeh*, a small quartz stone, would ward off the chumseh. Many adult SYs carried one at all times, and even kept one in the glove compartments of their cars.

One of the first things I did with my newly found clear-headedness was to shed myself of these fallacies and superstitions. It was vital for me to constantly remind myself that no one person's mind had control over another. I came to believe there was no such thing as the "supernatural," or the "evil eye," and that no human could see into the future or make contact with dead people. Gradually, a sense of self-esteem began to grow, driven by the love and camaraderie of AA members towards 'newcomers.' The achievement of remaining sober for each twenty-four hour cycle bolstered that new sentiment.

Thirty days after I had found AA, cigarettes had been removed from my life, and a new perception of women began to evolve. Abstinence from smoking happened in a strange manner. A good friend and supporter at meetings was Beverly Smith, an old timer with twenty years of sobriety. We were having lunch one day, and as we finished the meal, I began to cough. At that moment, I reached for a cigarette, lit it, took a drag, and then stared at the weed, still coughing. "This is insanity," I said, and squashed the cigarette in the ashtray. I never lit one again.

In examining my view of the opposite sex, it seemed to me to trace back to the misogynistic tendencies of the SY community, which, in my opinion, had its origins in the Jewish religion. Women had no obligation to pray; in fact, each morning men recited a prayer thanking Hashem for not making them a woman. Eve was the spoiler of the Garden of Eden. In Biblical days and right up to the 20th century, fathers decided whom their daughters would marry. One of the laws that continually puzzles me is of *Neda*, wherein a female is considered "unclean' during her menstrual cycle belittling a woman's natural physical existence, a function purportedly created by God.

Once, while attending a funeral of an old SY woman, her daughter wished to offer a eulogy, but was told she could not. When I inquired as to why she was prohibited from speaking about her mother, a rabbi said "Because she might be experiencing her menstrual cycle and would, therefore, be unclean to stand on the *"Tebah,"* the podium near where the sacred scrolls were kept stored.

I was grateful to the AA program in its ability to provide a safe place to recover from the disease, but two years after that first meeting the petty squabbling over procedures at meetings began to wear on me. There were people whose sharing went on and on which limited the number of members who could participate. I suggested we limit an individual's sharing to three minutes and have a bell ring to remind the speaker. After much acrimony, the new rule was adopted at that meeting by a majority of members during a "group conscious" vote. The change was soon adopted at other meetings as well. One member started what he called a "no bell" meeting to bring back the old custom of endless sharing, but the new standard was quickly adopted to overrule that idea.

Some old timers, many of them with twenty or more years of sobriety, but who still smoked pot, were not happy about the ruling from the AA General Service Office that they must go back to day one of their recovery after giving up all drugs.

As helpful as it was, there was something missing in AA. While many people, including me, kept sober by following the program, our general behavior had changed only slightly. People with years of abstinence were still smoking, womanizing, and gambling. Their moral structure had only slightly improved, even though the name of God was often mentioned in every other sentence of these men and women who had recovered from the disease. It became annoying for me to hear people relate how God had done this or that for them. It was difficult for me to understand what they were saying because of my lack of belief in a Supreme Being.

AA speaks about turning to a "higher power" which most members attributed to a male God. At the end of each meeting either the Lord's Prayer, "Our Father, who art in heaven…" or the Serenity prayer, "God, grant me the power…" was usually recited by all. There were a few meetings for atheists, but to me, even these groups treated their non-belief like a religion. In my case, the meetings themselves became my higher power because, as long as I was present, sobriety was maintained.

I was not judging anyone, but simply concluding that what was needed was something more than just being free from alcohol. It was imperative for me to discover how I got to need AA in the first place and to seek ways to heal myself from the life that led me to alcoholism.

One young man, Harold, who heard me sharing about the incidence in the movie theatre when I was eight years old, approached me after the meeting and suggested that another group, ACOA, Adult Children of Alcoholics, might offer some help in dealing with that and other past traumas. Harold offered to take me to a meeting, and I accepted.

Chills filled my body at that first gathering. Neither of my parents was alcoholic, although Becky was addicted to prescription painkillers. What struck me was the description of the dysfunctional home environment. Not only did my family fit into that narrative, to me the word "dysfunctional" characterized the whole SY community.

The fact that SYs were generous without limit when it came to supporting charities that helped others did not cover up the inherent prejudices against Blacks, Latinos and those groups that were not white and SY Jews. They support Israel over their country, America.

There seemed to be an unwillingness of SYs, in general, to move into the 21st Century, instead of falling back to the 12th. The persistence to hold on to superstitions and false prophets, and to value money above all else, these were the things I saw for the first time with my new vision, and I was an integral part of it. What freed me from the same shackles of delusions was the confession to myself that I was one of them, clinging to the same principles.

40

A SUDDEN BLAST OF SILENCE

One Sunday afternoon, near Labor Day, 1990, while sitting by Sammy's pool in Deal, Louie Shamah, Andy Dweck, Maxie Fallas and Ikey Salem popped in without invitation, as happened often with SYs. Sarah instructed the *khadameh*, Felicia, to bring out the lemonade, fruit, and cheeses. The boys sat down and immediately began complaining about the collapse of the commercial real estate business in New York. More than a few SY people involved in the business were nearly wiped out. Mr. Nowak and I avoided the crash due to our limited leveraging.

The conversation soon turned to the scandal that had happened the night before when two members of the Club were caught cheating at the high stakes Texas Hold 'Em poker game. It reminded me of the hand in which Sammy caught the dealer stacking the deck; but this caper was more sophisticated.

The two culprits had managed to sneak in a bunch of marked decks of cards and had been deceiving the other members on a regular basis. The main perpetrator, an import named Tofiq Schwecky, was able to see the almost invisible markings on the back of the cards and would know which hand to stay in on by reading his opponent's and the top card of the deck.

The underhanded ruse had gone on for months, and the losses of the honest members climbed into the tens of thousands. They were playing *Saldo*, a game similar to Texas Hold 'Em, and the scheme blew up in the culprit's face when one of the regular players, Mark Sasson, who was holding a full house of Aces over Kings, bet Five Thousand, increasing the pot total to Twenty-Two Thousand dollars.

Tofiq studied the man, and his eyes darted between the opponent's cards and the dealer's deck. Tofiq had a set of eights and should have folded his hand with such a large bet, but after slyly studying the back of the top card in the deck, he called the bet, and, lo and behold, the fourth eight fell, giving Tofiq quads. He showed his hand and started pulling in the money.

Sasson could not believe it. "You called looking for the fourth eight? You know what the odds are? Fifty to one! Damn it, how can you call that bet?"

Mark was so upset, he took the deck of cards home with him and studied each card under a magnifying glass. After several hours, he discovered the markings, a simple system printed into the deck. He was so furious that at five a.m. he called the Club President and related what he had discovered. The two sharks were called to the club the first thing that morning to receive the punishment: Tofiq had to turn over the amount won in that pot to Sasson, and each of the swindlers had to pay a Ten Thousand dollar fine to the organization. In addition, they received a lifetime ban from entering the club.

When Felicia served the fruit, we all gathered around the large table near the barbecue. Sammy brought out a bottle of Jack Daniels for the boys and poured them each a glass. Maxie noticed I didn't take a shot and brought up the subject of drinking.

"How long you been sober?" He asked.

"Almost eight years."

"Ever yearn for a drink?"

"No."

"Cigarettes?" chimed in Andy smoking a cigar.

"Uh-uh. Filthy habit," I added.

"How did you become an alcoholic?" Ikey inquired.

"Alcoholism is an insidious disease. It creeps up on you when you think of yourself as just a heavy drinker. I was always afraid of flying, couldn't believe that a plane the size of a building could get up into the air. I once took a fear of flying class sponsored by Pan Am. Didn't work. I saw a hypnotist who, after twenty sessions, *he* became afraid to fly. So, I had to get drunk before getting on a plane. Did that for years. Never drank during the day, except when flying. I had no clue what the problem was."

"How do you know?" Ikey asked. "What makes you an alcoholic?"

"It doesn't matter how much you drink; or how often. What counts is what the alcohol does to you. A normal drinker swallows the booze and pisses it out. An alcoholic experiences a personality change; he becomes another person."

"I give you a lot of credit," Sammy offered. "Don't know if I could give up drinking."

"You don't have to," I answered. "I've watched you. You don't even finish your drink. An alcoholic would not leave even one drop."

"So now you're normal?" Ikey said.

"What is normal? I don't drink, smoke, or gamble anymore. Does that make me normal? Who knows? There are so many things I need to fix before I become 'normal;' like working through the trauma of having been sexually molested."

A sudden blast of silence engulfed the table. Ikey's mouth dropped open. Only Sammy was not shocked, as he had heard this story before.

"Who did that to you?" Maxie inquired.

"An SY pervert; heard he died last year."

More silence until Ikey spoke. "Never told anyone this, but an uncle of mine did something to me. I was nine years old. After my parents were divorced, my mother's brother would pick me up from school. More than once, when he put me in the back seat, he would grab my crotch. He warned me if I told anyone it would hurt my mother."

"I can't believe I'm saying this," Maxie said. "This has been a lifelong secret, but one of the rabbi's in the Yeshiva masturbated in front of me while holding my hand during my private Bar Mitzvah lessons. I told my father, and he threatened to kill the rabbi if he ever touched another kid again. Eventually, the rabbi was arrested after another boy's parents called the police. Of course, the rabbi denied everything and was never brought to trial when community members swore that the rabbi was not capable of such horrors. A few months later, he was fired from his position and moved away from Brooklyn."

"God," Andy said incredulously. "Who knew this shit happened to SYs?"

"It happens everywhere, I said. "No group of people is immune to this. What I learned was that a large percentage of perpetrators themselves were abused."

Needless to say, these stories put a damper on the afternoon, but both Maxie and Ikey called me the next day to thank me for sharing my experience. It had given both of them permission to reveal their darkest secret.

ACOA provided me with the tools necessary to come to grips with the sexual assault I suffered at the hands of that pedophile in the movie theatre.

The more I talked about it at meetings, the more I was relieved of the pain and the shame that followed me my whole life. The side benefit of sharing led others to reveal similar circumstances that they had experienced.

Here's a tragic story. A thirty-two year old woman I sponsored in ACOA, let's call her "Mary," moved to New York from Minnesota when she was seventeen years old told me she that when having sex with any man the only way she could enjoy it was to picture her father during the intercourse. "Why?" I asked her.

"My dad used to come into my room at night and get under the covers with me. He would tell me how much he loved me, and then caressed my body."

"How old were you at the time?"

"It started when I was twelve and went on until I left the house on my seventeenth birthday."

"How often did this happen?" I asked.

"Three, sometimes four times a week. It felt so good when he touched me, and I would become aroused. Moments later, he would enter me, and I would have an orgasm."

"Have you ever spoken to a therapist about this?"

"About what?

"Mary, your father abused you repeatedly for years."

"Abused me? No. I enjoyed it. I wanted it."

"No, Mary," I insisted, "He took advantage of you. He should never have touched you."

"He was lonely after momma left us. I wanted him to be happy."

"Mary, what he did was a crime. If your father had been caught, he would have been put in jail for a long time. He broke a sacred trust."

She stared blankly at me for quite a while before the tsunami of tears rushed forward. I asked her if she needed a hug, and she nodded. My therapist recommended someone who might help Mary, and she began her long journey of recovery.

Working and sponsoring women in ACOA led to very special relations with women. I became known as a "safe man" because I made no move to engage in these relations in any way other than as a friend who might offer help in their recovery. I learned something new each day from these people, the cruelty and abuse they had endured, and the courage of most of them to face the pain and heal themselves.

"Anita" was raped when she was nineteen in her hometown of Metuchen, New Jersey by a guy she knew only casually from the neighborhood. She never reported it, and when I asked her why, she lowered her head and hesitated to answer.

"I… reached an orgasm," she said, apologetically.

"So?

"That meant I enjoyed it."

"No, it doesn't," I responded. "Orgasm during rape is fairly common. It comes about from the stimulation of your nerve endings." Anita was greatly relieved to hear this, and she, too, sought professional help.

The greatest tragedy for those who survive the abuser attacks is the shame we feel which leads to burying the pain in the darkest recesses of our emotions. The one road back towards healing is to let the pain resurface and walk through it with the help of other caring humans.

41

A WOMAN HAS TO DO SOME CHECKING

After celebrating my 8th anniversary of sobriety ACOA had taught me I was not responsible for my disease, but it was up to me to bring about my recovery. I did the Twelve Steps of AA, but repeated them in ACOA through a different perspective. Step 8 reads "Made a list of all persons we had harmed, and became willing to make amends to them all." I suggested a thirteenth step be added which might read, "Made a list of those who had harmed *me* and told them to go fuck themselves." Sadly to say, that idea was never adopted.

At meetings, women and men shared how they had been abused sexually, physically, and verbally as youths. There were stories of neglect by parents, some who terribly damaged the youngsters by pounding their own ultra-religious and obsessive beliefs into their children's heads.

Soon after that first ACOA meeting I began seeing a therapist, an intelligent woman with a Ph.D. who was aware of the kinds of trauma through which I had lived. She was a soothing voice, combating the shouting negative words reverberating in my head.

After two years of ACOA meetings and private therapy, a true sense of freedom filled both my heart and mind. The cords in my past were cut, and all the false gods began to dissolve, one by one. My attitude towards the opposite sex evolved into a clearer picture of being *people* first, females second, fully equal, if not superior in some ways. New relationships were born and blossomed with quite a few women, friendships wherein I could be a true supporter and collaborator in their recovery without any desire to seduce or to sleep with them. For the next three years, I remained celibate, which allowed me to deepen my respect for my new friendships and, as a result, for all women.

The greatest blessing of sobriety was the recovery of my daughter Tuni, who had become a cocaine addict even before I discovered my disease. Blinded by my own illness, it was impossible to see hers. My going to AA led to her asking for help.

One Sunday morning, Adele and I were attending the *bris* of our son Joseph's second child, a boy. The infant would be named Daniel, after me, according to custom. Since the baby was not his first-born, there would be no *Pidyon*. Joseph and his wife, Sheila, had put out a nice spread for the guests, and Adele approached me after the ceremony. "Isn't that baby adorable?" she said, more as a statement than a question, and I agreed. "He looks a little like you," she added.

"All babies look like shriveled prunes for the first few weeks. Wait until he's two or three months, then we'll see who he resembles."

"By the way, Danny, I ran into Sonia Franco the other day. She's still single, you know; lives in the city."

"Really? Wasn't she dating Ikey Sitt?"

"That's over. Want me to get you her number?"

"Why not?" I responded.

Three days later, I called Sonia. She barely remembered who I was and said she was seeing someone. I knew that wasn't true because of what Adele had previously said and because we spoke for nearly an hour. The call ended by my telling her if things changed to give me a ring.

Two weeks later, a Thursday night, she did call. "I want to apologize," she confessed. "There's no one special in my life right now."

"I kind of guessed that. Tell me, why'd you wait two weeks to ring me up?"

"A woman has to do some checking on a new fellow she might be dating."

"Is that what we'll be doing? Dating?"

"Isn't that why you called?"

"Well, yes."

"So there!" Her voice had the ring of a teenager.

"Okay, then, how about Saturday night, Abe's Steak House on the Third Avenue. Food's excellent. Oh, by the way, are you kosher?"

"Not since I was twelve."

"Great. Pick you up at seven-thirty?"

"Okey dokey,"

I took down her address, smiled as we hung up, and a good feeling came over me.

Sonia devoured a two and a half pound lobster at Abe's, sucking the meat out of each claw, putting the empty bones on a plate provided for just that. I was quite impressed by her ability to not miss a single speck of meat.

"That was delicious," she said, wiping her lips and removing the bib. "Did I embarrass you?"

"Not at all; it was a fascinating experience to watch. Care for another one?"

"Not on a first date."

We talked about trivial things, like popular songs and movies, and she even laughed at my silly jokes, allowing her to pass the first test. She asked about my business, and I tried to keep my success as low key as possible. She told me she had been working four days a week for an accountant earning One Hundred Twenty-Five dollars a day, and after five years had saved Thirty-Two Thousand dollars. I had to admit to being more impressed with that than her encounter with the lobster.

"So, tell me, Sonia, how come, at thirty-nine, you're still single?"

"That's because the right man hasn't found me yet. How long have you been single?"

"Way too long. Never thought I'd be solo eleven years after my divorce. Guess I needed the time to heal myself." The waiter appeared at the table.

"Dessert?" I offered.

"Uh-uh; just coffee. Black, please." I shook my head, and the waiter left.

"And have you healed?" she asked and stared straight at me.

"It's a work in progress; as the old cliché goes, 'one day at a time'."

We sat there for the next forty-five minutes sharing moments we each have been through, the failed relationships, the disappointments, the happy times, with me throwing in a bit of humor here and there. (Okay, here's one joke, with thanks to Henny Youngman: A man tells his friend, 'I've been in love with the same woman for 25 years. (Short pause) If my wife finds out, she'll kill me.')

As the evening went on, we both grew comfortable with one another. That night, my sleep was quite peaceful, and the dreams very pleasant.

Sonia lived in a small one-bedroom apartment on 78th off 2nd, on the fourth floor of a walk-up. After our third date, she invited me over for a home-cooked

Syrian meal. *Yebra*, grape leaves stuffed with ground meat and rice; *fasoulia*, navy beans in tomato sauce and served over rice, (much better than David's Restaurant) and a most delicious recipe for chicken and potatoes flavored with rosemary, olive oil, allspice, and cinnamon, cooked in an oven roaster. I complimented her on this lavish banquet, and our next date she confessed that her sister Rene had helped prepare the meal.

We saw each other three or four nights a week, and after a month, Sonia slept in my apartment. The sex was exceptional, but a sad reminder of what had been missing all those years with Adele. Sonia was willing to experiment during our encounters and taught me things I had not been aware of, the places in her sexual organ that were most sensitive. By the second month, she moved in permanently, and we were madly in love. We had become best friends along the way, which was an integral factor in our adoration growing ever deeper.

Sonia loved to laugh and have fun. She made even small occasions, like seeing a good movie, into a major event. She was star stricken by celebrities and watched all the gossip shows on TV. One afternoon, while having lunch at The Bagel Store on 2nd Avenue, her favorite male actor, Armand Asante, walked in. Her mouth dropped open and terror filled her eyes. I thought she had become ill.

"It's him!" she whispered to me.

"Who?"

"*Him*! Armand Asante!"

For the next few minutes, Sonia's eyes remained glued on *him*. Finally, she rose and walked up to the actor. "Excuse me, but I have been a big fan of yours," she said with a nervous quiver in her voice. "Ever since 'Little Darlings.' I think you are great!"

"You're very kind," Asante responded as he paid his check. He maneuvered his way around Sonia to leave the store and she followed him. She stopped at the phone booth on the corner and quickly dialed her sister Rene.

"I just saw Armand Asante! I told him how much I liked him. He told me…" She stopped and turned to me and asked, "What am I?"

"Very kind," I said and she repeated the words to her sister. She hung up and took small steps towards Armand which he quickly became aware of. He darted into a building, no doubt afraid Sonia was a stalker.

Over the next year, we traveled to London, Paris, and Rome with Sammy and Sarah, and took a cruise with them along the Mediterranean on a luxury liner. We lavished alone for twelve glorious days in Santo Domingo. Summer weekends were spent at Sammy's house in Deal, basking in the sun and putting on pounds from Sarah's cooking. At Friday's Shabbat dinner, she served one of my favorite dishes, *mahshi mishmosh*, hollowed out squash stuffed with ground meat and rice and cooked in a pot with apricots, spices, and the juice of tamarind seeds.

Sonia had a pleasant singing voice and enjoyed serenading me with love songs. She was a fan of Johnny Mathis and Englebert Humperdinck, even though they were not of her generation, and she would sing to me anywhere, any time, but especially while in the pool at Sammy and Sarah's house in Deal.

One Sunday, while sitting by the pool at the Levy house, Sarah blurted out "When are you two getting hitched?"

Sonia chimed in with, "Yeah, when are we getting married?"

Without hesitation, I directed Sammy to get a calendar. "Pick a date," I told Sonia.

She scrolled carefully through the months and stopped in December. "December 7th," she said with a smile, "Your fiftieth birthday."

The wedding was held at the Tavern on the Green on a cloudy, dismal Sunday with snow predicted for that evening. As it turned out, the mild white flakes covered the lighted trees, which were visible from inside the Crystal Room, giving it a look of a picture postcard.

We spent ten days honeymooning in St. Martin, but on the second day Sonia became silent and distant towards me, and unwilling to discuss what was bothering her. She had stayed in the room by herself that evening, refusing to join me for dinner. When I returned, she was lying in bed, still reluctant to discuss what was upsetting her. I sat next to her and took her hand.

"Sonia, I love you, but you must tell me what's bothering you so I can try to fix it. I cannot read your mind, sweetheart. Please tell me what's troubling you." She remained silent. "Look, we didn't get married through a *buzrah* that was forced on us, like my sister, Marilyn. We entered into this marriage because we care for each other and want to share a life. You're either in, or out, of that understanding.

After a long silence, she spoke hesitantly. "Today, when we were walking through the town, you stopped in a shop to look at wrist watches. I went in with you and waited as you looked over the collections. Later, when I walked into a fabric shop, you came in for a minute, then walked out."

"The reason was there was no air conditioning, and the dust from the fabrics was causing my asthma to act up. Sorry, I should have told you that at the time. Forgive me?"

She smiled, then leaned over and kissed me.

"We need to communicate these things that trouble us," I insisted. "If we don't, the marriage is doomed."

"I love you too, Danny," she whispered as she kissed me.

It's true; 'make-up' sex is the greatest.

42

BROKEN HEART

Claudia was in tears. She was sitting on my living room sofa, her face in her hands, failing to stem the flow. "Why does it have to end?" she sobbed, and I could not state a real answer.

"I'm too old to start a new marriage," I offered.

"What does that even mean?"

"There's too much baggage to bring along." I hesitated a moment. "I can't do it, Claudia."

"Okay, I get that. But why do we have to stop seeing each other?"

"You heard what our kids said; and Rabbi Judah, about us living in sin."

"Who cares what they said? I love you, Daniel."

That is what hurt me the most. We were deeply in love, but reality kept kicking me in the shins, reminding me how unfair it would be to Claudia to continue this relationship, one that could not end up anywhere respectable. I had wracked my brain over the past few weeks since that lunch with our daughters Tuni and Teri but kept coming up with the same answers: still in love with Sonia; too old to marry a woman twenty-five years younger than me, and whatever other lame excuse I could come up with. I had decided it would be grossly unfair to marry Claudia because, even though I am in relatively good health, who knows how many years would be left for me?

I moved closer on the sofa and put my arms around Claudia's shoulders to comfort her.

She was hesitant, but then turned to face me. "We've been so happy, darling. I want to thank you for bringing me back to life." Her words tugged at my heart. "I will not pressure you," she continued. "If you want to end this, so be it."

With that, she stood up and went for her coat. "I'll drive you home," I said as I helped her put it on and saw her to the door.

"I'll take an Uber," she responded, and did not turn back, but just walked out.

I was beside myself for the next half hour, pacing the floor and wringing my hands. Finally, I picked up the phone and speed dialed my sister Marilyn.

"You did what?" she said after I told her what happened. "Daniel, my baby brother, I thought you were a smart man. You're an idiot!"

"Marilyn, I just can't…"

"Can't what? Can't live out the rest of your life with someone who loves you, someone you love and want to be with? What on earth were you thinking?"

"This is not an easy thing for me, Marilyn. I'm completely confused."

"We've discussed this to death. You need this woman, Daniel."

"I know I do."

"Then count your lucky stars you found her. Hang up the phone and go after her." I fell silent until she came back on the phone again. "Danny! Listen to your big sister who wants nothing but happiness for you. Run! Chase after her!"

"We'll see," was the best I could offer.

Over the next few days I struggled to keep from calling Claudia. I knew if I heard her voice again, I would succumb to my feelings for her. I attended more ACOA meetings and confided with the women I was sponsoring. They all told me to call her, but I could not bring myself to pick up the phone.

My daughter Tuni invited me for Shabbat dinner, and after, when she served the coffee and parve cake, she and her husband Mark started in.

"Daddy, this is nonsense. If Sonia were here in spirit, she would insist you marry Claudia"

"Sonia cannot speak to me. Although, I must admit, I have had numerous conversations with her about this situation. Tuni, I appreciate your concerns, but…"

"Dad," Mark interrupted, "It's none of my business, but I've not seen you this happy in a long time. What is that worth? And why throw that away?"

"Look, kids," I countered, "there is a lot more to this decision than meets the eye."

"I get it, Daddy. Just promise you will think about it. Okay?"

"I will," I nodded. "I will give it serious consideration."

When I got home my sister Marilyn called me on the land line. "Danny, Claudia's aunt just called me. Your girlfriend is distraught with sadness. You need to do something."

"I will," I promised, but had no clue what to do.

Marilyn's prodding pushed my mind in circles. Coming from her, and because of the position my father had put her in when she was just a young girl, gave her words more weight.

43

TISHA B'AV

My sister Marilyn was born August 7, 1938, on *Tisha B'Av*, a date which is the culmination of three weeks of mourning starting from the day the Romans breached the first Jewish Temple before destroying it. It is also the date of numerous other Hebrew disasters which have occurred during this period, including the destruction of the second Temple.

Weddings and parties are not permitted, and it is customary not to eat meat or drink wine (except on Shabbat) and to observe other prohibitions such as not cutting one's hair or wearing new clothes. SYs are admonished to refrain from risky activities, which might include swimming and air travel, even in an age when the chance of being harmed on a commercial plane ride is miniscule. One must refrain from food and drink on this solemn day, and sex is not permitted. Bathing for pleasure, too, is restricted. The wearing of leather shoes is also prohibited.

My sister Marilyn was born on that day, and it portended her future. Marilyn was a beauty and sweet as a Charlotte Russe cake. She never raised her voice, kept a smile on her face at all times, and loved popular music. I remember running to her room with my brother Al on Saturday mornings after Pop left for *shul*, and Marilyn tuning her radio to Martin Block and the Make Believe Ballroom to hear the top songs of the day. My favorite was Vaughn Monroe's "Ghost Riders in the Sky."

Marilyn helped a great deal around the house and assisted Al and me with our homework. She was a good student in school and scored impressively on her report cards. In High School, she had an eighteen year old boyfriend, a

J-Dub kid named Davey Hertzendorf, who rode a motorcycle and whose wardrobe of jeans, a white T-shirt, black leather jacket and boots was fashioned after Marlon Brando in "The Wild Ones."

At this time, Pop was in a financial pickle. Becky's loose spending habits had caught up with him, and he was deeply in debt. He asked a friend for help, and the "friend" referred him to a Shylock. Pop borrowed Two Thousand dollars at a "special" rate, because of his friend, of only 2%, Forty Dollars, per week. Pop paid the interest only for six weeks, but with his weekly take-home pay of $110, he quickly fell behind in all his other payments. Pop was in dire straits until along came Rahmo Hussney.

Rahmo was an import from Lebanon having arrived only four years before. He brought some money with him, but had a well-to-do uncle, Abe Hussney. Abe, a friend of my father's, financed his nephew's opening of a small clip store on 42nd Street off 5th Avenue. Rahmo did very well, and now, at age thirty-nine, wanted to settle down and raise a family.

One Shabbat morning, after the prayers at shul, the elder Hussney approached Pop to arrange a *buzrah* for his nephew. My father invited Abe and Rahmo to come for coffee after Shabbat was over, and when they arrived, Pop had Marilyn serve the coffee. Rahmo whispered something in his uncle's ear, and Abe related the message.

"*Ya shreekie*," Abe began in Syrian. "My nephew Rahmo has been smitten by your daughter, Marilyn. He wishes to offer, with the utmost respect, the following for her hand in marriage: Four Thousand dollars as a cash dowry, and he will promise to buy a house for him and his new family to live in within one year after the birth of their first born. Also, he will supply his bride with a slightly used automobile, so she can run wifely errands. This is a fair arrangement, no?"

I watched as my father, with a pensive look on his face, hesitated a long while, struggling with the proposition. In his desperate state, he had no choice. He stood up from the chair and put out his hand in agreement of the *buzrah*. Pop got a bottle of *Arrack* from the refrigerator, liquor so strong it could melt a rock, and, in fact, as a kid, I used it as a remedy to kill the pain of my toothache. Pop poured three glasses to toast the deal, and after Abe and Rahmo left, Pop called Marilyn in to tell her the news.

"*Rohi*," he began, smiling and speaking slowly in a low voice, "I have arranged for you to marry a fine gentleman who will look after you and together raise a family."

I watched as the blood drained from Marilyn's face. "Poppa," she pleaded, "you can't do this to me! I'm only sixteen years old."

"In three months, you will be seventeen, and the marriage will wait until then. The man comes from a good family, *ya binti*, and will be a respectable husband."

"He's much older than me, and I don't even know him."

"Marilyn, trust your father. You will come to love him and be happy." He moved closer to her.

"I won't do it!" she protested defiantly.

Pop spun her around, and for the first time in my life, I saw my father hit one of his children. He smacked Marilyn hard, leaving a pink welt on her cheek. "You will do as I say!" he shouted. "I have given my word!"

Marilyn turned and ran to her room crying. I rushed to follow her, but she slammed and locked the door. I felt terrible for her, but there was nothing to be done.

The marriage occurred exactly one week after her seventeenth birthday. Of course, Pop had received the $4k the day after the deal was set and paid off the shy. Marilyn was now married to a man twenty-two years her senior.

I got a surprising gift out of this. Marilyn began spending Rahmo's money like a person who just found a suitcase full of hundred dollar bills. Clothes, shoes, a new TV set, and a drum kit for my fourteenth birthday that cost Six Hundred Dollars, including three of the finest Zildjian cymbals. Rahmo, thrilled with his new and beautiful young wife, did not utter a peep.

Marilyn carried two children for him. A boy, Moussa, and a girl, Allegra, two years apart, and both named after his parents. Six years after they were married, Rahmo was mysteriously pushed off a subway platform at the 42nd Street station. There were rumors that he owed a lot of money to Shylocks and bookies, but they never found out who had murdered him. In any case, Marilyn was silently joyous, though she felt the loss for her children. They would grow out of this tragedy, she reasoned, and she was right.

Weeks after Rahmo's death, Marilyn came across a steel box hidden in the basement of her house behind the water heater. She pried it open, and to her amazement saw bundles of hundred dollar bills wrapped in cellophane wrap. A quick count told her there was close to Two Million dollars in the container. This might have explained the murder of Rahmo, but she didn't care. She immediately opened an account with City Bank, leased a safe deposit box, and slowly moved the stash.

Two years later, Marilyn re-hooked up with her now divorced biker boyfriend, Davey, and they have lived together, unmarried, for nearly fifty years.

44

SONIA

The thing I loved most about Sonia was her unpretentiousness. She was not fazed by my wealth and continued her savings habits, such as cutting coupons from supermarket flyers.

"Daniel," she'd say while handing me a coupon to save fifty cents on one product or another, "use this at the supermarket."

"Yes, sweetheart," I'd respond, and then proceed to throw the coupon in the trash as soon as I left the condo. I gave her a Platinum Card from Amex and told her to keep the spending below ten thousand a month, but when the bills arrived, it showed she hadn't spent more than five hundred dollars. She bought most of her clothes from Thrift Stores and places like Lohman's and Daffy's, until they went out of business. She actually sat Shiva when Daffy's went out.

Once, while walking on Fifth Avenue we stopped into a Hermes store and she was looking at watches. She picked out one priced at Ninety-seven Hundred and fell in love with it. I offered to buy it for her birthday gift and she began to get the shakes.

"That's a lot of money," she said to the saleswoman. "Can you give us a discount?"

"We cannot," the Japanese clerk said with ice in her voice.

"What about that handbag there?" Sonia countered, as she pointed to a simple leather bag. "Can you throw it into the deal?"

"Madam," the clerk responded with disdain, "that handbag is fourteen thousand dollars."

Another time, soon after the marriage, and during a comped trip to the Trump Marina hotel in Atlantic City, I told Sonia to order anything she wanted from room service. In the morning she ordered scrambled eggs with bacon, pancakes, waffles, cream cheese and lox with bagels, a fruit plate, coffee, and a bottle of Perrier Jouet champagne because she liked the picture of it on the menu. Believe it or not, she ate eighty per cent of the food; and her weight has never been more than 115 pounds.

That night, we were invited to a party for Donald J Trump's fiftieth birthday. Sonia was standing near the dance floor watching couples dancing when Trump comes up from behind her, puts both his hands on her waist, and moves Sonia aside so he could get to the stage. He did so without so much as an "excuse me."

The amazement at and appreciation of the change in her lifestyle after we were married was never lost on Sonia. She valued every moment of it and thanked me profusely.

Sonia loved to have a good time and loved throwing parties. She would prepare the food herself with some help from her sister Rene. Her specialties were Syrian dishes, which she had learned how to cook from her mother. More help came from Poopa Dweck's (no relation to me) book, "Deal Delights."

Sonia took joy in everything we did: the vacations with the Levy's or the times we travelled alone. The parties we went to were enjoyed as much as the ones she gave.

She loved Christmas, not for the religious part, but for the way the department stores dressed their windows. She marveled at the Rockefeller Plaza tree and the holiday lights that lit up Fifth Avenue. She played the songs of the season over and over, even after New Year's had passed. Once, she noted, how Christians have beautiful songs for their holiday: "Jingle Bells," "I'll Be Home for Christmas," "Walking in a Winter Wonderland," "Have Your Self a Merry Little Christmas," and many more. "What do we Jews have?" Sonia complained. "Dreidel, Dreidel, Dreidel?"

Halloween was another favorite time of hers. She loved dressing up in ridiculous costumes (usually ones she had made herself) and go down to the village with her sister to join the massive crowds. Each year, I excused myself from that celebration.

Soon after we were married Sonia said that she couldn't wait for five years to pass so we could have a history together. Well, they did pass; then ten years, fifteen, twenty, and finally twenty-five. The blissfulness of those days together will forever be etched into my heart and mind. The twenty-five year honeymoon had come to a halt with the arrival of the disease that debilitated my Sonia.

The effects of Alzheimer's, memory loss, unable to remember family and friends, attacked Sonia early, but rapidly and viciously. Within months she did not even know who I was; but the disease did not diminish her beauty in my eyes. We did everything we could, including flying to the Johns Hopkins Medical Center for a consultation.

Watching this beautiful, sensitive and vibrant person's life deteriorating before me was a debilitating shock. Anger raged inside for being helpless to cure her. Her sister Rene innocently urged me to pray for her recovery. "To whom shall I pray? To God? He invented this disease. What would he do?"

The woman I loved was quickly slipping away from her existence. The only solace to be had was that Sonia had no clue as to what was happening to her. In the final days, as she lay in bed, she slept most of the time. I cried watching this tragedy happening and held her hand, more to comfort me than her. Ultimately, she contracted pneumonia, which finally took her life. I was devastated.

Sitting Shiva for Sonia brought me back to religion in that I said the Kadeesh for her repeatedly because I might have cursed God for taking her away from me, even though I did not believe in Him; but Sonia did, and it was for *her* soul I said the prayer. This wonderful, loving person, who had shared so much history with me, was gone, never to return.

45

TRUE LOVE

The blessings of my life, as well as the trials, have defined the quality in which I have lived. The toys one can buy with wealth has little value in determining one's esteem. Most folks look up to the rich, as did my mother, but only because they believe wealthy individuals have a power they themselves lack. Wealthy people are, in the final analysis, just people with a lot of money, who travel through life with the same ills and heartbreaks, the same good times and celebrations that people who are not as well off financially experience. The ability to write a large check for things you want is certainly freeing, but many times it is used to cover up the emptiness inside.

Some well-off people may have certain skills sometimes combined with a compulsive drive to succeed in the hope that by gaining a fortune, they will find the path to happiness. For those with wealth that I am familiar with, including me, that is just not the case. Happiness and self-esteem elude many of us. That is one of the reasons why many super wealthy people acquire expensive automobiles, yachts, jets, and multiple residences so that they can show the world how successful they have become in an attempt to inflate their self-esteem. It doesn't work; at least not in my experience. Those who were content before acquiring their fortunes remained content after they succeeded and did not require "things" to make them feel adequate. For those of us who were driven, as I was, no amount of riches can satisfy us, nor fill the empty holes in our emotional lives.

What amassing large amounts of money does provide is the false impression that you are smarter than those who have not achieved your level of affluence, which creates a trace of disdain towards those of lesser means. I know many rich people that believe they are never wrong about anything. Facts have little meaning if they are not in line with their opinions and beliefs. Wealth is also accompanied by an emotional detachment from those whose financial status is less than yours. It is not enough to make the Forbes' list of the world's richest people; if one's name is not at the top, a sense of inadequacy persists. I was one of those people, especially during my alcoholic years.

I have witnessed, sadly, that most wealthy people in my world do not have any real close friends. They are surrounded by sycophants and are constantly bombarded for money by relatives, acquaintances, people with "great" ideas, charities, or just plain scam artists. Moneyed people seek out other moneyed people with whom they can identify with, but in doing so, they invite competition for attention. If they are lucky, they may still have a relationship with a childhood friend that is based on love and equality, despite the difference in the amounts in their checkbooks. Such was the case with Sammy Levy and me.

Marriage offers hope that true love and friendship has been found. Not so, in my marriage to Adele. True love began when my son, Ezra, was born. However, a sense of impending failure arose with regard to my marriage to Adele and the subsequent reliance on alcohol to control the feelings associated with that. This prevented me from achieving that true love and happiness. When my son came along, I was on top of the world: money in the bank, a beautiful wife, and a bright future ahead of me. All of this, except for the money, began to collapse soon after his birth.

Ezra was a beautiful baby who grew into a precocious toddler. He had a way about him even during his "terrible twos" that enchanted you. The words coming out of his mouth were intelligent and coherent and well spoken. He had a habit of ending a phrase with a question mark. By the age of six, he was asking questions I had never thought of at his age.

"Daddy, why is the sky blue? Where do the leaves come from? How come you don't come home early?" It was easy enough to answer the first two with the help of Encyclopedia Britannica. The last one, I did not have an answer for.

Ezra was a prince. No trouble from this boy. His schoolwork was above his grade, and he was put into a "gifted child" program that succeeded in developing his talents. He had a great singing voice, better than his uncle Michael, and at his Bar Mitzvah, he read his Torah portion with such a beautiful melodic expression. He sang at high school events as well as at the SY-sponsored social productions of musical plays.

When the twins were born, the surprise of the beauty of these two infants was not lost on me. Neither one looked like a shriveled prune. Maybe it was because they did not have to squeeze their way into the world through such a small channel as their mother's vagina. Joseph, who came out first after Tuni, was also a delightful child; though he was a bit slow in starting to speak (he was three when the words began to flow from his mouth). He and Tuni were no trouble at all, although Joseph was not as bright or inventive as his siblings. The divorce affected him more than the other two children.

While Ezra graduated from the Wharton School of Business with honors, Joseph struggled through college. Tuni's drug habits were well hidden from me and Adele until the night she had called for help.

Ezra immediately went to work with a factoring company owned by the two Syrian Massry brothers. He loved his work and rose in the ranks of this small family-owned company displaying a natural knowledge of finance. By the time he was twenty-five, they offered him a partnership, but he decided to go off on his own.

Joseph could not hold onto a job so I took him into my company where he felt comfortable enough to carry out the relatively easy assignments given to him.

Ezra hooked up with a fellow Wharton graduate, Thomas Wingate, a bright and handsome young man from a well to do family from Saddle River, New Jersey. Thomas was as naturally attuned to the world of economics as my Ezra. With Thomas's father, George, and my backing they opened their offices on 7th Avenue and 48th Street. George and I each funded them with a loan of a million dollars after connecting them with our banks for lines of credits. That is one of the benefits of wealth: you can help your children ease into a business and, if they work hard at it, start making a living.

Ezra met and married an SY girl when he was twenty-seven. Janie was twenty-six. She was a bright college graduate working towards a PhD in psychology. Her goal was to become a psychologist and help children with problems, and she now runs a successful practice.

Joseph met and married Julie Mishan, daughter of an SY man who worked as a life insurance broker. Julie suffered from severe asthma and Joseph loved to care for her. Together they raised a fine family.

Ezra's business flourished, and he and Janie had two kids: a boy, Daniel, named after me, then a girl, a cutie named Adele, after her grandmother. Janie took time off from her studies for the crucial six months after the birth of each child, and then she and Ezra hired a nanny to help. Sonia and I had the pleasure of caring for our grandkids several times when our children went on vacations. Those were some of the most blissful days of our marriage.

At forty-eight years old Ezra is a content man. He has a sizeable income that he and his partner work hard to earn. The loans from his partner's father and I have long been paid back. My son is not showy. He drives a Range Rover, and Janie drives a Lexus. His son, Daniel, is heading off to Penn State to begin college in September.

Ezra and Janie's religious affiliation is with the Safra shul on East 63rd off 5th Avenue in Manhattan. He and his wife keep a kosher home, but will eat out un-kosher. They keep all the holidays, and I get to see the kids as often as possible.

Joseph and his wife, Julie, are orthodox. They keep Shabbat and are completely kosher. They are content with their lives and that makes me happy. Tuni and her husband also practice Orthodox Judaism, and, having recovered from her disease of addiction, now live a life of contentment as well.

The success of my children, despite my neglect during their formative years, is a huge reward for me, and one I hardly deserve. Sometimes, a man gets lucky.

46

POLITICS AND DEATH

Sammy and I argued over politics, all the time. He was a far right Republican, as were many SYs, and I was a flaming liberal. Truth be told, I rarely voted because I came to realize early in life that things wouldn't change much for me no matter who was elected president. America was greater than anyone who held the office of the most powerful position in the world. Maybe pay a little more tax under Democrats or a little less under Republicans. Agree or disagree with the leaders, they were all rational people (except maybe for Nixon) who did their best, which in some cases were good for the country and in others not so good. I liked Ronald Reagan, not so much for his policies, but more for bringing the country together in a light-hearted way. That's why I cast my vote for him in the second election.

Bill Clinton was a great President who balanced the budget under his watch for the first time since LBJ held the office. The last Republican to balance it was Eisenhower, in 1956 and 1957. Of course, Congress authorizes all spending, and the first year of his term a president inherits the budget of the previous president. For example, the balanced budget of Nixon's first year in office was actually the one Johnson signed off on.

The political arguments between Sammy and I were generally mild, although, on occasion, they became heated, like when the shit hit the fan over Clinton's extra-marital affairs.

Clinton was a fun guy who made everything seem possible, if only he could keep his fly zipped up. When the Monica Lewinsky debacle surfaced during a harassment lawsuit brought by Paula Jones, an independent investigator, Kenneth Starr, spent $70 million dollars of taxpayer money to come up with enough evidence that led to two counts for impeachment: obstruction of justice and perjury.

The Speaker of the House, Newt Gingrich, who, in my opinion, was, and still is, a mean-spirited politician (as, I believe, many Republicans are) had been one of the leading advocates for impeachment. He was counting on his party adding thirty seats in the House in the midterm elections, which would ensure the President would be impeached. When only five new members were added, the results were an embarrassment for Gingrich, and he resigned from his position on January 3, 1999. The Republicans did hold on to the majority, and right after the 106th Congress was seated, they voted to impeach Clinton. The Senate conducted the trial and the President was ultimately acquitted on both counts.

Bush was another character Sammy and I fought over, although we were in agreement about the Iraq war, for different reasons (I believe all dictators should be removed from the earth). The world has no place for these corrupt authoritarian so-called "leaders" who pillage their countries and treat their citizens viciously, particularly those who oppose them.

What was, and still is, true was that SYs support mostly Republican presidential candidates who are completely pro-Israel and anti-tax (unlike most Ashkenazi Jews who generally support Democrats). SYs would overlook the anti-tax part if the candidate showed a strong bias against the Palestinians. I believe most SYs did not vote for Obama; in fact, they spewed hatred towards him from the day he was elected, believing the Trump assertion that Obama was not born in the USA, or that he was really a Muslim. My brother Jakey called Obama an ahbud, and I admonished him for it.

"Maybe he was born here," Jakey said, "but he's a Muslim. According to Jewish Law," he went on, "if the mother is Jewish, the child is too. Muslim law says if the father is Muslim, then the child is as well. Since Obama's father was a Muslim…"

At that time, Sammy's wife Sarah began experiencing coughing fits and was coughing up blood. Sammy rushed her to their doctor who recommended they see a pulmonologist, which they promptly did. After extensive testing, the specialist's diagnosis was that Sarah had contracted a mutant strain of tuberculosis. How, or from where, they could not determine, and I was troubled when I read the disease kills 50% of the time.

She was put on a two-month regimen, taking four drugs, but did not respond well. So, the treatment was continued for another seven months after changing the mix of medicines. That did not help either. Sarah became bedridden, and, in early spring, Sammy moved her to the Deal house. He hired a full time sleep-in nurse named Martha Santamaria, a Mexican woman devoted to her work. She would soon become enamored by her employer.

Sarah would respond from time to time and feel up to taking a walk with Martha around the block. Most of the time, she was lethargic and weakened by the illness and would spend long hours sleeping.

After suffering along with his wife for nearly a year, Sammy became a basket case himself. His import business was failing due to many of his customers going directly to Chinese factories and cutting the middleman out.

One night, while Sarah was asleep, Martha had cooked a pot of *arroz con pollo* for Sammy, and as she was about to go to her room, he invited her to join him. She served the meal, and he complimented her cooking.

"This is delicious," he said.

"Thank you very much," she responded, a broad smile spreading across her face.

"How old are you, Martha?"

"Thirty-five." At age thirty-five, Martha was well below the criteria our man Eddie had set for girlfriends.

"You've been a great help to Sarah and me. Thank you." He reached across the table and put his hand on hers. She placed her other hand on top of his, clasping it tightly.

"This is a tough time for you and your family, Mr. Levy."

"Please, call me Sammy."

She blushed as he said that and then rubbed his hands. Presently, Martha slid her hands away slowly and lifted the dirty dishes. She put them in the washer and didn't move when Sammy came up behind her and put his arms around her waist. She turned around to face him. "We shouldn't…"

"You're right, we shouldn't," but he kissed her anyway. He led her to her bedroom well away from Sarah's room and began kissing her passionately. Her arousal was accompanied by rapid breathing and loud noises of desire, which

Sammy tried to hush; at the moment she reached her climax, Martha was almost shouting with ecstasy.

When the lovemaking was through, Martha quickly dressed and rushed to Sarah's room. She sighed with relief when she saw her patient had not moved since she had left her. The liaison between Martha and Sammy continued quietly until Sarah passed after two years of that debilitating illness. No one, his children or others, was aware of the relationship Sammy had with Sarah's nurse. I had no clue until he revealed it to me only after Sarah had died, and the *Shiva* was over. The two kept it quiet for four months after Sarah's passing when Sammy finally told his family. His two daughters approved, but his son, Isaac, had misgivings.

47

MR. NOWAK'S LITTLE SPEECH

It was the winter of 1996 when Sonia and I were invited to Mr. and Mrs. Nowak's home for dinner celebrating our fifth wedding anniversary. Mr. Nowak had been my partner in the real estate business for more than thirty years, and he said there was something important he needed to discuss with me.

Rivka went all out and cooked us a scrumptious Polish dinner that began with *Krupnik*, a thick barley soup with chicken and carrots, followed by Mushroom Pierogi. The main course was *Baranina*, juicy, tender, roasted mutton along with *Klopsiki*, ground meatballs in a tomato sauce, and *Sałatka z kartofli* on the side, a sweetened potato salad with celery and onions.

Mr. Nowak kept filling his glass with *schnapps* during the meal, a taste which he had acquired, oddly enough, in the *Sachsenhausen* concentration camp outside of Berlin.

He had used his skills as a tailor to mend the garments of the political refugees in trade for valuable items such as watches, jewelry, even cameras, which he would then swap with the Nazi guards for cigarettes and schnapps.

In Auschwitz, he revealed, now that he was a bit tipsy, how hard he had worked at the bakery and even volunteered for extra labor such as paving roads and building barracks. The German *SS-Oberscharführer*, Sergeant 1st Class Fingerhut, took a liking to Mr. Nowak and offered him the position of Capo, which Mr. Nowak cautiously rejected because he did not want to be an overseer of his fellow Jews.

Fingerhut arranged for passes to the women's compound now and then for liaisons with the female inmates. Rivka stopped clearing the dishes when hearing this for the first time and gave her husband a severe look. "This, of course, was before I met my darling Rivka," he said, to assuage her feelings.

"Did you not feel guilty taking advantage of those women?" Rivka inquired.

"No, I did not take advantage. The relations were consensual and temporarily filled an emptiness for them and me. I smuggled in bread to share with them and before long took a liking to one woman in particular. We had an oddly close relationship for several months. Eventually, she was sent to the gas chamber."

"Why did you conduct business with the Nazis?" I asked.

"Listen, Daniel, the one thought in mind every moment of my days in those camps, was to survive, to outlive that maniac Hitler and his regime; to see my mother again. I did what I had to do, without hurting anyone else. The bread I shared with others saved a few lives."

He took another shot of the fruit flavored brandy, and then looked straight at me. "And now, my *boobala*, I will tell you why I had you to come tonight, besides to enjoy your company. You know Rivka and I love you both. We have watched you, Daniel, become a *mensch* again, all because, we believe, of this wonderful lady you married." He raised his glass again to salute us and took another sip. "So, my little speech will be very short. Rivka and I have agreed to transfer our interest in the business to you, as our sole heir."

"Mr. Nowak…" I exclaimed, but he cut me off.

"No, no, no, Daniel. Hear me out. We have no relatives; all of them were killed by the Nazi bastards. You are our only family. So here are the terms. We will transfer our shares to you while we are alive so that we can use a lower evaluation of the properties to save on taxes. You will provide us with an income of $500 thousand dollars a year until both of our deaths. Also, you will donate $1 million dollars to the Holocaust Museum in Washington. He took another sip of the *schnapps, and then* looked up at me. "What you think?"

I was dumfounded. The old man's share amounted to more than One Hundred Million dollars, and he was giving it all to me. "What can I say?"

"Thank you would be nice," he smiled.

"You have no idea what this means to me."

"It means you will be a lot richer."

"It's not about the money. My family was poor and I could only dream of acquiring this kind of wealth. As a child, one of my fantasies was that a barrel of money would float down from the heavens and land in my bedroom. You have more than fulfilled that dream, my dear Mr. and Mrs. Nowak. More importantly, you have treated me like a son, and that is priceless."

Rivka's eyes teared up and I could see Mr. Nowak struggling to hide his.

"Are you sure you want to do this?"

"Absolutely," Rivka chimed in. "Knowing both of you has been a joy. Daniel, you have given me and Julius much pleasure; and some *tsuris* now and then," she laughed, "but you, your children and Sonia have brought so much to us."

"Our lawyer is already drawing up the papers for this transaction," Mr. Nowak said. "Do some good with it."

I stood up and thanked them both profusely.

"Come, Boobala," he said, "Give a hug."

I embraced both of them as did Sonia. Now there were tears in Mr. Nowak's eyes as he whispered, in Yiddish, "*Bentshn ir Mayn zun*. Bless you, my son."

Everyone was in tears now until the old man said, "Why we are crying? This is a joyous moment, for all of us. *L'chaim*," he shouted, and finished his drink.

We moved to the living room, and Mrs. Nowak followed us in presently with coffee, Rugelach, and a lemon sponge cake. Mr. Nowak waved for me to sit next to him.

"You know, Daniel, there is one thing we have never talked about." I looked at him quizzically. "I watched you go from being very religious to becoming an *apikoyres*. This is not good, my boy. One needs faith, which leads to hope, and that becomes the will to survive."

"I don't believe there is a God, sir, and you, Mr. Nowak, of all people…"

"Shush," he said, putting his hand to my mouth. "After the camps, there is no belief left in me for a God. Many times I have said If he existed, he would never have let that terrible time to happen." He shook his head sorrowfully. "All those persons: *mayn mame*, that poor, simple and harmless woman who raised me and never hurt a soul. Oy! And not only Jews: Gypsies, Poles, Czechs, Russians, even *fagelas*, those poor, poor people." He hesitated. "No, *boobala*, I do not speak of God. It is *faith* that matters; faith in yourself and who you are. *That* is what gets you through the toughest times in life. Please remember that."

"I will, Mr. Nowak. I will."

Over the next few days, we signed the necessary documents, and I immediately sent a check to the Holocaust Museum. I insisted on an addendum to the deal, and that was to write the Nowak's a check for five million dollars for them to have in case something should happen to me in the near future. They reluctantly agreed to accept it. In addition, recalling my mother Fortune's wishes to give to many charities, I donated another Five Million Dollars to fifty various institutions in her name.

As it turned out, in August of the next year, Rivka went first; then Mr. Julius Nowak followed her two months later. This beautiful couple that had survived the worst conflagration in history had finally met their ends, leaving this world a sadder place. In his last week of life, as if he knew death was close at hand, he made a donation of $5 million dollars to a fund for Holocaust survivors. He willed his home and all his "worldly possessions" to Sonia and me and we, in turn, turned them into cash, which we donated to the same holocaust fund.

There were two things I found in Mr. Nowak's house that I kept for myself. In the drawer of his small desk in his den was an old, worn sewing kit that he had probably used in the camps to help him stay alive. The other was a Hebrew and English book, "*Ecclesiastes*," which had hand written comments on each page, some in Yiddish, and others in broken English.

Through his notes, he appeared to be arguing or agreeing with the passages attributed to King Solomon. One comment hit me so hard it caused me to bawl like an infant. The book reads, "*One generation comes, and another passes away, but the earth abides forever*; and his comment was, "*Death will come, but there is no fear because I will live on through my son Daniel and his generations.*"

Here I was, at fifty-five, falling into a deeper depression after the death of Mr. Nowak than I had experienced when Pop died, struggling desperately to get out of it. That wasn't happening and therapy offered little help, so my family doctor put me on anti-depression medication, which alleviated somewhat the terrible sense of loss.

For weeks, I stumbled through the days just barely conscious of my existence, unable to work and not willing to socialize with friends. Sammy tried to snap me out of this mood by forcing me to go out to a restaurant, but I remained sullen throughout dinner. My children spent a good deal of time consoling me, and during those moments with my young grandchildren, the pain did subside; but, only temporarily.

The depression deepened even further. Sonia had become concerned; she contacted Rabbi Abraham Hecht, the Ashkenazi rabbi who now served as the spiritual leader of Congregation Sha'are Zion. Born in Brooklyn, he became the leading motivator in helping build the SY community grow to more than 3,500 families and become the largest Sephardic congregation in North America. Although there wasn't a trace of Sephardic ancestry in his roots, the Rabbi felt an inexplicable affinity with the community. Many saw Rabbi Hecht as the driving power behind the community's adopting the fact that Judaism must be part of contemporary society. He was also the Rabbi who wrote that letter for me to the Commanding General at Fort Dix.

Sonia had made the appointment for me to see him on a Thursday after the morning prayers. We met in his small office near the entrance to the synagogue. "I knew your father very well," he said, as he offered me a chair.

"In fact, he was one of the people who connected me up with the SYs."

"Interesting," I said, not really interested. My mind and heart were trapped in the devastating loss of the Nowaks.

"One summer, my wife and I spent our vacation at Fleishman's in upstate New York. Your father and mother were there, along with a group of other Syrian Jews. They asked me to speak at their afternoon lecture, and I did. Next thing I know, they made me the youth rabbi at Magen David Yeshiva."

I feigned a smile that cut his reminisces short.

"I understand you lost some very dear people."

"Yes."

He glanced at a notepad, and then said, "Julius Nowak. He was your partner, no?"

"More like a father," I nodded. "He had faith in me, loved me like a son, and loved me like my real father never did."

"Consider yourself lucky, Danny, to have had such a person in your life. *Hashem* gives you what you need to survive in this world. Let me ask you, do you pray?"

I shook my head and said, "No."

"Why not?"

"Because I don't believe."

"Don't believe what?"

"That there is a God."

"What has that got to do with prayer? Praying is a way to fulfill your spirituality, to create hope that you will be protected, and insert a sense of peacefulness in your heart. You loved these people. Pray for them. Say *Kadeesh*. You'll feel better, and you'll heal quicker. Trust me. Why not give it a try? What have you got to lose?"

I did try and did pray, not for me, but for them, even though Mr. Nowak was a non-believer himself. Rivka, on the other hand, lit Shabbat candles every week and observed all the major Holy Days. To my surprise, saying Kadeesh *did* help, and within weeks the damage to my heart became a scar; one that will be with me until I die.

48

A NOBLE JEW

From the day of Obama's election, I have heard many SYs condemn him for any and all reasons, whether well founded or not. To my mind, due to the continued use of the word *abbud* in the community, there was no doubt that their disrespect for the first African American elected in the history of the country stemmed from that stubborn thread of racism that permeated their beliefs. They ignored or belittled his accomplishments, including his efforts to save the country from the catastrophic recession that hit just before he entered the White House. He saved one million jobs by bailing out the automobile industry, prevented the banks from failing after their disastrous dealings with the housing market, added new jobs for seventy-five straight months (a record), and brought health insurance to millions of people who never had any. He had Osama bin Laden tracked and killed, and oversaw a period where the stock market reached an all-time high. When the deal with Iran was signed, they vilified him even more, many SYs seeing that pact as a serious threat to the safety of Israel.

Then, along comes Donald Trump, with his bombastic bullying and his impoliteness for others; his megalomaniacal ravings and his pathological lying, beginning with his "Birther" falsehood questioning where Barrack Obama was born. Never in the history of America has a President been forced to show his birth certificate to quell the lies being promoted by Trump. The fabrications Trump has created are far beyond belief, yet they are ignored or excused by his followers, as he garnered the support of most SYs, who, in turn, attacked Hillary Clinton viciously.

Sammy and I were sitting by his pool the weekend after Trump announced his candidacy. "He's my man!" Sammy said. "Hillary's been screwing the country ever since Whitewater. Have you seen the list of the forty-nine people that were connected to the Clintons and mysteriously died?"

"What are you implying? That they had something to do with the deaths of these people?"

"I'm just saying…"

"You're just saying nonsense," I interrupted. "Remember, my poor, uninformed friend, that Bill Clinton was impeached for lying about a blow job. And you want to believe that your malicious Republicans will let the Clintons get away with mass murder? Sammy, you are a bigger fool than I thought if you buy into that crap."

"She's a liar," he claimed, as he lit his fourth cigarette within ten minutes.

"So, you don't like liars? If Trump's lips are moving, he is lying."

Sammy remained silent for a moment. "He is going to be our next president."

"No way," I countered. "The guy's a bigoted, racist, xenophobic, misogynistic anti-Semite."

"Anti-Semite? His daughter's Jewish. So are his grandkids."

"He can still be an anti-Semite," I insisted. "Even a Jew can be anti-Semitic, like that Queens kid, Daniel Burros, who hid his identity and joined the KKK. Here's a story few people are aware of. When Adolf Hitler's mother was dying of cancer, a Jewish doctor, Eduard Bloch, was caring for her and the Hitler family. Hitler called him an "*edeljude*" – a noble Jew – and never forgot the kindness he showed his mother Klara. On Hitler's orders, Bloch was protected by the Gestapo, was able to keep his apartment in Vienna, and got coupons for clothing and other things – the only Jew in that city to do so.

"When Hitler annexed Austria, Bloch wrote to him for help in migrating out of the country. Hitler arranged protection for him and, ultimately, in 1941, the doctor went to America. Does that mean Hitler was not an anti-Semite, because he helped a Jew?"

Sammy stood up from his chair and put his hand out to me. "That's bullshit."

"Look it up"

"Never mind. Trump's going to win. How much you want to bet?'

"You are a first class idiot, Levy."

"How much?" He insisted. "I'll take four to one he wins the primary."

"Against sixteen others more qualified? A sucker bet. You got it: my Four Thousand to your One Thousand." We shook on it, and when Trump did win the primaries Sammy refused to take the money. "I don't need your *flooce*. It was the principal. Now, how much he beats Hillary?"

Three weeks after that conversation, Sammy, during a medical exam with a pulmonologist, got the news that he had Stage 4 lung cancer. Surgery was performed, and the doctors said it went well. He started chemo immediately after, but continued to smoke.

One afternoon, while sitting by his pool Sammy lit a cigarette in front of me, and I grabbed it out of his mouth. "You can't be smoking, you moron!" I reprimanded him. "You have lung cancer!"

"Doesn't matter," he responded softly as he lit another. "It's going to kill me anyway"

"What are you talking about? The doctors say they got out the cancer."

Sammy shook his head. "Don't listen to what they say. Sammy knows better. It's just a matter of time."

"Stop that! Don't talk that way. There's a lot that can be done."

"We'll see," he said, lighting another cigarette.

The maid brought out coffee and desserts.

"More importantly," he went on, "your girlfriend Hillary's going to eat crap with those emails."

"Trump is making a mountain out of a piece of turd," I insisted.

"'Crooked Hillary', my man says, and he's right."

"What did she do wrong? For twenty-five years the Republicans have attacked this woman and her husband, accusing them of everything, but nothing ever comes of these accusations. Have they ever been charged with anything? No!"

"What about Benghazi?"

"What about it?" I shouted. My patience was fading. "They held nine congressional hearings, *nine!* All of them led by your offensive Republicans, and they came up with nothing. That Trey Gowdy takes the cake for his nastiness. What are they going to say next, that the Clintons are part of the Russian mafia?"

"Who knows what will pop up? They are looking into her foundation. 'Pay for Play,' my man says. They gave away state secrets for donations."

"They never took a penny for themselves."

"I read the papers, too, you know, you jackass. Fox News says they are investigating it. Sean Hannity…"

"Hannity? That idiot?" I shouted back. "He is the most mean spirited asshole of all time. He asks a question and steps all over the answer if he does not hear things his way."

"Look," Sammy went on, "Trump has turned off this 'political correctness' nonsense and speaks what's in is heart. He tells the truth."

"Only if you spell the word 'truth' 'l-i-e-s.'"

"Trump has started a movement to speak for the angry middle class, the 'forgotten people' he calls them."

"The only thing these people were angry about was having to keep their racist, anti-American views to themselves for so many years. I'll admit one thing, though. Trump has allowed them to bring these hateful feelings to the surface. If he died tomorrow, they would still support him because, for them, a vote for Trump is really a vote for themselves."

"That's a stupid thing to say." Sammy said, giving up the argument. "Let's go to AC for some poker."

"Now, that's the most intelligent thing you've said all day."

49

THE BOY'S GOT TALENT

My brother Michael needed help. He was living in Vermont with his wife Edith, an Ashkenazic woman five years older than him. The age difference didn't matter when they first hooked up. Michael was thirty-two, Edith thirty-seven. They met while performing in an off-Broadway production of a play written by my brother, and partially financed by me, dealing with the Salem witch-hunt. It was morbid, not one line to smile at, with scene after scene condemning the world and everyone in it. That was forty-six years ago, which is, for some who die young, a lifetime.

They were married and moved to Vermont to run a summer stock theatre. With my help in the funding, he eventually bought it for fifty thousand dollars. He and Edith were blissfully happy.

They had a boy, Edward, they called him; Michael was breaking with the SY tradition of naming the first born son after his father. He did use the first initial of Pop's name, "E", as many other SY's do these days, and reluctantly, had Edward circumcised "for health reasons," Michael said. But he absolutely refused to have a *Pidyon*. "I'm not buying my kid back from some greedy high priest."

Michael's career had not gone where his talents should have taken him. He refused to compromise on his writings and acting. He had given up singing professionally, and after he had told me a story that happened when he was twelve years old, it became clear why he never pursued that art.

When he was twelve Michael had entered himself into a talent contest being held in summer school at P.S. 205, the school across from the apartment we grew up in. He sang Perry Como's version of "Because," and won. There was a talent scout present who walked Michael home to talk to our parents. My father's brother, uncle Moussa, was present.

"My name's Huckerby, James Huckerby," the agent said as he sat down at the kitchen table. "I want to tell you, folks. You've got a very talented boy here."

"What you mean?" Pop asked.

"I mean your son has a great voice, and a terrific stage presence. This lad has charisma!"

"*Ishoo kar-is-ma?*" my father asked.

"*Eckal charah,*" Uncle Moussa said, meaning bullshit.

"Michael needs training. We have a school, right here in Brooklyn, where he can be taught everything he needs to know."

"*Cam?*" Pop asked. "How much?"

Huckerby stood up and handed his business card to my father. "Call me to set up an appointment, and we can discuss the details." He smiled at my brother. "Yes, sir, this boy's got talent." He patted Michael on the back and left.

Pop studied the man's card, but Uncle Moussa grabbed it out of his hand and tore it up. "This is a crook," he said in Syrian. "They want to steal your money."

Michael ran to the bedroom and cried. He never thought much of Uncle Moussa after that day.

My brother was content running his little theatre. He loved being amongst actors and spent a great deal of his time writing plays, none of which he had success in selling. He would produce one of these works each summer at his theatre, receive mixed or poor reviews, but the young actors in his workshop loved the opportunity to emote using his words.

Edward worked for me for a short time, then headed out to California to work for a producer. He shimmied his way up the ladder and eventually was hired by a production company to develop TV shows. He wrote episodes for cable series and, apparently, was more talented than his father because the first script he wrote, a horror story, was sold, produced, and enjoyed moderate success at the box office.

Edward married and gave my brother a grandson and a granddaughter. They would come back east every Thanksgiving for a week to spend the holiday with his parents.

Michael died from pneumonia and heart failure at the age of 74. He had it in his will that he be cremated, which, of course is in violation of the Hebrew religion. His son followed his father's wishes, much to the chagrin of my brother Al and sister Marilyn.

At a eulogy service for Michael, held in Vermont, Edward gave an emotionally charged speech that moved everyone in the audience. I had flown up there with my sister but Al sent his condolences by email to Edward, who spoke of Michael's tenacity and his dedication to the arts. He expressed with tribute his father's love of him, and how he was showered with much affection. Edward revealed how he learned so much from my brother about acting and writing.

"My father was a kind and decent person who lived his life as he chose. His favorite song was "My Way" because it spelled out his existence. I used to hear him sing it when I was growing up, and it always sent a chill through my body when he held the last two notes, singing them loud and proud, "My Wa-a-ay."

That was my brother, Michael. Loud and proud. I miss him terribly.

50

LOOK AT YOUR FEET

I got a burning phone call from my son Ezra one evening. "Dad" he said, "what the hell are you doing!" I remained silent. "Just hung up from Tuni; she said you broke up with Claudia; is that true?" More silence from me. "Why would you do that?"

"It won't work out," I said, meekly.

"What won't work out? You love her; she loves you. Tell me dad, why would you throw that away?"

"It isn't fair for her to be married to an older man whose time on earth is quickly ticking away."

"Which book did you read that from, Dad? You can't throw away this chance at happiness." He paused for a moment, and then said, "I'm coming over."

"Don't…"

"I need to try to talk some sense into you."

Forty-five minutes later all three of my children were there along with their spouses. Joseph was the first to speak. "Pop, we are all aware of the struggles you went through in your life. That is more than enough punishment for any one person to endure."

"I've had many years of happiness as well," I replied. "The years with Sonia were wonderful times."

"So who says you can't have more 'wonderful years?'" Tuni chimed in. "Why give up a joy that is staring you in the face?"

Ezra's wife, Janie, joined in. "Dad, you deserve this. Don't let it slip away."

For the next hour and a half this went on, each of my children and their spouses preaching and pleading for me not to give up Claudia. On top of their appeals, a phone call came from Claudia's daughter, Teri, telling me how unhappy her mother was.

All this was too much for me to fight and an agreement was reached whereby I would call Claudia the next day to discuss the matter further.

That night I tossed and turned debating with myself about what to do. The next evening, Claudia and I met at Due, our favorite Italian restaurant. She ordered a glass of Merlot and we both exchanged pleasantries as she sipped the wine.

"I heard you got a good working over from your kids last night."

"It was rough," I nodded. "They all love you and are urging me to marry you."

"My children feel the same about you. They say they've never seen me happier."

"You know I love you, Claudia, right? This situation is not about you."

"But it is, Daniel. My life is being affected by the ghost of Sonia." I lowered my head as she went on. "She was a great lady, from what you've told me and from what I've heard about her. But, sweetheart, she is not here anymore and I *am*."

I reached for her hand and held it. "You *are* here, darling, and I am very glad to have found you. But, after all, the age difference…"

"Shouldn't I have the right to make that decision for myself?"

We were quiet through much of the dinner until I finally made the offer. "We shall continue to see each other for the next three months and make the final decision then."

"Is dry humping allowed during the three months?" she quipped and we both laughed easing the tension.

"Agreed?"

She leaned over to kiss me. "Agreed."

Thar night, as I slept alone in my bed, I reviewed the situation of my life. My son, Joseph, works with me in the real estate business. Ezra has established himself along with his partner in the field of finance. Early on in their lives, I made it a point to teach my children a work ethic. All three worked in my office a couple of days a week after school. All three have graduated from college, unlike me, who was a "high school throw-out".

We are a family that loves and respects each other. Sonia, who had no children of her own, took well towards my kids and they grew to love her as a kind, decent, stepmother. Right up until today, even after Sonia's death, the whole family gets together at Tuni's house in Brooklyn on the first nights of Rosh Hashanah and Passover. The second night they go to their respective in-laws for the Holiday meals, and I attend the lavish setting of Claudia's holiday repast. Mere mortals cannot measure the pleasure of grandchildren. Every one of my eight amazing jewels is a sublime gift that brings me joy each time we are together.

I have amassed a far greater fortune in business than ever imagined, which was doubled when that wonderful human being, my dear, dear, Julius Nowak gave me his share in the business. As a child, I could only wish for such wealth in pipedreams and fantasies.

Claudia and I shared all the material comforts one could ask for. Coming up on the ridiculous age of seventy-six I have found new love with a wonderful woman. My children and grandchildren are taken care of, and the emptiness inside has been reduced considerably over the years of my sobriety. Therapy has helped me through the rough moments. Yet, since the end of life is closer than the beginning, one still wonders what it was all about. I recall learning the first commandment of the Torah is to procreate, "Be fruitful and multiply," it says, and I have fulfilled that. But in the short span of life, years that have flown by without warning, the words of "Is That All There Is?" as Peggy Lee sings it, ring in my head.

Rabbi Judah met with me again at David's soon after I called him. During the meal, I poured out my feelings about life and death and described the hollowness that had been in my soul. "What has my life been about? What have I accomplished besides making money? What will be my legacy? In the end, a hundred years from now, who will care that I ever existed?"

Judah listened intently and remained silent for a moment after I finished asking those questions. He then spoke in a harsh tone. "Danny, you should be ashamed of yourself! Besides the obvious answers, i.e., you raised a good family, you are a decent, charitable man, an honorable business executive, something that is rare to find these days. You need to acknowledge how you have overcome the struggles of your life."

"That's a great speech, Judah. You'll get a check for 10k from me today."

"You may want to tear it up when I'm finished with what I have to say. Despite all your attributes, in the final analysis, you are a fool. You think that one can plan one's life in advance thinking that all the strategies you develop will happen as anticipated? Only Hashem knows the results of an individual life. Only *He* is aware whether any of us can face the challenges he has put before us. Hashem gives us these problems to solve, because it makes us better people. He never gives us more than we can handle. The Gemara teaches us…"

"There's the problem, Rabbi," I interrupted. "You've heard me say I don't believe in God or religion any more. Look at the damage it has caused in this world."

"Humans have caused most of the damage, not God."

"We were supposedly created in his image. He has caused lots of damage. The Flood, the slavery of Hebrews in Egypt and black people in later years, wars throughout the history of the world that could have been stopped by a simple wag of His all-powerful finger. What about the diseases and the 'natural' disasters that occurred throughout the millennia; events that have destroyed tens of thousands of people? It's all God's handiwork. Please, Judah, don't tell me only humans are to blame for this."

"It is impossible for you or me to figure these things out" the Rabbi said. "The only answer is to believe someone or something greater than you is in control and has a master plan for each of us. Faith is all we have."

"My former partner, who did not believe in God, said the same thing."

"Don't deny people their beliefs, Danny. To paraphrase John Lennon, it gets them through the night."

"Well said, Judah. Well, then, let them believe what they want as long as they don't push it on me."

"Fair enough," the Rabbi said as he stood.

"But I'm not giving up trying to bust through that SY wall of racial intolerance," I persisted.

"Every group of people has some level of intolerance."

"My goal right now will be to enlighten the community I love. We'll go after the next group after we've succeeded with the SYs."

"There is your legacy, Daniel. That is God's handiwork at play."

We shook hands and he left.

Was I aware of my life? Was I present in my existence? Not always. Not until the alcohol freezing my brain was removed, and the true feelings of my youth were brought back to the surface. The pain and suffering from the neglect and abuse have finally been healed because they have been allowed to surface, becoming scars that shall be with me until that last moment but that can longer affect me. The years with Sonia were wonderful and could only have been enjoyed because healing the early pain allowed the current bliss to fulfill me. I had the rare second chance to be a good father, helping my children, especially Tuni, heal their own wounds.

My sobriety helped me to weather the death of Sonia, but it also allowed me to experience that awful pain, to process it, and let it scar my heart; but, not shut it down.

That evening I called my sister Marilyn and told her about the deal I made with Claudia.

"My baby brother," she said, "now there is something smart coming out of your mouth. The main lesson here is to remember life does not end until it ends."

"You sound like Yogi Berra."

"Who?"

"Never mind; I love you." I hung up the phone and stared down at the floor, something my AA sponsor, Nicky, had instructed me to do whenever there was doubt about what was happening to me. "Look at your feet," he said, "and if they are still standing on the ground, you are okay." And I am.

The End

EPILOGUE

I am proud of my heritage, both religious and communal. Much good has been accomplished by the community and the practice of their faith has been a strong bond for its members. There is always room for improvement in the evolution of society and leaders who stand in the way of enlightening those they lead do a disservice to the entire world.

I am a lucky man to have my wife, Linda, in my life who has patiently tolerated my time writing this book and have been equally rewarded with my two children, Raquel and Marcus, and my grandchildren, Shane, Luna and Minnie.

The names of the characters are fictitious except for public figures, the billionaires and certain Rabbis. My thanks to the late Mr. Sam Catton's book, "Men of Faith," published in 2001 by Sephardic Heritage Foundation, for some of the historical facts herein about the community. I knew Mr. Catton and his son, Harry very well, as well as his younger son Eddie, who passed away too early. The Catton family personified the best of the SY community.

Zev Chafets' article in the New York Times, "The SY Empire" (October 14, 2007) was helpful in explaining the ban on converts.

Wikipedia was an invaluable source for particulars about the Jews in Poland and other facts about SYs.

David Meager's article, "Slavery in Bible Times" (Cross†Way Issue Autumn 2006 No. 102) filled in details in the discussion of "ahbeed" and slavery.

Brigitte Hamann's "Hitler's Vienna: A Portrait of the Tyrant as a Young Man" (Tauris Parke Paperbacks) was helpful in explaining the Nazi warlord's special attention given to Eduard Bloch, the Jewish doctor who cared for Hitler's mother as she was dying.